[handwritten inscription] To Erin —
Hope you enjoy how it all comes together!

TWELVE

BOOK THREE IN THE
MORE
TRILOGY

By
T.M. Franklin

[handwritten signature]

Cover image by: © stock.adobe.com / yblaz
Cover design by: T.M. Franklin

Enchanted

PUBLICATIONS
www.enchantedpublications.com

Visit the Author's web site at
www.TMFranklin.com

CHAPTER ONE

A block of ice smashed against the wall above Ava, raining down a shower of freezing crystals. She cursed under her breath and made a dash for the adjoining building—a detached garage—and pressed her back against the wall next to Caleb.

"I thought you said she'd be reasonable," she said, sneaking a glance around the corner and ducking back with a gasp as another bowling-ball-sized block of ice shot their way and landed at their feet.

"That's what the intel said," Caleb replied and clenched his jaw as he scanned their surroundings.

They'd received word of a possible Half-Breed named Sophie near the border in Minnesota, and Caleb was supposed to get to her before the Council did. Ava had begged to come along, after going crazy with boredom while holed up at the Colony for almost a month. He'd agreed only because there'd been no time to argue and no one else to go with him. Since his kidnapping and manipulation, the Guardians had instigated a strict buddy system. Even Caleb was subject to it.

There had been a plan, of course. There was always a plan. But as Ava was quickly coming to realize, when it came to the Race, such plans often fell apart.

They'd driven to Minnesota but had left the car at the gate so they could shift into the neighborhood where Sophie lived. Caleb had been careful to materialize out of sight of the house, only to find the girl standing at her mailbox, staring at them wide-eyed and obviously scared out of her mind. When Caleb had stepped toward her, she took off running toward the house, and the ice bombardment had commenced.

"We should have brought Adam," she said, shivering as the ice crystals in her hair melted and dripped down her collar.

"He was needed back at the Colony."

The dampener could mute gifts, sometimes block them altogether, but Gideon was leery to let Adam go too far from the Guardian Colony ever since the Rogue attack. Caleb had assured his father that he and Ava could handle it. It was supposed to be a routine mission, after all.

"Well, he sure would have come in handy with Miss Ice Ice Baby over there," she said with a disgruntled frown. Ava spotted a couple of garbage cans propped against the house and an idea began to form. "You think you can shift us behind that tree on the other side of the yard without her noticing?"

Caleb snuck a quick peek. "Yeah. What are you thinking?"

"I need to get where I can see her so I can try and bind her."

Caleb stiffened. "No way."

Ava bristled with a familiar nudge of frustration. "Come on, Caleb, it's no big deal." He'd been such a mother hen lately, and she was *fine*.

"You can't use your gifts. You promised. Not until we figure out—"

Another ball of ice ricocheted off the corner of the building, and they fell to the ground, covering their heads.

A cryokinetic—that's what they'd called her. Someone who used cold and ice like a pyrokinetic used fire.

More like a human snow blower.

Ava still couldn't believe this was her life.

"We need to do something!" Ava snapped. "I'm open to other ideas."

Protectors would be coming soon—within a day or two if their intel was correct, not that Ava was counting on that—but Caleb and Ava had yet to get to the front walk, let alone the front door. Ava knew their only chance was to bind Sophie long enough to convince her they weren't there to hurt her. Convincing Caleb of that, however, was easier said than done.

"We can wait her out," he said as a burst of smaller ice pellets hit them. He pulled Ava into his arms and rolled closer to the wall to shield them from the worst of the blast. "She's panicking . . . afraid . . . and her gift is lashing out. She can't keep it up for long. When she calms down, or gets tired, we'll be able to get to her."

"And how long will that take?" At his silence, she pushed away from him. "You have no idea, right?"

Caleb rolled over to sit braced against the wall and glared at her with a mulish expression but said nothing.

Ava took a deep breath and crawled on her knees to sit between his sprawled legs. She touched his face, and the mingling of their power settled them both. "I'll be okay," she said softly. "I won't use a lot. You know it's only bad when I try to do too m—"

"We don't know that."

"I'm fine," she said, willing him to believe it and ignoring the ache behind her eyes. "We have to do something. It's only a matter of time before a neighbor calls the cops."

As if emphasizing her words, another ice ball crashed into the garage door.

Caleb frowned in the direction of the noise, and she knew he was desperately trying to think of an alternative plan of action.

"Come on." She got to her feet and held out her hands. "We need to do this. Now."

Caleb tried to stare her down, but when she didn't look away, he took a deep breath and let her pull him to his feet. "You sure you're okay?" he asked, reaching out to touch her cheek, his gift sparking along her skin.

"I'm sure." She stepped close and wrapped her arms around his waist as another ice ball flew past. "Let's go." Ava closed her eyes as Caleb shifted them across the yard and took a second to steady herself before peering around the trunk of the tree. She spotted the girl peeking out from the living room blinds.

Ava used her gift to rattle the garbage cans by the garage and smiled when another ice ball flew in that direction. She reached out for Caleb's hand, using his gift to boost her own and to ground her. "Okay, I'm going to bind her so she can't run then you shift us inside," she said.

"I really don't like this." He squeezed her hand, though, so Ava knew he was with her.

"I can deal with anything she throws at us." She glanced back at him with a wry smile. "You do the talking."

"Great."

"Hey, you're the one with all the experience."

Another chunk of ice crashed into the garage, but it was smaller.

Ava hoped that was a good sign.

Caleb yanked on her hand a little. "First sign of trouble and I'm shifting us out. She'll just have to take her chances with the Council."

"I'll be fine," she said with a reassuring smile. "Ready?" He gave a curt nod, and Ava turned back to the window. She let her gift flow up and out, willing it to wrap around the cryokinetic and visualizing ropes lacing around her in a tight web.

When they heard a muffled shriek, Caleb pulled Ava close and they shifted inside.

When Caleb released her, Ava swayed on her feet and tried to stay focused on keeping Sophie bound.

The girl screamed, and a small ice ball shot toward them that Ava deflected easily.

Caleb maintained a safe distance, holding up his hands in a placating gesture. "Please, calm down," he said. "We're not here to hurt you. We want to help you."

The girl struggled against Ava's grip, tears streaming down her cheeks.

She was young—maybe Ava's age, possibly a little older—with warm brown skin and black hair wildly curling around her shoulders. She wore jeans and a red sweatshirt tattered at the sleeves.

The room was cold, ice crystals forming around the windows, and Ava shivered as she watched the girl's panicked eyes search for an escape.

Eyes like mine.

"Caleb," Ava murmured.

"I see it."

There wasn't time to contemplate the discovery, however, as another spray of ice shards flew toward them.

Ava stopped them in midair, and they fell to the ground as though they'd hit an invisible shield.

The girl choked out a sob.

"Don't be afraid," Ava said in a quiet voice as she stepped around Caleb.

Sophie whimpered, and the temperature dropped a little, but there were no more ice balls.

Thank goodness.

"I'm going to let you go, but don't run, okay? We just want to talk. We're not going to hurt you."

After a moment, the girl nodded jerkily.

Ava pulled her gift back, and Sophie slumped to the sofa.

"What do you want?" she asked, wiping away tears with the back of her hand. "Who are you?"

Ava smiled and eased down to sit on the other end of the sofa. "I'm afraid that's kind of a long story."

Ava closed the bathroom door quietly, leaned back against it, and closed her eyes against the pain in her head. Once Sophie had calmed down, Caleb began to explain about the Race and Half-Breeds, and Ava had been able to excuse herself without much notice.

She left the light off and fumbled in her jacket pocket for the little container of painkillers she'd taken to keeping close at all times. She popped a couple of the pills in her mouth and swallowed them dry, followed by a couple of R-cubes. With a heavy sigh Ava turned to the mirror and winced at her washed-out appearance. She prodded at her nose carefully, glad that she'd at least managed to avoid a nosebleed. There was no way she would have been able to hide that from Caleb.

She'd been hiding a lot lately.

But with the ongoing threat of the Rogues, and the upcoming trip to New Elysia, she knew she was needed. Her gifts were needed. If they were to come under attack, Ava had to be able to fight. If Caleb or the others found out that her headaches were getting worse—that she'd started having them even when she wasn't using her gifts—they'd leave her behind, and she couldn't let that happen. She couldn't let them face the Council, not to mention the Rogues, without her. She couldn't let Caleb face that kind of threat alone. Not after she'd come so close to losing him.

Ava bent over the sink and splashed some cool water on her face, swiping it over the back of her neck as she sagged against the counter. She'd see Talia again once she got back to the Colony. Hopefully, she'd be able to help, and since she was bound by the same confidentiality as a human doctor—Ava had made sure of that before she had ever approached the healer in the first place—she'd keep her secret.

It was only for a short time, anyway. Once they got to New Elysia, the doctors there would figure out what was causing her problems and she, and everyone else, would be able to focus on figuring out how to stop the Rogues.

"Ava?" Caleb's muffled voice at the door made her jump. She'd been so lost in thought she hadn't even felt his approach. "Are you all right?"

She turned off the water and wiped her face quickly with a towel. "Yeah. One sec." She checked her appearance once more and brushed her fingers through her hair. The headache had eased, thankfully, and her face had regained its color. Ava reached for the door and forced a relaxed smile before opening it.

Caleb searched her face. "You sure you're okay?"

"Of course," she said, widening the smile a bit. "Everything okay with Sophie?"

"Yeah. We really should get out of here, though."

"Well, let's go, then," she replied, patting his chest as she squeezed past him in the narrow hallway. He trailed behind as she made her way into the living room, which had warmed to a normal temperature, the ice on the windows melted and dripped onto the carpet.

Sophie emerged from a bedroom on the other side of the living room, carrying a small duffle bag and a backpack.

"You ready to go?" Ava asked.

Sophie took a deep breath. "I think so." Her lip trembled slightly, and Ava crossed to her.

"It's going to be okay," she said, reaching out to gently squeeze the girl's shoulders. "We'll keep you safe. I promise."

Sophie nodded and swiped away a few errant tears.

Ava led her to the front door as Caleb opened it and poked his head out to scan the yard before waving them through. He grabbed Ava's arm to hold her back.

"Are you sure you're all right?" he whispered, glancing at Sophie a few steps ahead on the walkway. "No headaches?"

Ava ignored the curl of guilt in her stomach. She hated lying to Caleb, but she didn't see an alternative. Not if she was going to keep him safe.

"I told you, I'm fine," she said, popping up to kiss him lightly.

He caught her around the waist and studied her for a moment, focused and intent as he looked into her eyes.

She forced herself to meet his gaze—not to flinch, even as her heart thumped heavily in her chest.

"Okay," he said finally, sliding his hand down to squeeze hers. "Let's go."

Ava let out a slow breath as they took off at a jog toward the road. It was probably nothing anyway. Her powers were new, and her body was still getting used to them. Even the Colony healer couldn't deny the possibility. Her body and her brain simply needed to adapt to her new abilities and the headaches would stop. She'd be fine.

Ava picked up the pace and turned right toward the gate.

She'd be *fine*.

The drive back to Red Lake took about eight hours. Caleb could have cut some time off that if he'd been able to shift, but with two passengers, it wasn't possible. Ava had tried to convince him to shift Sophie and leave the car with her, but he didn't feel comfortable with Ava out of his sight. She'd rolled her eyes, muttering about the bond, but it wasn't that.

Well, it's not only that.

He was worried about her. No matter how many times she insisted that she was fine, that the headaches had tapered off, he couldn't shake his concern. It was better for them all to stay together anyway, he reasoned. Ava could relate to Sophie in a way he couldn't. Especially if the suspected Half-Breed was really what they thought she was.

"So let me get this straight," the girl in question said as they approached the border crossing at International Falls. "You're saying you can somehow get this guy to let us across, even though I don't have a passport?"

Ava turned and grinned. "Caleb's really good at this. Trust me."

Sophie shrugged, but Caleb spotted her fingers twisting nervously in her lap through the rearview mirror.

"It'll be fine," he said as they crawled forward in line. He held his and Ava's passports and tapped them lightly on the wheel as they pulled up to the checkpoint. Caleb rolled down the window, a bright smile on his face.

"Morning. Where are you headed?" the guard asked as he took the passports.

"Red Lake." Caleb reached out with his gift to touch the man's mind.

Just a little push.

"How long will you be visiting?"

"Oh, couple of weeks, I think. Going to see family."

The man nodded and ran the passports under a scanner. "Bringing anything into the country?"

Caleb heard Sophie's sharp intake of breath and cast her a warning glance in the mirror. "No. Nothing."

"No alcohol, tobacco, or firearms?" The guard sounded as though he'd asked the questions so many times he could probably do it in his sleep.

"Nope. Just us. The two of us." Caleb willed the man to accept his words. The guard froze for a moment, his gaze drifting slowly to the backseat, and Caleb reached out to touch his forehead. "Only two of us in the car. Just a routine check. Nothing special to see here."

The guard nodded slowly and turned to face Caleb, his eyes still a bit blank. "Nothing?" he mumbled.

"Are we finished?" Caleb asked, pulling his hand back.

The man started and shook his head as if to clear it. "Sorry, yeah." he said, handing back the passports. "You two have a nice visit."

Caleb saluted the man with the passports and drove through the checkpoint, turning off the main highway almost immediately. He preferred the back roads, for obvious reasons.

After a few minutes, Sophie burst out in laughter. "Okay, you *have* to tell me how you did that."

Caleb smiled at her in the mirror. "Practice. Lots of practice."

"Don't let him fool you," Ava said, turning sideways in the seat to face Sophie. "I've been practicing a ton and I can't do it."

Caleb reached out to squeeze her knee. "You can do plenty of other stuff."

Sophie perked up. "Oh yeah?"

They'd talked about the Race in general terms but hadn't got to specific gifts yet.

"Like what?" she asked.

"I can move stuff around . . . you know, with my mind," Ava said, waving her hand around as if to illustrate. "And make stuff."

"Make stuff?"

"They call it *manifesting*. I can manipulate—" She sat up suddenly and grabbed Caleb's hand. "Do you feel that?"

"What?" He instinctively checked the mirrors, but there was nobody behind them.

"Someone . . ." Ava's eyes glazed over. "Someone's coming. Fast."

Caleb stepped on the gas, searching the horizon. "Who? Anyone familiar?"

"What's happening?" Sophie asked.

Ava shook her head. "I can't tell. Not yet anyway. You think it's Protectors?"

Caleb's jaw tightened. "Or Rogues."

"You think they know?" Ava glanced at Sophie.

"*We* don't know. Not for sure."

"Would somebody *please* tell me what's going on?" Sophie shouted from the backseat.

The temperature in the car dipped as frost formed along the edges of the windows.

"You've got to calm her down," Caleb muttered, taking a turn too fast and swerving to correct. "Now."

Ava didn't argue, instead scrambling over the seat to take the girl's hand. "Sophie, listen to me. You need to stay calm, okay? Try to breathe with me."

"But—"

"I'll explain everything, but first you need to calm down. You see what's happening?"

Through the mirror, Caleb saw her glance up at the roof of the car as snowflakes began to drift through the interior.

"I . . . I don't understand," Sophie murmured. "What's—why is it snowing?"

"It's you," Ava said quietly. "You're upset, and your gift is reacting."

"I don't understand what's happening to me." Sophie choked on a sob, and Caleb felt the telltale prickle of another Race signature along the edges of his consciousness.

"I feel them now," he said, sitting taller in the seat and leaning forward as if willing the car to go faster.

Ava didn't respond but remained focused on Sophie.

Caleb felt Ava's gift and knew she was letting it flow into the girl a little, helping calm her.

"We'll help you." Ava sounded so calm and soothing. "We'll help you learn to control it, but for right now, you need to calm down. Breathe with me, okay?"

Sophie nodded and swallowed tears as she tried to match Ava's inhale and exhale.

The snow stopped.

"That's good." Ava nodded encouragingly. "Keep breathing. I need you to stay calm. Someone's coming, and I'm guessing they're after you."

Sophie's breath caught, and the ice gathering on the dashboard cracked.

"It's okay," Ava hurried to say. "Keep breathing. Stay calm. We're going to keep you safe."

Sophie gripped Ava's hand, but she kept breathing slowly in and out. "How?"

Ava smiled. "You asked what I could do? Well, I'm about to show you." She turned backward and knelt on the seat, her eyes focused on the stretch of road behind them.

Caleb felt his heart race as he looked back and forth between the rearview and side mirrors to watch for what they knew was coming.

It didn't take long before a speck appeared. All too quickly, the speck grew to the size of a black SUV and filled his driver's side mirror.

"What are you waiting for?" Caleb growled. "They're right on top of us."

"Objects in mirror are closer than they appear," Ava said under her breath, her fingers digging into the back of the seat.

Caleb sensed a swell of her power and then, just as quickly, a blast smashed the car forward, as though a large object had hit them.

"What was that?" Ava shouted as Caleb fought to keep the car on the road.

"Must be Devon." Caleb checked his mirror and saw the SUV closing in again. "Protector. Moves air."

Another blast hit the car.

Sophie clutched the door handle, her knuckles white. "He's doing that with air?"

The snow started again.

"Stay calm," Ava said distractedly.

"Easy for you to say."

Ava turned again to focus on the people behind them as Caleb flicked his gaze from the road ahead to the rearview mirror.

The SUV was almost on their bumper.

"Now would be good, Ava," he said through gritted teeth. "He's going to hit us again."

With a loud boom, the front of the SUV jumped up then hit the road again, the driver fighting to correct a swerve.

"What did you do?" Caleb didn't let off the gas, but he couldn't take his eyes off the rearview mirror.

With another boom, not quite as loud, the SUV shuddered to a stop in the middle of the road.

Devon shot one more blast their way, but it barely hit them, a quiet smack echoing through the frame and breaking a shower of ice loose from the windows before they sped away.

Ava twisted and collapsed into the seat, pressing her fingers to her nose.

"Are you okay?" Caleb asked.

She nodded, fumbling to get a tissue out of her jeans. "Fine. It's not bad."

"You sure?"

Before she could answer, Sophie held up her hands. "Okay, what exactly just happened?"

Ava swiped at her nose and showed the tissue to Caleb with a roll of her eyes. "See? Nothing," she said, waving it around.

It wasn't much blood. That was true. Still, Caleb wasn't really reassured.

"It was Protectors, sent by the Council we told you about," Ava explained. "They must have picked up our trail from your house."

Sophie looked out the rear window. "Can they still track us?"

Ava shot a glance at Caleb, who was already reaching for his phone. "I'll call ahead for Balaam," he said.

"He can lure them away," Ava told Sophie. "You don't have to worry."

Sophie nodded, but her eyes were wide. "And the car? What did you do to it?"

Ava smiled. "I blew the tires. Well, technically, I changed the *air* in the tires."

"Changed it?"

"Into gravel."

"Gravel." Sophie stared at Ava, and Caleb noticed her gripping the door handle, her knuckles white.

He smirked.

"It was the first thing that came to mind," she said, a little defensively. "And it's pretty easy."

"Easy?" Sophie squeaked.

"Yeah, well, they're rocks, you know? No moving parts. No complicated bits and pieces." Ava wiggled her fingers and grinned.

"So . . . how?"

Ava shrugged. "I just concentrate and picture what I want to be there and—poof—it's there."

"Poof?"

Caleb scoffed. "Well, it's a little more complicated than that."

"I can rearrange atoms and stuff," Ava said, waving it off as if it was nothing. "But I can't make things that I don't have personal experience with."

Sophie swallowed and nodded, saying nothing. She released the door handle and took Ava's hand between hers. "Can you make me a margarita? Because I think I really need one."

Ava laughed, and Caleb kept one eye on the road as he placed a call to the Colony.

CHAPTER TWO

After meeting Balaam in Kenora, it had been almost midnight by the time they arrived at the Colony. Balaam's ability to impersonate any Race signature was exactly what they'd needed to keep everyone safe, but he had to make at least brief physical contact with the signature he was imitating. The diversion had added another hour and a half to the trip, but Ava felt a lot safer when they'd left the mimic to guide the Protectors away.

"What happens if they catch him?" Sophie had asked as she watched Balaam jog down the block and disappear around a corner.

"They won't," Caleb had assured her. "Balaam is very good at what he does."

Gideon was waiting for them when they arrived, but he held off asking any questions, personally showing Sophie to her quarters next to Ava's instead.

The girl was brimming with questions herself, but Ava had assured her they'd all be answered in the morning, and Sophie had been too tired to argue.

They were all exhausted, and Ava's head had been lightly throbbing ever since the incident with the Protectors. She swallowed another couple of painkillers dry and laid back in her bed, hoping sleep would bring her some relief.

Instead, she found herself in a dark forest, the moon a mere sliver overhead, and a cool wind whistling through the trees. Ava knew it was a dream, but she also knew it was something more.

Since her experience with Emma, she'd come to identify the feelings, the instinct, that came with dreams influenced by her Race intuition. They were clearer, sharper, and also sparked a *knowing* deep inside her.

That knowing told her that she needed to move through the trees toward an unknown force pulling her forward, but with every step she took her legs grew heavier, as though they were bogged down in heavy mud. The trees grew thicker, barely enough space for her to squeeze between them, and she struggled with sharp branches scraping against her skin. Still, the pull continued, demanding she keep moving . . . keep pushing.

A sharp pain shot through her head, and she pressed her palms to her skull as if she could force the pain away. She fell to her knees and started to crawl, knowing she needed to get . . . to get to . . . she needed to get to *him*.

A branch swept across her face, and she shoved it away, gasping when her palm came back covered in blood. She swiped at her nose only to discover more blood running down her arm and dripping onto the ground. She shook her head and pushed forward, crawling along the damp—

No, not damp ground. Wet *ground.*

The muddy bog splashed around her as she struggled to keep moving, the water growing deeper and deeper, pulling her down, sucking her in.

She stopped to push her hair out of her face and gaped as she inspected it closer.

That's not water.

Thick red flowed in a river of blood around her, and the current pushed against her in ripples of sticky crimson.

"No!" she shouted as she struggled to her feet only to have them swept out from under her. She tried to swim, choking on the liquid heat as it dragged her down. She had to keep moving. She had to fight, to breathe. She had to—

One last gasp and a wave crashed over her, yanking her under the surface into the thick, swirling darkness.

Ava awoke with a start, blinking and squinting to focus as early morning sunlight filled her room with a soft glow. She panted, trying to catch her breath as she ran her hands over her face, her arms.

No blood?

Nothing but a sheen of sweat sticking her clothes to her skin. Her head still throbbed slightly, but other than that, she was fine.

She collapsed onto the bed as her breathing eased. This was why she'd wanted her own room.

Well, one of the reasons.

Gideon had assumed that she and Caleb would share, and Ava suspected Caleb had as well, but he'd hidden any surprise and simply nodded when Ava had moved her things into her own quarters.

She couldn't let him witness one of her attacks, or worse, see her like this afterward.

It was still early, barely after six o'clock, so Ava slipped out of her room to the communal bathroom for a quick shower to erase the last remnants of the troubling vision. She had no idea what it meant and, not for the first time, cursed her intuition, which seemed to want to tell her things but not in a very clear manner.

Her headache intensified a bit as she brushed her teeth and slipped in her contacts, and she frowned when she noticed she'd taken the last of her painkillers the night before.

Talia. I have to find Talia.

Ava dressed quickly, hoping to catch the healer before the rest of the Colony woke, especially Caleb.

Her shoes crunched on the ground as she made her way through the outer ring of buildings to the residences in the center of the Colony. Talia's office was also her home, and after all this time, Ava knew the way well.

She rounded the corner of the squat building, checking over her shoulder before she knocked on the back entrance and slipped her hands inside the sleeves of her sweatshirt. She clutched her arms across her chest and bounced a little in the early morning chill while she waited.

After a moment, the door opened and Talia greeted her with the familiar rise of one perfect eyebrow. "Didn't know you were back."

"Got in late last night." Ava blew into her fists. "I know it's early, but can I come in?"

Talia stepped back, gesturing with one arm and a slight nod. "I was about to make some coffee. You want some?"

Ava nodded, intentionally avoiding looking in Talia's direction as she shrugged off her coat and hung it on a hook by the door. The healer hated when people stared, and it was something that Ava had been working on. She followed the woman into the small kitchen and took a seat at the island, picking at the cuffs of her shirt.

Talia made the coffee with quiet efficiency, not saying another word until she'd poured two cups and slid one across the countertop toward Ava. "So what's up?"

Ava lost herself in the soft grey eyes and sighed. Talia lifted her cup to sip from it, and Ava jumped at the movement. "Sorry," she mumbled, taking a scalding gulp from her own cup.

"Don't worry about it."

"I know it bothers you."

Talia arched one shoulder delicately upward in a half shrug. "How are the headaches?"

This time it was Ava who shrugged. "I'm out of the pills."

"I can give you some more. I don't suppose you've changed your mind about telling Caleb?"

Ava set her cup down a little too forcefully, and coffee sloshed over the lip. "No."

Talia sighed. "I think that's a mistake."

"You've made that all too clear." Ava immediately regretted sniping. "Sorry," she said, reaching for a napkin to clean up the spill. "I just don't want to worry him."

"And you don't want him to make you stay with us when they go to New Elysia."

"They need me." Ava avoided Talia's knowing gaze. "You know they do."

"Which is the only reason I haven't forced the issue."

Ava's eyes widened. "This is you *not* forcing the issue?"

Talia laughed, shaking her head. "Come on. Let's go into the clinic. I should at least examine you before I drug you up and send you on your way."

Ava followed the healer into the small examination room off the living room, which also served as a waiting room for the clinic. She hopped up onto the exam table, used to the routine by this time.

Talia had been away from the Colony when the Rogues attacked but had returned shortly after. She had trained with physicians in New Elysia before joining the Guardians when she was no longer able to reconcile her Hippocratic oath with what had been done to the Half-Breeds. It was that oath and the promise of confidentiality that had led Ava to trust her.

Gideon had told Talia about the headaches and nosebleeds, of course. That was no secret. But only Talia and Ava knew how bad they'd gotten, and Ava aimed to keep it that way, at least until the Rogue threat was dealt with.

"Anything new?" Ava asked, as she always did.

Talia had been conducting her own research into Ava's condition.

"Nothing," she said, shining a light into Ava's eyes then checking her ears. "You know the Council has bet—"

"No."

"Ava—"

She looked the healer in the eye. "I promise. I'll talk to the doctors in New Elysia when we get there. Just . . . not yet."

Talia's mouth tightened, but she nodded and continued the examination. "Headaches worse?"

"They come and go." At Talia's suspicious look, Ava sighed in resignation. "Yeah, they're worse. And it's not just my head."

"What else?"

"Muscle aches. All over, really. Like I've got the flu or something. Nausea sometimes."

Talia hummed and made a note in Ava's chart. "Have you noticed anything in particular bringing on the attacks?"

"Well, when I use my gifts, of course," Ava said. "Sometimes when I have the dreams. Sometimes for no reason at all."

Talia frowned. "That's new."

"I know."

Talia grabbed her stethoscope off a hook on the wall and warmed the chest piece with a few breaths. "Breathe in and out, slowly," she said as she listened to Ava's heart and lungs and made a few more notes.

"Can I ask you a personal question?" Ava shifted a little on the table, the worn vinyl creaking with the movement.

Talia nodded, still writing in Ava's chart.

"Do you ever miss, you know, going out there . . . into the world?"

Talia glanced at her then looked back at the chart. "Not really."

"Sorry, I know it's none of my business," Ava said quickly. "I was just curious. I mean . . . I've never really met anyone like you before."

Talia sighed, closed the chart, and tapped it on the edge of the table. "I know it must seem strange to you."

"To be too beautiful to go out in public? Yeah, kinda."

She smiled, and Ava was stunned by it for a moment. "You know we have to keep under the radar," Talia said. "For people like me, it's difficult."

"I would think that someone like you could do whatever you wanted," Ava said. "Be a model or an actress or . . . *anything*, really."

"But I wanted to be a healer," she said quietly. "I wanted to help my people. And being noticed isn't part of who we are."

Ava braced herself and looked directly into Talia's eyes. She still hadn't gotten used to the full impact—the carved cheekbones, golden skin, light-and-dark grey eyes. Even with the Veil, the woman was unearthly . . . ethereal. There was no way she could walk down the streets of New York or Paris and not stop traffic.

"At least here, I can be myself. I don't have to try to hide."

"Do you ever . . ." Ava swallowed nervously, but she was so *curious.* "Lift your Veil completely?" Talia was mesmerizing even with a Veil. Without? Well, Ava couldn't even picture it.

Talia shrugged. "No need. It's part of me. Like all of us, I don't even have to try to keep it up."

"Well, not like *all* of us."

Unlike the others, Ava had no Veil. It was all part of her father's plan to make her look ordinary—human.

"True." Talia tapped her pen against her lips. "Sorry."

"It's no big deal. I can handle being, you know, normal." Ava wiggled a palm back and forth. "Ish."

"Well, at least in one respect," Talia said with a wink before moving toward a tall cabinet and scouring the shelves.

Ava handed over her medicine bottle and waited as the healer refilled it and handed it back. "Thanks," she said, hopping down from the table. "Oh, by the way, I'll probably be by later."

"Oh?"

"Yeah, I'm sure Gideon will want you to take a look at the woman we brought back."

"The Half-Breed, yes." Talia nodded. "He told me."

Ava chewed on her lip. "Well, that's what we thought. I'm guessing she's a little more, though."

Talia arched a brow. "Really?"

"We have the same eyes," Ava said. "And . . . I don't know . . . I could feel a *connection*, somehow. Like with Emma."

"You think she's one of the Twelve?"

"I'd almost bet money on it."

Talia reached for her coffee cup and took a long sip. "This should be interesting."

"You have no idea," Ava replied with a sigh. "I better get back before Caleb wakes up. I'm sure Gideon's going to want a debrief. We'll bring Sophie by after."

"I'll be here."

Ava paused halfway out the door. "Thanks, Talia. Really."

"Just doing my job," she said lightly and grinned. "But you're welcome. Keep me posted, okay?"

Ava nodded and headed back toward her quarters at a jog, stopping long enough to swallow a couple of the pain pills dry and take a deep breath before yanking the door open and walking inside.

She nearly jumped out of her skin when Caleb stepped out of the shadows. She'd been so lost in thought she hadn't even sensed him nearby. "You scared me to death!" she said, hoping he'd believe that was the cause of her racing heartbeat.

"Where have you been?" he asked, looking over her shoulder as if he'd find the answer entering behind her.

She'd learned partial truths were better than lies. "I woke up early and went to see Talia."

Caleb stiffened, concern evident on his face as he reached out to cup his palm around her neck. "Are you all right?"

"Fine, yes. I'm fine," she said, feeling him reach out with his gift. It was second nature now, the mingling of their power. "Just . . . after last night, I wanted to check things out, and I let her know about Sophie."

Ahh, truth. Much safer ground.

He nodded. "Probably a good idea. Speaking of which, Gideon wants to see us."

"Should I get her?"

Caleb leaned down, kissed her softly, and looked into her eyes, searching for . . . something.

Ava forced herself to hold his gaze.

He kissed her again. "Let her sleep, I think. I'm sure yesterday took a lot out of her. Gideon wants our report first, anyway. He sent me to find you."

"Sorry," she said as they turned to walk down the hall toward Gideon's office. "I didn't think anyone would be up for a while."

"I don't think Gideon ever sleeps," Caleb said wryly.

He was huddled over his computer when they walked in, and if the dark shadows under the Guardian leader's eyes were any indication, it didn't look like it. He leaned back and waved at the chairs across from his desk in invitation. "Balaam led them west and lost them near the border to Montana. He's circling south a bit to make sure, but he should be back in a day or so."

"That's good," Caleb said. "Don't know what we would have done without him."

Gideon rocked back in his chair. "So tell me about Sophie. How's she doing?"

"As well as you'd expect. Better, actually," Caleb said. "She's a cryogenic, although her gift is highly unstable at the moment."

"We can help with that."

Caleb shot Ava a glance. "That's not all."

"Oh?" He looked between them, waiting with his fingers tented against his lips.

"I . . . *we*," Ava clarified, "think she may be like me."

Gideon sat up, alert. "Full-blooded Race? Or do you mea—"

"I mean, like *me*. I think she's one of the Twelve. I think she's my sister."

"I appreciate you taking the time to see me." The demure comment felt foreign on Tiernan's tongue, but it was the way things were done. If anyone had told him a few months ago he'd be acting as an ambassador to the Council, he'd have told them they were crazy.

But desperate times and all that.

He was doing what he had to do, and in this case, it meant coming to Kaeden Cross with hat in hand, so to speak.

"I only have a few minutes," the Council member told him, waving toward a chair before taking a seat behind his desk, his golden gaze watching expectantly.

For a moment, Tiernan entertained the idea that they could almost pass for twins—both tall, muscled, and shaved bald—if not for the scar marring Tiernan's face and his blue and green eyes. "Rafe told you why I'm here?"

Kaeden nodded and leaned back in his chair, lacing his fingers over his stomach. "An alliance with the Guardians. Not an easy feat to accomplish."

"Yeah, well. That's an understatement."

Kaeden's lips quirked. "Who do you have so far?"

The Protector let out a heavy breath. "As you know, Rafe supports the alliance. Naomi will go along with whatever the majority decides. Andreas is . . . thinking about it."

"And Madeleine?"

"I won't need Madeleine if I can get you and Andreas."

Kaeden laughed, loud and full. "Oh, Protector, when did you become such a politician?"

Tiernan asked himself the same question on a daily basis. Hourly. Sometimes more.

"Borré and the Rogues pose a real threat," he said instead of replying. "The Council will need all the help it can get if it's going to defeat them."

"The Rogues have never been much of an issue before."

"Not one at a time. Not when they weren't organized. Not before the Twelve." At Kaeden's stoic silence, Tiernan rolled his eyes. "I know the Council is aware, at least to some extent, of what's going on. The fact of the matter is, the Twelve are powerful—more than you or me or any Race before, I'd hazard to say." He recalled the destruction Ava had wreaked on the Guardians' training field. "You know they've set their sights on the Council." It was a guess, but when Kaeden's stare broke, Tiernan knew he'd guessed right.

Kaeden stood and turned toward the window. "I'm with you," he said quietly. "But I won't cross Madeleine."

Tiernan grunted in frustration, and Kaeden turned to face him, smirking.

"You need it to be unanimous, Protector. For something like this, there can be no dissension. Take my word on it."

Tiernan knew he was right. "She's going to be difficult. You know how she feels about the Guardians."

"She'll listen to reason. It will simply take some convincing." He glanced sidelong at Tiernan. "You might want to get on her good side."

Tiernan laughed humorlessly. That was easier said than done, but he knew the Council member was right. Madeleine was the key to everything. And it was up to Tiernan to win her over.

God help us all.

CHAPTER THREE

Caleb leaned against the wall of the examination room, watching Ava as she talked with Sophie and held her hand for reassurance. Talia was running the blood sample she'd taken, and they, along with Gideon, were waiting, even though they were pretty sure what it would show. Ava was sure, at least, and Caleb tended to trust her judgment.

Well, for the most part.

He reached out for her through the bond, a trickle of familiar relief going through him when their gifts merged.

She looked at him with a small smile, obviously feeling it as well.

He smiled back, wishing he could shift her away someplace quiet. Someplace private. Someplace where they didn't have to think about the Rogues or the Twelve or conspiracies that put the world in danger.

Someday. When this is all over.

Talia clicked a few keys on her computer and turned to Sophie. "You probably should see this," she said. "But perhaps you'd prefer the others lea—"

"Hold on a second." Gideon took a step forward, scowling.

"Rogue plot or no, this woman has a right to privacy, and I will not reveal her medical information without her consent." Talia tilted her chin slightly higher and firmly stood her ground.

Silence hung heavy in the room until Sophie said quietly, "It's all right."

She took a deep breath. "This is . . . I get that this is bigger than me."

"You're sure?"

Sophie exchanged a long look with Ava, who squeezed her hand and nodded. "Yeah. Lay it on me."

Talia's lips lifted slightly. "All right, then. Well, to put it simply, Ava was right. You are sisters. Well, half sisters anyway."

Sophie's eyes widened. "Really? Are you sure?"

"As sure as we can be." Talia rose gracefully from her chair and crossed to them. "Without getting too technical about it, the tests show the two of you share a parent. And, from what we understand, it's your father."

"Our father." Sophie stared at her and Ava's clasped hands, her voice a stunned whisper. "We're sisters?"

Caleb cleared his throat. "Well, I'm afraid there's a bit more to it than that."

Ava glanced at him nervously before turning back to Sophie. "It's kind of complicated."

Sophie shook her head with a wry snort. "More complicated than a tribe of superhuman beings living in secret and hunting down any half humans they may come across, only to come up against *other* superhuman beings who want to protect those half humans?"

Shocked silence filled the room followed by a burst of laughter.

"Okay, good point," Ava said, still half giggling. "But yeah. It's even more complicated than that."

Sophie took a deep breath, straightened her spine, and ran a hand over her hair. The curls bounced back instantly, refusing to be tamed. "Well, this sounds like a bit of a story," she said, sucking on her tongue with a loud pop. "And I think I'll need to hear it on a full stomach. What do you all do for breakfast around here?" She looked at Gideon expectantly, and he blinked at her in surprise before a slow smile lit his face.

"I think we can rustle up something," he said.

They left Talia's and headed toward the common area. They loaded up plates in the kitchen, and Caleb had to smile at the way Gideon cleared the room with a look as they took their seats.

Ava sat next to Caleb and leaned in for a moment, and he sighed softly at her warmth—both from her body and the gift curling through him.

Sophie chewed on her toast and looked around the table, waiting.

Caleb had expected Gideon to take the lead, but his father deferred to Ava with a nod.

Ava started a little but took the bull by the horns. "Okay, then. So we've told you about the Race and the Council," she said. "But there's another group of Race, called the Rogues."

"Rogues."

"Yeah." Ava took a deep breath. "They're Race who don't really want to live by the rules, see? They do their own thing, chase after power and pleasure, and pretty much mow over whoever gets in their way."

Gideon leaned forward, elbows propped on either side of his plate. "In the past, they've always been a nuisance, easily dealt with by the Protectors," he said. "Since they are, essentially, selfish, they worked alone and were therefore quickly contained."

"But what does this have to do with me?" Sophie asked, pushing away her plate.

Caleb felt for her. He'd kind of lost his appetite, too.

"A group of them have banded together," Ava explained. "They want to overthrow the Council and seize power. Their leader is a man named Elias Borré." She watched Sophie carefully. "Borré is our biological father."

Sophie collapsed back in her seat. "Whoa."

"Yeah. Whoa. But there's more," Ava said, licking her lips. "Borré is a scientist, some kind of genetic genius, or something, and he set out to create these super Race soldiers—genetically engineered to be even more powerful. He took the best of the Race and he bred them to be even more." She watched Sophie, and they all waited for what Ava said to sink in.

They didn't have to wait long.

"You mean . . ." Sophie lifted a finger to point at Ava then herself.

"Yeah," Ava replied. "He made us to—as cliché as it sounds—take over the world."

"Holy—" Sophie rubbed her hands over her face. "So . . . he's crazy?"

Gideon snorted. "Well, that's up for debate, but sanity aside, Borré is very, *very* smart. And *very* dangerous."

"But we're here," she said, flicking a glance at Ava. "We're not going to help him."

"There are more of us," Ava said. "Twelve, all together."

"How many does he have with him?"

"We're not sure yet," Gideon replied, frustration leaking into his voice. "We're behind the eight ball on this one. We know Borré's general plan but no specifics. We don't know when or how, or who the rest of the Twelve are. We lucked out in finding you."

Sophie leaned forward on the table and rubbed at her temples. "I can't believe this."

"I know it's a lot to take in," Ava said, touching her arm. "I was you a few months ago."

"And I was *normal* a few months ago." Sophie continued to massage her temples. "I had a job. I was going to college. Next thing I know, I'm causing hailstorms and freezing the pipes in my bathroom."

Caleb sat up, exchanging a look with his father. "Any idea what caused it? I mean, can you pinpoint something that may have jumpstarted your gift?"

Sophie shrugged. "Not really. I mean, I didn't hit my head or anything. I was on the phone with my mom and we got into an argument, and before I knew what was happening, there was ice on the windows."

"Your mom?" Ava asked. "Were you adopted?"

"Foster mom," Sophie explained. "The last of many. I was a bit of a problem child. Why?"

Ava sighed. "They put me with adoptive parents, *human* parents, and they blocked my Race gifts. It makes sense they'd do the same with you."

"But my gifts aren't blocked. At least not anymore."

Gideon leaned back in his chair, assuming his familiar position with his fingers tented in front of his lips. "You're older than Ava. Emma, too. It's possible that the block is simply wearing down. Maybe yours wasn't as strong, or it could have weakened with time."

"There's something I don't get. I live alone. Why wouldn't this Borré have come for me before now? If he's collecting these . . ." She waved a hand.

"The Twelve," Ava said.

"Creative." Sophie rolled her eyes. "If he's collecting the *Twelve,* why not take me?"

"Maybe he lost you," Ava replied. "If you've been shuffled around in foster homes, maybe he lost track of you."

"Or maybe he has his own reasons," Caleb said. "Like Gideon said, we don't know what's going through Borré's mind right now."

Sophie stood up and rubbed at the back of her neck as she walked across the room. After a moment, she turned to face them. "So Ava and I share a father. And we were bred to help him with this plan?"

Gideon nodded.

"And this, this . . . Emma, she's one of his kids, too?"

"They all are," Ava said with a wince. "Borré's the father of all the Twelve. But we all have different mothers."

Sophie froze, and when she looked at Ava, her eyes were wide with shock, or maybe fear. "Not all," she said.

"What do you mean?" Caleb asked.

Her lip trembled and Ava took her hand. "It's okay, you can trust us," she said.

"I haven't seen him in years," Sophie said quickly. "We were separated when we were little."

"Who?" Gideon's voice cut through the rising tension.

She replied as if in a daze, her words low and running together. "They wanted a little boy, but two kids were too much—"

"Hold on a second," Gideon said. "What are you talking about?"

Sophie blinked and focused once again on the Guardian leader. "Isaiah," she said. "And if having the same father means I'm part of the Twelve, then he is, too."

"Holy crap," Ava murmured. "You mean—"

"Yeah. Isaiah. He's my baby brother."

Elias Borré sipped his double espresso, wincing at the bitter taste as he checked his watch one more time. He frowned.

Unacceptable.

Being late was something he wouldn't ordinarily tolerate, but given the venue—the young couple in the corner, a businessman tapping at his laptop, the bored barista leaning on the counter playing some game on his phone—there was little he could do.

No, it would be too much work to deal with Emma's tardiness here. Too much to clean up, and Elias really hadn't the time nor the inclination to deal with it. So he'd let it slide.

He checked his watch again.

I'll give her ten minutes.

He rarely met his people in public, preferring to stay on the more private estate on the edge of town, but once in a while, he needed a double espresso or a *pain au chocolat*. The coffee shop in the middle of downtown Kalispell, Montana, created a fair rendition of his favorite pastry. The coffee wasn't bad either.

For peasants.

Elias shook his head and sighed. Perhaps he was losing his taste for the finer things. He hated the idea of it, but it really couldn't be helped. He was where he needed to be.

For the moment.

He fought the urge to rub at his eyes. The contacts irritated him, and he seldom wore them, but out in the world it was best not to stick out. He had to admit that he was looking forward to the day when his people could lose the contacts and lift the Veils for good. When they could step out of the shadows and take their rightful place.

Elias sensed her halfway down the block and took another sip of his espresso, schooling his expression into one of cool disappointment. Emma needed a firm hand, they all did, but his daughter was eager to please. It was a benefit, but also made her careless, on occasion.

The girl in question burst through the door, eyes frantic as they settled on him. She took a deep breath and dropped her gaze as she approached. "I'm sorry I'm late, Father," she said, her voice a quiet tremble. "Traffic was—"

"Excuses, Emma?" he said reproachfully. "Really?"

She swallowed, head dipping in acknowledgment of the reprimand. "I'm sorry, Father."

He let her stew for a moment, taking another sip of the cooling coffee, then he nudged the chair across from him with the toe of his shoe in invitation.

Emma relaxed ever so slightly and took a seat.

A waitress approached, and Elias fought off a scowl of irritation, instead ordering his daughter a latte and chocolate chip cookie with an indulgent smile.

She didn't speak, simply kept her head bowed and hands folded in her lap.

Elias waited until the waitress delivered the order before he addressed her. "How have you been, daughter?"

Her eyes flashed up in surprise. "F-f-fine. Thank you, Father."

"You've been enjoying Billings?"

She couldn't keep the frown off her face, but she tried. He had to give her that.

"It's . . . nice. Quiet." She hesitated and he waved a hand, gesturing for her to continue. "It's just difficult," she said. "Being away for so long."

"I see you every week," he said. "I do have other commitments, you know?"

"Oh, I know, Father. I'm not complaining," she said, the words tumbling out. "And I appreciate you taking the time. It's just . . ." She rubbed her forehead.

"Ah, poor thing," he said, clucking his tongue. "Is it painful?" She straightened, putting on a brave face, and a rush of pride made Elias smile gently.

"It's not so bad. I only want to be useful. I could help, Father. If I was here, I could—"

"Shhh," he said, reaching across the table to sweep the hair out of her face. "Hush now."

She leaned into the touch, her eyes fluttering closed, and he pulled his hand away. She whimpered.

He arched a brow. The girl needed to learn more control.

Emma blushed and dipped her head.

Better.

"The time away was for your own good," he said. "Time for you to contemplate your actions and learn from them."

She nodded, eager words falling from her lips. "Oh, I have, Father. I've learned. I promise, I won't let you down again."

"Your actions in relation to your sister have had serious repercussions. I've had to adjust my timeline and make other changes to compensate for your failure."

Emma's shoulders fell as she curled into herself. "I know, Father. I am so sorry."

He heard the tears in her voice and felt her anguish through their link.

"I swear I'll do better if you'll give me another chance."

He studied her for a few minutes, allowing her to wallow a bit in her guilt and regret. They were powerful emotions, especially when it came to Emma. Finally, he eased closer and cupped his palm over her head. "Relax, daughter," he said, giving her what she needed.

She sighed, her muscles relaxing as the pain retreated, relief oozing into her muscles and nerves . . . the very cells of her being.

It didn't take long after all these years. He knew her so well, and she accepted his help so easily. Thirty seconds, maybe less, and he leaned back and picked up his cup to finish his coffee.

Emma's eyes fluttered open, glazed and dreamy, until she blinked a few times and focused on him. "Thank you, Father."

"You're welcome, Emma. You know I'd do anything for you."

"I know."

"And, of course, you'll do anything for me."

"Yes, Father."

"That's what family's all about, after all."

"Yes, Father."

He set his cup on the saucer and smoothed his napkin in front of him before leaning back in his chair. "Speaking of family, I think it's time you remedy the Ava situation."

She stiffened and attempted to cover it, but little escaped his notice.

"Is there a problem?" he asked.

"No." She cleared her throat and shook her head. "Of course not, Father. What do you want me to do?"

"Your sister is quite stubborn," he said, a little fondly. "I'd underestimated what would be necessary to persuade her to join our cause."

"It wasn't your fault. It was mine."

Elias waved a hand, feeling generous. "That is neither here nor there. It's in the past, and it's time to focus on the future. *Our* future." He reached across the table to pat his daughter's hand. "And you're—" His phone buzzed, bouncing slightly on the table, and he frowned at the name on the screen.

He knows better.

Holding up a finger toward his daughter, Elias answered the call. "What is it?"

"The cryo is gone."

"Sophie?" The name came out in a near-growl, and he watched Emma freeze, her latte halfway to her lips. "What do you mean she's gone?"

"House was empty," Sloan Bartok said, obviously just as frustrated as Elias. He didn't handle failure well. "We missed her by an hour. Maybe two."

"What do you mean, you missed her? How could you miss her?"

"She wasn't at her last known address. She'd moved twice, and it took some time—"

Elias cursed, his fingers digging into the edge of the table. "Who has her? The Council?"

"Protectors were there when we arrived, but they didn't have her."

"Did they see you?"

"With all due respect, you know me better than that."

True.

Bartok was nothing if not careful, and his training made him especially difficult to detect.

"So Guardians, then," Elias said, half to himself.

Bartok murmured agreement. "There's more."

"Oh, let me guess. Foster."

"And your little girl. Well, your *other* little girl," Bartok replied.

"Ava?"

"She was all over the place."

"Interesting." Elias pursed his lips, thinking about that. "I didn't think they let her leave the Colony."

Bartok didn't reply. He tended not to, when the answers were obvious. Instead, he asked, "What now?"

Elias considered his next move, mind racing as the pieces fell into place. "We'll need to move up the timetable. Obviously, my children are not as secure as I'd hoped." He reached across the table to run a finger down Emma's cheek. "Go after the boy, as planned."

"Are we going to move against the Colony?" Bartok asked.

Elias scoffed. "Wasted effort. The Guardians pose no threat to our plans."

"What about Ava?"

Elias eyed his daughter across the table. "Oh, I have a plan for Ava," he said. "If she doesn't come of her own free will, she'll have to be convinced."

"How do you plan to do that?"

"Easy enough," Elias replied. "Hit her close to home."

CHAPTER FOUR

Outside a nondescript brick building housing a nondescript high school in a nondescript town in the middle of nowhere, North Dakota, Tiernan Ross leaned against a scraggly elm tree and cursed his life.

He could have done anything, really—moved to Europe, spent some time on a quiet beach, and ignored anything and everything that stank of politics and power plays and the ridiculous mess he'd gotten himself involved in.

Katherine had said he was getting soft, and although he'd greeted the statement with his trademark glower, deep down he had feared she was right. He felt a strange sense of responsibility to the band of outlaws hiding out in the Canadian wilderness, and to the girl who pushed all his buttons, but still managed to get under his skin.

Tiernan let out a heavy sigh and checked his watch again. School would be out in three minutes.

Finally.

It had been almost a month, and he didn't know what he had been thinking, offering to be an ambassador to the Council on behalf of the Guardians. It was a delicate proposition, and Tiernan, as a rule, didn't do delicate. Still, he'd been meeting with Council leaders, first Rafe and Naomi, to help ease the way, then Kaeden, for what good it did him. It was slow going, and Tiernan was going insane with the waiting, so he'd taken an assignment, in no small part to get on Madeleine's good side, as Kaeden had suggested, which was what led to standing outside a high school, cooling his heels, and waiting for a Half-Breed. It was strange. A few months ago, it would have been business as usual, but now . . .

A feeling of unease combined with a strange twist in his stomach he couldn't identify left him antsy and riddled with—

Okay, maybe I can identify it. Guilt. It's guilt.

Tiernan, as a rule, didn't do guilt either.

He'd been fine—doing his duty, living his life—until Ava came along and started to break down the walls that kept out irritating things like guilt and compassion and . . .

Well—

The bell rang, driving away the unsettling thoughts, and Tiernan straightened, eyes zeroing in on the door of the school and the blue Honda he'd already identified as belonging to one Isaiah Bennett.

He scanned the uniformed teenagers streaming out of the building for the face he'd committed to memory from a series of recon images he'd received earlier.

Tall, thin, dark-skinned with hair trimmed close to his scalp . . . there.

Of course, it was the middle of the afternoon, so he couldn't just grab the kid and make a run for it. Instead, Tiernan started the motorcycle he'd liberated from a Walmart parking lot in Bismarck and waited as Isaiah waved to his friends and tossed his backpack into the car before climbing in. He knew where the boy lived but tailed him anyway, hoping for a detour along the way that would make it easier to apprehend him.

Take him. Kidnap him.

Tiernan's jaw clenched, and his fists tightened on the handlebars, the motorcycle engine revving in protest. He took a deep breath to steady his nerves.

It's just an assignment. Another job. Grab the kid. Take him to the Council. Let them deal with the rest. Like dozens before.

It was all part of maintaining the peace. Rafe had said it would be a show of goodwill to the Council.

Tiernan wasn't convinced.

The Half-Breed—Isaiah—pulled into the driveway of his suburban home, and Tiernan let the bike slow to a stop across the street.

The neighborhood was quiet, but not empty. The hum of a lawnmower two doors down mingled with the swish of a woman sweeping her porch at the end of the block and the incessant yapping of a small dog that Tiernan couldn't quite pinpoint.

Isaiah hitched his backpack up onto his shoulder and turned to walk toward the road.

Toward Tiernan.

"Crap." He yanked the phone from his pocket and looked down at it as though he was texting, or GPS-ing, or something other than stalking a teenage boy. He almost dropped it when it buzzed in his hand with an incoming call.

Gideon.

He debated answering, casting a quick glance toward Isaiah. The boy was looking directly at him, so he took the plunge and hit the call button, hoping it would be make him a little less conspicuous. "Yeah?"

"Any progress?"

Tiernan feigned interest in the sky, watching the boy out of the corner of his eye and only letting out a relieved breath when Isaiah turned to check the mailbox at the end of the drive.

"Everything okay?" Gideon prompted.

"Yeah. Yeah," Tiernan replied. "Sorry. Kind of in the middle of something here."

Isaiah tucked the mail into the crook of his arm and walked back to the house.

A little of Tiernan's tension eased. "What about there? How's the relocation going?"

Gideon sighed. "It's taking some time to find the right places," he said. "We're splitting up the group, placing them in different safe houses, all relatively close to New Elysia so it's easier for them to move once the Council gives the go-ahead." There was a heavy silence. "They *are* going to give the go-ahead, right?"

This time it was Tiernan's turn to sigh. "I'm working on it. You know how politicians are."

"Yeah, that I do." Gideon chuckled. "There's been another development you probably should know about."

"Yeah?"

"Caleb and Ava rescued a woman before Protectors could get there," he said. "We thought she was a Half-Breed. Turns out, we were wrong."

Tiernan stiffened and kicked his boot against the motorcycle tire. "You're kidding."

"Yeah. Ava's got another sister."

A low growl escaped from deep in Tiernan's throat before he could stop it. "Do you have her locked up?"

"She's not a prisoner, Tiernan. She's given us no reason to distrust her."

"Yeah, well, that's what we thought about Ava's *other* sister," Tiernan snapped, still a little—

Okay, more than a little.

He was still incredibly angry that he hadn't acted on his suspicions when it came to Emma. "Do I have to remind you of how *that* turned out?"

"No. You don't," Gideon said curtly. "But we can't penalize Sophie for what Emma's done. They're two different people, and as far as we can tell, she's had no contact with Borré or any of the Rogues. She only came into her powers a f—"

"What powers?"

"Nothing that can influence others," Gideon assured him. "She's a cryo. Seems to be her only ability, at this point. Although, we'll know more once her block is fully lifted."

"Who's going to do that?"

"Not sure yet," Gideon admitted. "We don't have anyone with the necessary skills here. I think we might have to wait until we get to New Elysia." He took a deep breath. "Ava's fighting us on it."

At least someone at the Colony has some sense.

"Maybe you should listen to her."

"That's beside the point."

"Well, what *is* the point?" Tiernan growled, glancing toward the house again, irritated with the entire subject. He had things to do. Places to be. Alliances to negotiate.

"The point is Sophie told us she has a brother."

Tiernan stilled. "Brother? You don't mean . . . "

"Yeah, I do. Biological brother. They were in the foster system but were separated when the boy was adopted."

Tiernan cursed.

Gideon echoed the sentiment.

"So does the Council know?"

"About the boy? I don't know," Gideon replied. "But I'm willing to bet that Borré knows we have Sophie by now, so we need to get to Isaiah before the Rogues do."

Tiernan froze, the weight of expectation heavy in his chest. "Isaiah?"

"Sophie's brother."

It was too much of a coincidence, and Tiernan didn't believe in coincidences. "I don't think the Rogues are who you need to worry about."

"What are you talking about?"

"The kid," Tiernan said. "Is his last name Bennett?" He heard nothing but the sound of soft inhales for several beats, and then the almost whispered question.

"The Council knows about him?"

"I'm standing outside his house right now."

Gideon's tone turned icy. "And why would that be? I thought—"

"I'm greasing the wheels with the Council," Tiernan said, kicking the tire again as if it were the wheel in question. "Like I was supposed to. I'm trying to clear the way, but I'm no damned politician. I have to work with what I've got."

"So you're going to turn a kid over to them? You know w—"

"No, I'm not!" Tiernan shouted as he kicked his bike a little too hard and had to reach out to steady it. He took a deep breath to calm himself and spoke in a quiet, steady voice. "I'm not, but he'll need a safe place."

"I can get you one," Gideon said quickly.

Tiernan scrubbed a hand over his shaved head. "The Council's not going to be happy that I let him slip through my fingers."

"You sure you know what you're doing?"

Tiernan laughed. "No. You?"

He heard Gideon chuckle. "Not really, but one thing at a time. Get the kid, and I'll get you the location of a safe house. You have to keep him out of the Council's hands. At least until we get them on our side."

"I'm still not convinced that's going to happen."

"Yeah, well. Hate to say it, but that's on you, too. At least for now."

No pressure.

"Thanks." Tiernan glanced up and down the quiet street—even the lawn mower and the yappy dog had gone silent. "I'll call you when I have him," he said, jogging toward the house as he hung up the phone and stuffed it in his pocket.

He would have preferred to wait for dark, but with this new development, he didn't have the luxury.

He just hoped Isaiah Bennett wasn't a screamer.

Ava wasn't sure what exactly led her out to the playground so late that evening. The moon was full, lighting the path as her breath frosted before her. A cold blast forced her to huddle deeper into her winter coat, cramming her gloved hands in the pockets.

The Colony grounds were all but deserted, everyone escaping the chill either in their own quarters or in the common room, laughing over hot chocolate and board games. Some had already left the Colony altogether, headed for safe houses picked out by Gideon personally. The rest would be moved within a week or two. After that, it was on to New Elysia, if everything went as planned. If everything went as they hoped. Nobody talked about what would happen if the Council refused them. They knew there really wasn't any other option.

Ava rounded a corner and was surprised by exactly how unsurprised she was to see a familiar figure on the swings, her feet dragging along the ground. Perhaps Ava had finally become accustomed to her Race intuition, or maybe she knew how Sophie was feeling. Ava had spent a lot of time on that same swing considering her life and her options. To find her half sister doing the same thing spoke to either the power of genetics or the simple draw of childhood comforts when dealing with adult problems.

Nothing beats a swing for clear thinking.

Sophie looked up as Ava took the swing next to her, watching as she pushed with her feet to twist the chain over her head.

"How are you doing?" Ava asked.

Sophie sighed. "Well, that . . . that's a question."

Ava laughed as she picked up her feet and let the swing spin one way, then the other, before bouncing to a jerky stop. "It's a lot to take in. I know."

"How did you deal with it?"

Ava smiled and shrugged. "Not well, to be honest."

"I just . . . I've gone through my whole life knowing who I am—who I *thought* I was. Even if that person wasn't perfect. Even if that life wasn't perfect. And now . . ."

Ava pushed off the ground and started to swing. "And now you feel like you don't know who you are. You don't even feel like you're in control of your own life. Like you're some pawn in this global chess game and somebody else is running the board."

"Yes!" Sophie exclaimed, shoving with her feet and leaning back as she matched Ava's rhythm. "It's frustrating. Disconcerting."

"Terrifying."

Sophie didn't respond, dropping her gaze to the ground.

They glided back and forth for a while with nothing but echoing squeaks from the swings' chains and the sweep of their feet on the gravel breaking the silence.

"I'm not even sure what I'm supposed to do," Sophie said finally, her voice almost a whisper.

"What do you want to do?"

Sophie's gaze sharpened. "Like I have a choice!"

"Of course you have a choice." Ava planted her feet and faced her sister, a kind of indignant rage simmering up her spine. "Nobody is going to make you do anything," she said. "*You* are in charge here. This is *your* life. It doesn't matter who your father is or where you came from. Borré may have mixed up some crap in a petri dish, but that is not *you.*"

Sophie straightened, her chin lifting. "And if I decide to go home? To pretend all this never happened?"

Ava sighed. "Well, you have that option." She shrugged.

"But this Council will find me eventually. Or the Rogues."

"Most likely." Sophie's despondency and confusion raced across their link, and Ava hastened to reassure her. "Right now, right here, you're safe."

"It's not all about *me.*"

"They'll find Isaiah. He'll be okay."

"And then what?" Sophie's eyes sparkled with unshed tears in the moonlight. "What will we do?"

Ava reached out and took Sophie's hand, feeling her power in the touch. "You'll decide if you want to ask Gideon to protect you. He'll keep you and Isaiah together in a safe house and then, hopefully, if we get this alliance with the Council, you'll be able to stay in New Elysia until this is all over."

Sophie clenched her jaw. "Or?"

"Or." Ava squeezed her hand and released it. "Or you fight. You come with us when we try to take down Borré and the Rogues. We'll need all the help we can get."

Sophie nodded and swiped at her eyes. "I don't like the idea of hiding, but I need to protect my brother."

"He'll be safe. No matter what you decide, he'll be safe. You can trust these people."

Sophie took in a deep breath and let it out slowly. "Well, first things first, right? What can you tell me about this block?"

Ava frowned, remembering the moment Emma lifted her block in this very same spot—the feeling of power. Of freedom.

Before it all went so wrong.

"Gideon says we'll need to find someone to lift it the rest of the way. Hopefully, there will be someone in New Elysia."

"Does it hurt?"

Ava swallowed, unsure if she should tell her sister the whole story. "Not really. Not when it's lifted."

Sophie raised a brow. "But?"

Ava chewed on her lip, debating. "I need to tell you this. You need to know what you're getting into. But I have to ask—this has to stay between us, at least for now, okay?"

Sophie half laughed. "Who am I going to tell?"

"Just . . . nobody can know. Not even Caleb. Not yet."

Sophie's eyes were dark in the dim light of the moon, and Ava couldn't even see the hazel gold that matched her own. But they were earnest, honest, when Sophie said, "All right."

Ava cleared her throat, unsure where to start. "Since the block's been lifted, I'm able to do . . . a lot. A lot more than before. It freed up all my Race gifts, and they're, well, not to toot my own horn, but they're pretty incredible." She grinned, and Sophie returned the gesture. "But there's something wrong, too."

Sophie sobered. "What do you mean?"

"I'm not sure why exactly, but I get these headaches . . . nosebleeds. It's only when I push myself, use my gifts too much, for the most part. Although, lately, it seems to be getting worse."

"And you think . . . you think the same thing will happen to me?"

"I don't know. Not really," Ava replied. "But Emma said—she told me that Borré could stop it. That it happened to the others, but he could help."

"The others. You mean the others like us?"

Ava nodded. "I don't know how, and I don't know why. I haven't told anybody what Emma said. Only Talia, the Guardian healer, knows how bad my symptoms have gotten. She's been helping me manage them."

"But you said Gideon is trustworthy. Shouldn't you tell him? Maybe he could—"

"No. He can't." Ava yanked herself to her feet and kicked at the gravel.

"He's already said whatever's happening to me is beyond what they can deal with here. My only hope for answers is in New Elysia. Their medical facilities are better. They have doctors there who might be able to figure things out."

"And if they can't?" Sophie watched her intently, obviously expecting the answer.

"Then the only one who can help me—help *us*, possibly—is Elias Borré," she said. "So, in more ways than one, it looks like we're in this together."

CHAPTER FIVE

"Focus on the leaf. See each rib, each vein." Audrey's soothing familiar voice lulled Ava as she guided Sophie through the training exercise. It wasn't long ago that Ava had done the same thing, although sometimes it seemed as though it had been another lifetime.

Everything in the Colony was sparse and efficient, and the living quarters were no exception. Ava sat at the kitchen table of the small eat-in off Audrey's humble living room, quietly observing. Caleb had disappeared before dawn, so she'd agreed to go with Sophie, not only to distract herself from wondering where he was but also for moral support. Ava seemed to be failing at that, however, as Sophie threw her hands up after only a few minutes.

"It's not working. I don't see anything. Just a stupid leaf." She tossed the offending flora onto the table to emphasize the point.

"It didn't work for me either, at first," Ava said. "You have to be patient."

The room chilled, and Ava tucked her hands up into the sleeves of her sweater. "You need to get a handle on that, too, by the way," she said with a wry twist of her lips.

Sophie took a deep breath, closed her eyes for a moment, and the cold dissipated. "Sorry."

"Don't apologize," Ava replied, reaching out to touch her arm briefly. "Your control's getting better already."

"She's right," Audrey said with an encouraging smile. "Pyros and cryos typically have more difficulty with their gifts since they are so closely tied to their emotional state. You're really doing very well."

"But that's it." Sophie sat back in her chair and picked up the leaf, twirling it in her fingers. "I have my freeze ray, or whatever, but nothing else that you say I should have. No super senses or speed or strength. I'm just a human air conditioner."

"For *now*," Ava said. "Once the block is lifted—"

"*If* the block is lifted," Sophie interjected.

"If the block is lifted," Ava relented. "You'll probably get it all. Like me."

They exchanged a significant look, both realizing exactly what that entailed.

"Perhaps we should set this aside for a bit," Audrey said, tucking a strand of red hair behind her ear. "You're making progress with your cryokinetic ability, so maybe we should focus on that." She stood up and motioned toward the door. "Not in here, though. I'd prefer to keep any snowstorms out of doors, if you please."

Sophie rolled her eyes but the tension in her shoulders eased, and the three of them grabbed their coats and made their way outside toward the training field.

The field had been cleared of blocks and cones—even the obstacle course had been dismantled in anticipation of the Colony move. The damage Ava had wrought when she'd first unveiled her power had been cleaned up for the most part, the fence repaired and grass starting to grow over the cracks in the ground, but she still felt a wave of guilt when she walked through the gate.

Audrey seemed to sense her discontent and reached out to squeeze her hand. "No point living in the past," she said quietly as they reached the center of the field, and she turned her attention to Sophie. "All right, your gift seems to be threefold. You can affect the temperature around you. You can apparently condense the moisture in the air, creating miniature snowstorms, for lack of a better word."

"Don't forget the ice balls," Ava said, grinning at Sophie. "Those are pretty awesome, you know, when they're not flying at your head."

Sophie laughed, deep and loud. "Well, that's more of a reflex, actually."

"And that's what we need to work on," Audrey said. "I've only worked with a couple of cryos, but like most Race gifts, it comes down to focus."

"Like the leaf?" Sophie asked skeptically.

"Yes, like the leaf. Don't look at me like that." Audrey clapped her hands together once. "Let's start small. Adjusting the temperature right around you, perhaps?"

"Just like that," Sophie muttered.

Ava laughed. "You sound like me. It sounds harder than it actually is. You have to become familiar with your gift, learn to recognize it. You should feel it inside you. Mine's kind of like a tingle."

"Yeah," Sophie said slowly. "I think I know what you mean."

"Try to feel it." Ava took her hand. "I'm going to use my gift to try to help you. Close your eyes and take a few deep breaths. Try to be calm. Your gift wants to work for you. So try to just . . . let it."

It took a while, but Sophie was finally able to lower and raise the temperature around them with more control and even create a light snowfall.

Sophie's power stirred under Ava's fingers—different than her own, or even Emma's—and she began to understand the uniqueness of each person's Race signature.

They tried for the ice balls, but seemed to hit a wall.

"Maybe we're going at this wrong," Audrey said, rubbing at her chin. "I want you to think back. How do you feel when you create these ice balls?"

Sophie's eyes narrowed as she concentrated. "Panicked. Afraid. Kind of . . . I don't know . . . trapped?"

"Like you'd run away if you could?"

"Yes." Her eyes lit up. "It only happens when I can't. Run away, I mean. Like when Caleb and Ava came for me. I knew I couldn't run or they'd catch me, but I couldn't get to my car in the garage."

"So you fought back the only way you knew how." Audrey nodded, a small smile on her face. "It makes sense. Your gift was simply trying to protect you, even if you didn't do it consciously."

Sophie deflated. "So how do I do it consciously, then? It's not like I can make myself feel threatened if I'm not."

Ava held out her hand and reached for her gift. In a moment, an apple formed, shimmering into existence in her palm. She smiled at Sophie's sharp inhale and tossed the apple to her.

She fumbled with it a moment before examining it closely. "It looks real," Sophie murmured.

"It *is* real," Ava said. "If I'm understanding this right, what I do and what you do really aren't that different." She looked to Audrey for confirmation, and the older woman nodded in encouragement.

Ava reached for the apple and it disappeared, the molecules transforming back into thin air. "You need to picture in your mind what you want to happen," she said. "See the ice forming around you. Visualize it flying toward your target."

Sophie closed her eyes and tried, but nothing happened. "I don't know what I'm doing," she admitted. "It's different, somehow. I can't seem to make it happen."

"It might be the block." Audrey rubbed her bottom lip as if she were considering all the possibilities.

Ava stared at Sophie, gaining her focus once more with a long, slow exhale, turned, and strode away, whirling back to face her when she was halfway across the field. She eyed a soccer ball tucked in a box next to the shed and reached for her gift.

The ball flew across the yard and into Sophie's stomach.

"Hey!" she shouted, clutching at her belly.

"If you can't access it any other way, we'll have to work with what you've got," Ava shouted back. "Try not to think about it too hard." She picked up the ball again, drew it back toward herself, and let it fly at Sophie once again.

The other girl ducked, and the ball flew past her to bounce on the grass.

Audrey moved to the side to watch. "It's a reflex," she told Sophie. "You said it yourself. So let it happen." She turned to Ava. "I think you need more of a threat."

Ava grinned and used her gift to pull a few more balls from the box. The soccer ball joined the group, whirling around Ava in a wide circle. "I'm going to send them your way," she told Sophie. "You ready?"

Sophie squared her shoulders. "Ready."

"Don't overdo it," Audrey warned.

Ava waved her off with a grin.

It wasn't pretty.

Ava started off slow, lobbing balls toward Sophie and hitting her about half the time. At Audrey's insistence, she increased the pace and the impact, but Sophie simply dodged the balls, or got hit by them.

Finally, Audrey huffed in frustration and went to stand behind the girl, pinning her arms to her side with her Race strength. "Don't fight it. Now there's nothing you can do to avoid the hit, so you either need to take it, or fight it off."

Sophie gritted her teeth, and the air chilled as she lifted the balls once again. She tossed the soccer ball and laughed when a gust of heavy wind blew it off course.

"That's it!" Audrey exclaimed, tucking her face behind Sophie's back to protect it. "A little harder, Ava!"

Ava followed instructions, and this time, the gust came right toward her, shoving her back a step. She shivered at the icy wind but couldn't keep the smile off her face. "Try to focus it on the balls, okay? I don't want frostbite!"

Sophie laughed but seemed to take the advice in stride.

When the gust focused into a spray of icy fog followed by a piece of marble-sized hail, the little group erupted in cheers.

Sophie collapsed onto the grass. "I'm exhausted. How do you guys keep doing this?"

"It gets easier with time," Audrey said.

"And as you get more familiar with your gift. Not to mention when the block—" Ava jolted, her whole body spinning toward the gate as she felt Caleb approach. Not only Caleb . . . Tiernan, too, and Gideon, and someone . . . else. Someone unfamiliar.

So close and I didn't even notice.

The thought left her oddly unsettled.

"What is it?" Sophie got to her feet and moved to Ava's side, watching carefully until the gate creaked open and drew her attention.

Caleb, Tiernan, and Gideon filed in, along with a teenage boy—tall, black, and gangly—who seemed somehow familiar. Ava wasn't certain if it was his appearance or his gift that sparked recognition deep within her.

Sophie gasped. "Isaiah?"

She ran across the field, and the boy's eyes widened as his step faltered before he dashed toward her. They met in the middle and embraced, a chorus of, "What are you doing here?" and "Are you okay?" filling the air.

"Isaiah?" Audrey whispered.

"Sophie's brother," Ava replied, unable to pull her eyes from the tearful reunion. "*My* brother."

Audrey took her hand and squeezed it gently as they walked toward the little group.

Ava eyed Tiernan and Caleb. "I take it this is where you disappeared to?"

Caleb leaned down to kiss her, his palm warm on the back of her neck.

"Sorry. It was before dawn, and Gideon was worried Tiernan might need my help."

"I had everything under control," Tiernan grumbled.

"Just a precaution." Gideon's response left no room for argument.

It didn't keep Tiernan from glaring at him, however.

"So what's going on here?" the Guardian leader asked, clearly ignoring the look.

"We're working with Sophie, trying to help her hone her gift," Audrey replied.

"And?"

"It's going well, actually," she said. "Only the cryokinesis right now, but she seems to be gaining some control."

"Really?" Gideon glanced at Sophie. "Do you think I could see? I haven't seen a cryo in action for more than twenty years."

Ava eyed her sister and saw how tightly she clung to her brother's hand. "Maybe this can wait."

"No, it's fine," Sophie said quickly. "Now that I know Isaiah's safe, I need to make sure he stays that way. I need to be able to protect him—both of us."

"Hey!" Isaiah elbowed her. "I can take care of myself."

"Hush, now," she said with a smile, and his returning grin showed it was a frequent admonishment in the past. "Watch this. You're going to love it."

Isaiah looked a bit confused, but the smile didn't leave his face as his sister turned to Audrey expectantly.

"You ready?" she asked.

Audrey frowned for a moment. "Perhaps Isaiah would be a better choice," she said, eyeing the boy. "If you're protecting him, it might even be more motivation."

Sophie looked her brother over from head to toe, took his hand, and led him to the center of the field.

"What's going on?" His voice cracked, and he cleared his throat nervously.

"You'll see," she replied, pulling him behind her. "Just stay there, okay?"

He obeyed but kept a hand firmly in hers, peering over her shoulder toward Ava, who'd taken her place down the field.

She heard him gasp when the balls flew up to circle around her, but she kept her focus on Sophie. Ava could feel her sister's power, even across the field, and something . . . different.

Without warning, Ava shot the balls across the field at high speed, one after another.

Sophie let out a distressed squeal of sorts, and to Ava's surprise, an ice ball the size of a baseball knocked the first rubber ball out of the way and flew toward her.

Ava reached for her gift to deflect it, the other balls falling harmlessly to the ground as she lost focus, and the ice ball shattered three feet before her, showering her with icy spray.

A heavy silence fell over the field, broken a few seconds later by Gideon's booming laugh. "I think that's more than a *little* control!" he exclaimed.

It took a moment for Ava to catch her breath. "That's the first time she's been able to do it."

The group converged on the middle of the field, all eyes turned on Sophie, speculative and more than a little impressed.

"The threat to Isaiah, you think?" Gideon asked Audrey.

"Perhaps. Not really much of a threat, though."

Ava snorted. "I'm not going to throw rocks at her."

"Thanks," Sophie said wryly.

"Maybe more of the block fell," Caleb offered.

"Maybe," Gideon replied, darting his gaze back and forth between Sophie and her brother still huddled behind her and clutching her hand.

Without thinking, Ava laid her own had over their joined ones. She gasped at the feeling of power that shot up her arm and yanked it away as though she'd been shocked.

"What is it?" Caleb reached for her, half pulling her behind him.

"It's . . . I'm not sure." Ava took a step forward, drawn by some compulsion she didn't really understand. When Caleb stiffened, she tore her eyes away to look up at him. "It's okay."

Caleb didn't release her, his gaze flashing to Gideon. "What's happening?"

Ava knew he was remembering the last time, and she could imagine his frustration when she was under Emma's influence. His fear when she was no longer herself.

This is something else entirely.

"It's okay," she said in a firmer voice, taking his face between her hands. "I'm here. I'm okay. I promise."

Caleb looked into her eyes, and she felt his gift pushing, testing, almost probing, before it withdrew, and he nodded.

Ava smiled and reached out to touch Sophie's hand again. She expected the jolt this time—the surge of power that raced up her arm and through her body. Still, she gasped, her mouth dropping open a little at the sensation.

Sophie watched her with wide eyes.

"Do you feel that?" Ava whispered.

"I feel . . . something," she replied. "More than before."

"Ha!"

That's an understatement.

Ava turned to Isaiah. "Do you feel anything?"

The boy shrugged. "I don't know. I don't understand what's happening. I don't understand any of this."

Ava reached for Caleb, drawing him forward and laying his hand atop theirs. "Do you?"

Caleb closed his eyes for a moment then looked at her with a slight frown. "I feel you. And faintly, what I assume is Sophie. That's it."

Ava pulled away, shaking her hand a little and flexing her fingers. "I think I know where Sophie's sudden control came from."

"A link," Gideon murmured. "A link between the Twelve."

She nodded.

Tiernan grunted. "Anybody care to translate for those of us who have no idea what's going on?"

Isaiah giggled, and the bigger man smirked at him.

"It appears Elias Borré created some kind of link between the Twelve," Gideon said. "A link that can boost their power."

"A boost?" Tiernan eyed Ava warily. "How much of a boost?"

"I'm not sure," she replied. "I've felt it with Caleb before, but not as strong as this."

"It's not uncommon for bonded couples to share a link to varying degrees," Gideon explained. "It doesn't always happen, but it makes sense with your superior abilities that Caleb's power could strengthen your own."

"I've never heard of such a thing outside of bonded couples, though," Audrey said.

"I felt it with Emma, too," Ava replied slowly. "I didn't realize it was out of the ordinary at the time. I mean, I've felt other people's gifts before, but . . ." She was lost in memories of a forest clearing and Emma's encouraging voice.

"Don't you feel it? The power coursing through you? It wants you to

push it. It wants to do it."

"I thought it was part of her compulsion," Ava said finally. "But there was more to it. She was using the link. She didn't even have to touch me."

Caleb frowned, and Ava knew he was lost in the same troubling memories. "That's why you were so strong."

"I think that was part of it, at least."

"So let me get this straight," Tiernan said, rubbing a hand over his shaved head. "Not only did Borré create a Race hit squad, for want of a better word, but he made it so that when you're all together, you're even *more* powerful?"

No one said anything as the weight of it settled around them.

"Well, that's perfect," he all but growled. "How are we supposed to fight that?"

Gideon let out a heavy breath. "You forget we have three of the Twelve right here," he said.

"Hardly!" Tiernan threw up his hands then pointed at Sophie. "She's still partially blocked, and the boy has no power at all." He glanced at Isaiah. "No offense."

"None taken."

"If he's one of the Twelve, he's got power," Gideon said.

Sophie looked outraged. "*If?*"

"Borré could have lied," Ava explained. "Isaiah's Race, I can feel that, but it might not come from Borré. We have to test him to know for sure."

"There's no need," Sophie said, lifting her chin. "He's my brother. The rest doesn't matter. He's not getting involved."

"Agreed," Tiernan said with a nod, crossing his arms over his chest.

"If he's one of the Twelve, we're going to need him," Gideon replied, frowning. "We'll help Sophie and Isaiah hone their gifts—"

"Oh, no." Sophie pulled her brother closer, and the air chilled around them. "Me, fine. But not Isaiah. I want him somewhere safe."

"But if I can help—"

"Hush. You're just a kid. You d—"

"I'm sixteen!"

"Isaiah!"

"Hold on a second," Gideon said, raising his hands. "I think we need to take this one step at a time."

"I agree." Audrey stepped forward to touch Sophie's shoulder. "I think maybe Isaiah could use something to eat. We all could," she said with a pointed look that encompassed the rest of the group. "Let's take some time and get to know each other a bit, shall we? There's time enough for all this later."

Sophie nodded, but her shoulders remained tense, her hand still clutched tightly to her brother's.

Ava knew this fight was far from over. The testing would need to be done, but Ava already knew the truth. Isaiah was one of the Twelve. As soon as she'd felt that surge of power, she'd known the truth.

They made their way back to the common room where conversation was forced and stilted as they talked about anything but the Rogue threat and their newest recruits.

Caleb took her hand as they lagged behind the others. "You okay?"

She nodded. "A bit overwhelmed, I guess."

He smiled and leaned down to brush his lips over her ear.

She shivered.

"I love you," he whispered.

To Ava, those simple words were a promise, a gift of strength and reassurance that, no matter what happened, Caleb would be at her side. Guilt poked at her, reminding her of what she'd been keeping from him, but she quickly pushed that aside. If she was going to be there for *him*, to have his back, she had to.

"I love you, too," she replied.

CHAPTER SIX

Lunch was a tense affair with Sophie and Isaiah making excuses to sit at a table of their own under the guise of catching up with each other. They eyed the rest of the group periodically and spoke in low tones even though everybody else could hear them.

Caleb tried not to listen in and focused on his chili and corn bread and Ava sitting next to him. It calmed him having her near, although he knew she was holding back. Keeping something from him. Ava wasn't the only one with instincts, after all.

He knew it was a lot to take in—the appearance of another sister and now a brother—and the realization that they were all connected more closely than any of them had realized.

Caleb watched her out of the corner of his eye as she stirred her chili absently, lost in thought.

She pushed away her bowl. "So how did it go in New Elysia?" Ava asked Tiernan. She caught the look he exchanged with Gideon. "I guess everybody else knows already?"

Tiernan shrugged. "About as well as could be expected. In the end, it came down to Madeleine, and on my way here, I got the word she's agreed to speak to a Guardian contingent."

"What about the others?"

"It all depends on how things go with this initial meeting," Tiernan replied. "I think the rest of the Council will follow her lead, so it's up to us to convince her that an alliance is the only option. Of course, she doesn't know yet that I snatched Isaiah and ran."

"How do you plan to deal with that?" Ava asked.

"I told her the Guardians beat me to him," he replied. "She wasn't happy about it, but she gave me the go-ahead to come here and negotiate."

"So." Ava eyed Gideon briefly. "Who's in this contingent?"

"The four of us—you, me, Tiernan, and Caleb," the Guardian leader replied before turning to his left. "Audrey, I'll need you and Tyra to go with the rest of the refugees. Keep things under control."

"Of course."

Gideon cleared his throat. "I think it's wise to allow Sophie and Isaiah to remain with the refugees, at least for now. We can take a sample of their DNA to the Council doctors for testing."

Ava winced. "Sophie isn't going to like that."

"Madeleine wants them both in New Elysia," Tiernan said. "This is as much of a compromise as you're going to get at this point."

Gideon shrugged. "She wants as much information on the Twelve as she can get. It's what I would do in her position."

Caleb wondered if anyone else sensed that his indifference was a show. He expected so.

"It's all so ridiculous," Ava said, crumbling a piece of corn bread between her fingers. "We all need to work together on this. It's the only way."

"Madeleine will come around," Gideon reassured her, not for the first time. "In any case, the first step is DNA testing to find out if the boy really is your brother. If he is, it's a matter of removing his block as well, and we need the Council's resources for that."

"Do you sense a gift in him?" Caleb asked. His father had a strong skill for detection, but the block sometimes made it difficult, as it had in Ava's case.

Gideon shook his head. "I can't be sure. I think there's something there, but if his block is at full strength, it would make sense that I couldn't get through it." He turned to Ava. "What do you think?"

Ava chewed on her lip, frowning slightly and staring at the table as though the answers were carved into the top. "I think he's Race, and I think he's my brother."

Gideon nodded, unsurprised. "Well, the testing will validate that, although my gut tells me to trust your instincts on this one." He pushed away his bowl and wiped his mouth with a napkin. "Audrey, maybe you could show Isaiah to quarters close to his sister. Maybe ease the way a little?"

"I'll go with you," Tiernan said, getting to his feet as Audrey rose. At her raised brow, he shrugged and sniffed. "What? The boy doesn't know you. He seems to trust me, for whatever misplaced reason."

Ava snickered. "You're not as scary as you pretend to be, you know."

Tiernan looked insulted, but he turned on his heel and headed toward Sophie and Isaiah's table, Audrey in his wake.

"You two should get ready to go as well," Gideon said. "I want to leave for New Elysia as soon as we get confirmation on Isaiah."

"I'm all but packed," Ava said, distracted as she watched Sophie and Isaiah leave with Audrey and Tiernan. "But I was going to stop by and see Talia. Someone should probably let her know what's going on, anyway." She stood to leave, eyes widening a little when Caleb stood as well.

"Thought I'd keep you company." He couldn't explain the flush on her cheeks or the nervous twitch of her fingers. "Is something wrong?" he asked.

"No," she said quickly with the flash of a smile as she took his hand. "Of course not. Let's go."

They walked through the compound, dappled sunlight breaking through the trees and warming the air.

Ava was quiet, but she leaned into him, her free hand gripping gently at his elbow.

"Are you going to tell me what's bothering you?" Caleb asked.

"Me? Nothing. I'm fine."

"Come on, Ava. You know that's not true."

She sighed, looking off into the distance. "I don't know. It all feels so real now, I guess. Being here . . ."

"Feels safe," he finished quietly.

"Yeah."

"They won't do anything to you. My mother has her faults, but she'd never go back on her word."

"I'm not worried about that." Ava waved her hand dismissively. "I can't explain it, but I feel like it's all coming to a head, you know? And faster than we expected."

"You think Borré will act soon?"

Ava frowned and gave a frustrated shake of her head. "I don't know. Not really. It's just a feeling I have that we need to be ready."

"Maybe Borré put a countdown clock in you all as well." Caleb was half joking, but Ava didn't laugh.

"Maybe." She slowed as they reached Talia's quarters. "We need Sophie and Isaiah on our side, though. We need to find any others and get to them before Borré can."

"That's not going to be easy," Caleb replied. "Finding Sophie and Isaiah was pure luck."

Ava frowned. "There has to be a way . . ." She started toward the door and stopped abruptly. "You told me once that the Council keeps track of medical records, looking for Half-Breeds, right?"

"Right. They monitor a lot of things. The signs can be anywhere."

She nodded and released his hand, pacing for a moment as she thought. "If there's a DNA link between the Twelve, wouldn't they be able to target that?"

"Maybe. If they knew what they were looking for."

"So it's a possibility?"

"I would think so. But who knows how long that would take?"

"Well, we've got to try something," Ava said, throwing her hands up. "All this advanced technology has to be good for *something*. If we can find even one or two—"

"I hear what you're saying." Caleb rubbed her upper arms, and her tension eased, her muscles relaxing under his touch. "If the Council agrees to work with us, we can try at least."

Ava let out a sigh and moved closer, burrowing into his coat, her cheek against his chest.

Caleb held her tight, her presence filling him with peace. The bond was growing stronger between them every day. It was something that both thrilled and frightened him.

"Is there more?" he asked.

She pulled back and looked up at him. "What?"

"Is that all that's wrong?" he asked. "You know you can tell me anything."

Ava opened her mouth as if she was going to say something but shut it quickly, smiling as she shook her head. "No. That's it. I only want to make sure we're ready, you know? For whatever comes our way."

Caleb touched her cheek, fingertips grazing her skin as he tucked a piece of hair behind her ear. "You sure?"

She popped up on her toes and pressed her lips to his. "I'm sure. I'm fine. Don't worry so much."

Caleb tried to follow her instructions as he deepened the kiss. He was finding, however, that it wasn't that easy.

Ava was definitely hiding something. Whether it was simply the depth of her own fears or something more, he wasn't certain. That was something he'd come to learn, though—Ava would not be pushed. She'd come to him when she was ready. He'd have to be patient, whether he liked it or not.

When the kiss broke and she smiled up at him, cheeks flushed and lips swollen, he forced a smile. "We'll get through this," he promised. "And when it's all over—"

"When it's all over, we're taking that vacation," she said smartly.

He grinned. "Sounds good."

"Then I'm going back to school."

"I'll carry your books."

Neither one of them said what they both were thinking—there was no guarantee anything would be over soon. And that there was every chance that in the end, Borré and the Rogues would win.

It was a couple of hours before Ava made it back to the healer's quarters on her own. She'd smiled and played along as they'd told Talia about the plans to test Isaiah, but she'd been forced to hold on to the real reason for her visit until she was alone.

"Back so soon?" Talia said with a smile as she let Ava in.

"Caleb's meeting with Gideon," she replied. "Making the final plans for the trip."

"I take it you need more medication."

"Stock me up, doc," Ava said with forced lightheartedness. "And maybe you can work some of your mojo? Give me a little booster before we leave?"

Talia nodded and led her into the exam room. "Hop up on the table." She washed her hands and lowered the lights in the room.

They'd done this a few times before, but Ava usually didn't like the grogginess that came after one of Talia's treatments. She wasn't sure exactly what the healer did—some kind of visualization that boosted her immune system or something. All Ava knew was it gave her some respite from the headaches and gave her energy for a couple of days afterward. It was something she figured would come in handy since Talia wouldn't be accompanying them to New Elysia.

She lay back on the table and closed her eyes, giving herself over to the healer's ministrations. Ava's tension eased as Talia smoothed cool palms over her head and down her shoulders, over and over again in a gentle rhythm. A wave of calm and relaxation seeped into Ava's skin from the healer's fingers, flowing through her body and washing her pain away.

A few minutes later, Talia shook her gently to draw her attention.

Ava sat up, blinking against the rush of dizziness that she'd come to expect.

Talia handed her a bottle of medication and a glass of water. "Better wait a few minutes before you try to stand up," she advised.

Ava nodded and sipped at the water, eyeing her host. "Can I ask you something?"

"Hmm?" Talia made a few notes in Ava's chart and filed it in a large cabinet.

"Have you ever done a tattoo?"

Talia's eyebrows shot up. "A few. Why do you ask?"

Ava shrugged. "I know it's an acquired skill, you know, because of the healing."

"Yes, that's true," she said slowly. "Actually, it's not that different from what I just did."

"So . . . you think you could give me one?" She hadn't been sure she would even ask until that moment, but suddenly, Ava knew she wanted it.

"I could." Talia leaned against the counter and crossed her arms over her chest. "Do you know what you want?"

Ava reached for the cord that always hung around her neck and pulled out the pendant hanging beneath her clothes. "This," she said, tapping the Celtic knot between the blue and green symbolizing humanity and the First Race.

"That's the Guardian symbol."

"Yeah, I know," Ava said, running her finger over the hammered metal. "Caleb told me the knot is for unity. And I . . . with everything that's going on, I guess I want a more permanent reminder. That this is what we're fighting for, you know? Not human or Race or Half-Breed, but everyone coexisting and living in peace."

Talia nodded, smiling. "I can see that." She turned to rummage in a cabinet, drawing out what looked like a tattoo gun and some other supplies. "Do you know where you want it?"

Ava had considered placing it over her heart, or on her shoulder, but she recalled Emma's wrist—the symbol for the Twelve peeking out from under her sleeve.

Huh. Almost . . . poetic.

Two sisters with conflicting loyalties, fighting on different sides—one for power, the other for right.

Ava had to believe she was fighting for right.

"Here," she said, running a finger along the inside of her left wrist. "Do it here."

Andreas Petrov often lost track of how many decades he'd served on the Race Council.

Ten? Twelve?

Sometimes it seemed as if the years flew by. Conversely, sitting in Madeleine Foster's living room with the other Council members reminded him of how hours . . . minutes . . . seconds could drag interminably.

"Are you certain they can be trusted?" Naomi asked, twisting her fingers nervously in her lap.

It wasn't the first time the question had been asked, and he knew the answer would be the same.

"Of course not," Kaeden replied. "But someone has to take a leap of faith here. We've suspected the Rogues were planning something, but from what Ross says, they could act sooner rather than later. We need to be prepared. We need every tool at our disposal."

"Even if they're traitors to the Race?" Madeleine eyes flashed, and Andreas fought back a smile. Madeleine put up a stoic façade in public, but behind closed doors she often wore her heart—and her fury—on her sleeve.

"It's a little late for second thoughts," he said, examining his perfectly buffed fingernails. "You've already said they could come."

"What else was I supposed to do?" she asked, glaring at the group. "You all but forced my hand."

"Don't be ridiculous, Madeleine." Rafe sat slouched in a low armchair, watching the conversation with a slight smirk. "You know as well as we do there was no other option. The Guardians have information we need. More important, they have some of the illustrious Twelve."

"The Twelve," Madeleine spat. "Borré's arrogance knows no bounds. And now he plans to turn these children of his against us? Against his own people?"

"Borré has never been one of us. But this is all beside the point, isn't it?" Andreas raised his brows and met every gaze.

Silence hung heavy in the room for several moments.

Andreas waited, patient as always.

"I want them watched," Madeleine said, her voice quiet but firm. "Twenty-four-hour guard on Ava Michaels and her apparent siblings."

"I'll take care of it," Andreas replied. "What about Gideon?"

At mention of the man's name, Madeleine's jaw tensed. "Tiernan Ross will be charged with keeping him in line. As for my son . . ."

Everyone turned toward her, waiting for the conclusion to that sentence. It was no secret that Caleb Foster had been aiding the Guardians, but it was a fact that had not been addressed publicly until now.

Madeleine sighed. "Well, if we do decide to move forward with this, I suppose his . . . indiscretions are the least of our problems. I'll deal with Caleb myself."

"What about a public statement?" Naomi asked. "If people see Gideon Campbell walk into town, they're going to start asking questions."

"It's our job to make sure they *don't* see him," Madeleine replied. "At least not until we're ready to put forward a united front on this and gain the people's support. Although how that will be accomplished is beyond me at this point." She rubbed her temples, eyes fluttering closed.

"They'll unite in the face of a threat," Kaeden pointed out.

Madeleine laughed humorlessly. "Yes, but how do we explain that threat without inducing a mass panic?"

"It's simple," Andreas said. "As you say, we need to keep things quiet for now, at least until we know more about these Twelve and about the Rogue plot."

The response was immediate and heated, voices escalating in frustration.

"But our people have the right to know they're in danger!"

"We don't know the extent of that danger."

"—find out we lied—"

"Nobody's lying—"

"Lies by omission are still—"

"What's the alternative? Panic in the streets?"

"—not giving them enough credit."

"She's right. They should be able to defend them—"

"All right, enough!" Madeleine drew to her full height and fixed each of them with a quelling look. "Andreas is right. We can't go public with this until we know exactly what we're dealing with." She turned to Rafe. "You meet them at the gate when they arrive. Make sure they are shown to private quarters and that they're kept out of the public eye."

Rafe nodded.

"Andreas will handle security," Madeleine said, pacing across the room slowly. "We'll keep them isolated to the medical wing for now, at least until the testing is complete. Naomi, perhaps you can try to befriend our guests. You're the most diplomatic of us all."

Naomi pursed her lips. "You mean the least threatening."

Madeleine only acknowledged the comment with a slight tilt of her head. "I'll deal with Gideon and Caleb and try to get more information. That means exploring our outside resources falls to you, Kaeden. Turn over every rock. Look under every bush. I want to know what Borré is up to and when he plans to make his move."

"What about the rest of the Guardians?" Kaeden asked.

Madeleine sighed heavily. "If we do agree to an alliance, we will need to provide protection for them as well. But let's cross that bridge when we come to it, shall we?"

"I can speak to the Housing Authority," Naomi offered. "I'll make some discreet inquiries to see what's available."

"Good. All right. Any questions?" Madeleine observed the room silently, eyes flicking from one to the next.

No one would say anything else. Yes, they governed together, but they also followed Madeleine's lead in most things.

"Fine. We'll meet again tomorrow." She dismissed them all with a weary smile and turned to Andreas, tipping her head toward the kitchen. "Andreas, a word?"

As the others left the house, he followed her and leaned against the kitchen counter.

She retrieved a couple of water bottles from the refrigerator then seemed to rethink it and replaced them, pulling out a half bottle of white wine instead. She held it up, arching a brow at Andreas in question.

He nodded. Wine was almost always a better option, in his opinion.

She poured them each a glass and took a long sip, swirling it in her mouth before she swallowed and asked, "What do you really think of all this?"

He pursed his lips and frowned. "I think . . . I think Gideon is probably right. If this threat is real, we'll need to work together to neutralize it."

Madeleine swirled her wine, lost in thought. "It will mean changing the way we've done things for decades—*centuries*. Allowing the Guardians into New Elysia will basically be admitting we were wrong."

"Or simply that we can adapt when the need arises."

Madeleine's lips quirked. "Ah, yes, the proper spin. You were always good at that, Andreas."

He lifted his glass in a silent toast, and she mimicked the movement.

Madeleine drained her glass, refilled it, and moved toward the window over the sink.

Andreas watched her carefully. "There's something else."

She glanced over her shoulder. "Perceptive, as usual." She crossed her arms, turning back to the window. "Kaeden may need your . . . assistance."

Interesting.

"Any particular reason for your concern?"

Madeleine shrugged. "You know as well as I do that Borré has been moving too quickly and too efficiently to be working blindly. Our sources say there could be a sympathizer right here in the city. Perhaps a Protector or someone on the Council itself."

"And you suspect Kaeden Cross?" Andreas said with a laugh. "He hardly seems the type."

"Who does?" she asked sharply. "We cannot take any unnecessary risks. I'm merely suggesting that you make sure any information Kaeden uncovers makes it back to all of us. Completely."

Andreas swirled the last of his wine in the glass before swallowing it. He approached her and set the glass down on the counter next to her. "I'll take care of it," he said quietly.

CHAPTER SEVEN

Elias Borré frowned at the paperwork on his makeshift desk, plans upon plans racing through his mind as he adapted, consulted, and adapted again. He hadn't gotten where he was by not being able to think ahead and guess his opponent's move three or four miles down the road. He leaned back in his chair and tapped his lips, smiling slightly.

It won't be long now.

A knock at the door drew his attention, and Sloan walked in, a grim expression on his face.

"What is it?" Elias asked.

"They got the boy."

Elias pursed his lips, nodding. "Not entirely unexpected." He couldn't resist chastising the man to keep him in place, however. "Losing your touch, Sloan?"

Bartok squared his shoulders. "No, sir. I'll—"

"You'll do what I say and no more." Borré got to his feet and gathered the documents on the table. "I've received word that the Guardians are on move."

Sloan frowned. "But we've known that for some time. We've had people monitoring the Colony."

"I don't mean them," Elias snapped. "The refugees are not important. I mean Gideon. I mean my *children*."

"Oh. Yes. Of course, sir."

"They've been given sanctuary, however temporary, in New Elysia. I expect they'll leave the Colony tomorrow, the day after at the latest."

"They don't dare wait any longer."

"No. No, Gideon will want to move quickly." Elias slid the papers into a folder and tapped it against the table to get the edges straight.

Neat, orderly . . . everything in its place.

"Ava is to go with the contingent to meet with the Council, but the other two are not expected in New Elysia. I suspect Gideon wants to keep them somewhere safe."

"There are half a dozen Guardian safe houses within a day of New Elysia."

"Pick the one nearest the city," Elias said, circling the table to perch on the edge. "He'll want to have Sophie and Isaiah close. I suspect Tyra will be the one to accompany them. He won't leave it to one of his lesser soldiers."

Sloan opened his mouth, and Elias could tell the man wanted to offer a plan of attack. Instead, however, he simply squared his shoulders and asked, "What are my orders?"

Elias smiled.

Ahh, he's learning.

"Ava will have to wait, for now. As for the other two, when the opportunity presents itself, I expect you to retrieve what's mine."

Sloan nodded, head bowed under Borré's glittering gaze. "Yes, sir."

He left the room and Elias took a moment to breathe, relishing the idea that it was all coming together as he'd planned. Sure, there'd been challenges along the way—and he knew there would continue to be—but in the end, he'd adapt. He'd survive.

He'd win.

Early the next morning, Sophie and Isaiah headed south, following Tyra's booted footsteps down the muddy trail. The trees dripped a quiet pitter-patter that splashed up rich and earthy scents around them as they dodged puddles and climbed over tangled roots.

Sophie held her brother's hand tightly and adjusted the bag on her shoulder as she eyed the little group around her nervously. She'd been glad when Gideon told her he hadn't expected the two of them to go to New Elysia —a city of super men, thank you very much—and instead would go with some of the other refugees to a safe house near Kalispell.

Safe house. She liked the sound of that.

So it was the two of them, along with a half dozen of what Sophie had dubbed "ordinary people." Although, the schoolteacher trudging along slightly ahead of her was able to make things grow, as the trail of little pink flowers popping up in her wake attested. So ordinary was relative, but it separated those people from the six Guardian soldiers who stomped in formation around the group carrying weapons and an aura of danger. Tyra walked point, and someone named Adam brought up the rear. Sophie hadn't discovered what his gift was, but like the others, the guy kept his gaze constantly on the move, always alert for any sign of danger.

Isaiah rubbed absently at his arm.

The spot where they'd drawn several vials of blood the night before had already healed, but Sophie knew he was thinking about what they'd learned. No one had really been surprised about the DNA testing. It was one of the reasons that Sophie had eventually relented and let them conduct it. Isaiah was her brother. She'd never had any doubt, and apparently, like Ava and herself—she was still having trouble wrapping her head around all *that*—he was also one of the Twelve.

"You okay?" she asked in a quiet voice.

He shook his head. "Just thinking. About everything, you know? It's . . . weird."

Sophie laughed. "Which part?"

"All of it. Having another sister—*sisters*—not to mention brothers, and all these people with powers?" He waved a hand to encompass the entire group moving through the forest. "It's like a comic book or something."

"Yeah. I know what you mean."

"And you." Isaiah looked up at her, his gold and brown gaze the same but opposite of Sophie's. And Ava's. "What you can do. It's pretty cool, actually." He frowned. "You think I can do the same thing?" He turned to face forward, brow creased in concentration, and Sophie suspected he was trying.

"I don't know," she said, squeezing his hand. "They say everyone's different. You might be able to do something even cooler."

Isaiah grinned, his eyes crinkling at the corners. "Cooler. Heh."

Sophie rolled her own eyes. "You know what I mean."

"Maybe when they figure out how to lift this block." He tapped at his temple and Sophie's stomach sank.

After what Ava had told her was happening to her—a side effect of lifting the block—she wasn't sure she wanted it herself, let alone her little brother. She couldn't stand to see him in pain.

"I'll be fine," he said.

Sophie started. "What?"

He blinked, his pupils dilating but quickly shrinking back to normal. "You said you didn't want me to be in pain."

"I didn't actually say that."

"But I heard you—"

"I . . ." She swallowed. "I didn't say it out loud, b-but I *thought* it." She looked up at her brother.

When did he get so much taller than me?

"Try it again," he said.

"Try what? Thinking something? I never stopped."

"Think something specific," he said, yanking on her arm. "Think something *at* me."

"How in the world do you think something *at* someone?"

"Sophie!" He pulled her to a stop, only to start walking again when one of the Guardian soldiers looked at him with a scowl. He lowered his voice. "Just try, okay?"

She sighed, a mixture of fear and excitement racing through her. "Okay. What sho—"

"Anything," he hissed. "Just think something over and over, and I'll try to guess what it is. Maybe a number?"

Pfft! Too easy.

She tried to come up with something even better but got distracted by the pink flowers blooming behind the teacher's shoes. She wondered if they grew naturally in the area or if they were something unique, created by the woman's power.

The color's so bright. Almost Pepto-Bismol or Barbie Dream Hou—

"Pink," Isaiah said firmly.

Sophie gasped. "I wasn't ready!"

Isaiah laughed. "I was right, wasn't I? I couldn't make out specific words—not like before—but I could hear 'pink.' Or maybe see it? Feel it? I don't know. I just knew it was pink."

Sophie forced a grin through her trepidation.

This is real.

Isaiah, apparently, had a gift as well, which meant he really was one of the Twelve.

Which means . . .

She didn't like to think about what it meant, so instead, she bumped his shoulder with her own and whispered, "Let's try again."

By the time they made it to the SUVs concealed in the metal garage off a dirt road leading to the Trans-Canada highway, Isaiah could pick individual words or numbers out of Sophie's head with little or no effort. Complex thoughts were a little more difficult, although it seemed as if he could also sense emotions to a certain extent. It only worked one way, though. He tried to push words into Sophie's head, and at one point even tried to get Tyra to scratch her nose, but to no avail.

It reminded Sophie of when they were kids sharing secrets—the two of them against the world.

They'd been on the road for about six hours when Isaiah nudged Sophie out of a near-doze against the window.

She cast him a questioning glance, and he nodded toward Tyra, who was in the front passenger seat, talking quietly on her cell. Isaiah opened his mouth, but something made Sophie hold a finger to her lips. She rummaged in her bag for a small notebook and pen and held them out to him.

He tilted his head and stared at the back of Tyra's head, his eyes narrowing in concentration. After a brief moment, he scribbled in the book and turned it so Sophie could read it.

Something's wrong. She thinks we're being followed.

Sophie started to take the pen, but Isaiah apparently knew what she was going to ask.

Not sure who. Tyra thinks Rogues? Council? He paused then added, *She's worried.*

Sophie didn't know Gideon's second-in-command that well, but she knew enough to know the woman didn't get worried, at least not easily. She took the notebook and tucked it back into her backpack, glancing over her shoulder out the back window of the SUV. She saw the second car close behind them and a third in the distance, but nobody beyond that. A shiver of unease settled between her shoulders. Not fear, at least not for herself. Her little brother, though . . .

"Are you okay?" Isaiah whispered.

Sophie nodded and took his hand. "Don't worry. Everything will be fine." She fought to believe it herself, but as she snuck another look out the back of the car, she knew she'd do whatever it took to protect Isaiah.

Ava had said that others would want her, would want Isaiah. Whether it was the Rogues or the Council, it didn't matter. Sophie knew that if there was someone following them, and that someone was after Isaiah, they'd have to get through her first.

And something Sophie was quickly learning was how to put up a good fight.

"Five minutes and I'll be good," Caleb said, collapsing on a fallen log to catch his breath. "Maybe ten."

They'd been shifting all morning, taking short breaks in between for Caleb to chew on R-cubes and regain his energy. Gideon and Tiernan opted for a helicopter out of Winnipeg, but Caleb preferred not to fly unless absolutely necessary, so shifting it was.

Ava was enjoying having Caleb to herself for a while, and if she got to spend most of that time in his arms, well, all the better.

"How much farther?" she asked as she took a seat next to him and leaned into his side.

Caleb consulted the GPS on his phone. "Another six or seven shifts should do it," he replied. "We should get there a little after Gideon."

Ava nodded, sliding an arm around his waist as she curled into him.

Caleb popped another R-cube into his mouth before stretching his arm over her shoulder and pressing a kiss to her temple. "You okay?"

She hummed, closing her eyes and basking in Caleb's warmth, his scent. She could almost fall asleep like this. Her night had been frustratingly short and interrupted by vague nightmares that she couldn't remember once she'd awakened—flashes of shadow and blood, fear and fury. The dreams had left her exhausted and unsettled with her intuition on edge ever since.

As if sensing her discomfort, Caleb pulled her onto his lap. He traced light fingertips over her cheek, lifting her face so he could kiss her.

She sighed into the touch, melted into the kiss, and wished this was it—that everything else could just fade away while they lived in this moment forever. She was hyperaware of every place Caleb's skin touched hers, his palm against her cheek, fingers tracing lightly over her ear, his lips moving softly against hers, reassuring and firm. She slid her own arms around his neck to hold him close, the mingling of their power comforting her in her very core.

But . . .

There was something else, too. Another niggling sensation pushing through. An echo of her nightmare, perhaps, or maybe something more.

Ava broke away and drew a shaky breath.

"What is it?" Caleb asked.

"I don't—I'm not sure."

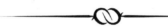

Sophie's heart raced as the SUV sped around a wide curve and Tyra shouted into the cell phone, "Get Adam on that pyro or something! We've got to get—"

The crash of a fireball next to the car cut off her words, the resulting explosion rocking the vehicle.

"We've got to get off the highway," Tyra told the driver. "Get out of this damned car so we can fight back!"

"You want to face that pyro head-on?" he replied, swerving around a slow-moving car in front of them.

"A bullet will take him out. Doesn't matter what his gift is." She pointed to the right. "There—take that exit. Try to shake him through town." She turned her attention back to the cell. "We need to split up. They can't follow us all. We'll rendezvous in Medicine Hat—but only if you know you're clear. We can't risk exposing the safe house." She listened for a moment, grim-faced, then disconnected the call, and pocketed the phone without another word.

Sophie saw one SUV continuing down the highway while the third chased them into town—Moose Jaw, according to the sign that whizzed by. They split again at the first light. Their car turned right as the one behind them sped left, tires squealing. For the first time, Sophie saw a car chasing them—a black sedan with dark windows—and she held her breath as it neared the intersection and turned right to follow them.

"They're behind us," Sophie said unnecessarily. She wasn't surprised. She knew what they were after. Her heart sped up, pounding in her chest as she gripped Isaiah's hand, both their palms slick with sweat.

"Sophie?" Isaiah's voice was small.

Sophie was vaguely aware of the tingle of her gift. Frost edged the car windows.

"I see them," Tyra muttered.

Another fireball hit wide to their left.

Warning shots.

They don't want to kill us.

Sophie knew that wouldn't serve their pursuers' purpose, but it didn't slow her racing heart or ease the grip she had on Isaiah.

Tyra braced her hand against the seat and cursed as the car swerved wildly. She asked Sophie, "Can you—do you think you can do something?"

"I don't know. I can try."

Another fireball hit, and the explosion threw the SUV sideways.

The driver fought against the wheel, tires squealing as it slid across the road on two wheels.

Oh, g—we're going to flip.

"Is someone coming?" Caleb asked.

Ava's face had taken on a pale, sickly cast, her eyes glazed as she breathed shallow and fast. "No. Not here," she said. "Not here."

Sophie grabbed Isaiah's hand with both her own, her gift flaring inside her.

A gust of wind came at the SUV from the opposite direction and knocked it back onto all four wheels. It skidded into a couple of garbage cans before jolting to a stop at the curb.

"Everybody out!" Tyra shouted. "Take cover in the alley!" She ushered Sophie and Isaiah out, putting herself between them and the coming threat as they ran for the dark space between two brick buildings.

People along the street had stopped to stare, and Sophie couldn't help wondering how the Race or the Council or whoever would go about hiding this from the world.

Not my problem.

Not for the moment, at least.

Their pursuers screeched to a stop behind the SUV, and four men stepped out of the vehicle. They seemed to be in no hurry, walking slow and purposeful toward the alley, like they hadn't a care in the world. Sophie even saw one of them nod and smile at a gaping child standing astride a bicycle.

Sophie backed into the alley and yanked Isaiah behind her as she reached for that feeling, that spark she'd accessed back at the training field. The men appeared in the mouth of the alley, and Sophie glanced behind her, looking for a way out. There wasn't one.

Tyra and the driver didn't waste any time. They fired toward the mouth of the alley.

One of the men grinned, cold and terrifying, and nodded to the man next to him.

The young man lifted a hand and a fireball shot toward the Guardian driver.

He never had a chance.

The driver fell to the ground, his screams cutting through the air.

A gunshot—two—and the screams were silenced.

Sophie shuddered.

"Sophie," Ava murmured, a drop of blood bubbling at her nose.

"Ava?" Caleb wiped it away while panic clawed in his chest. "Sophie's going to the safe house. She's fine."

Ava's eyes cleared as she looked into his. "No. She's not."

The temperature dropped and the air turned to icy frost around them. Sophie recognized the tingling electricity of her gift racing along her nerve endings and sparking at her skin.

Another fireball hurled toward Tyra, who dove to the ground and rolled into the brick wall.

With a thought, Sophie diverted the fireball with a ball of ice, the combination sizzling in the air and filling it with a cloud of steam, and the remnants dripping to the ground.

Everything seemed to speed up.

One moment, Tyra was rolling over to get to her feet. The next, she had a knife to her throat, and the pyrokinetic was bouncing another fireball in his palm next to her.

Two other men—one strawberry blond, one dark-haired—approached Sophie and Isaiah, slow and easy, both moving with a confidence that had Sophie's instincts flaring.

"Stay back," Sophie warned, another ice ball forming before her. Isaiah trembled behind her, feeding her fear, feeding her gift.

The blond man stepped forward and tilted his head. His eyes flashed— one blue, one brown—pupils blowing wide as he smiled softly.

Sophie was barely aware of the ice ball falling to the concrete before her knees gave out and darkness enveloped her.

"What is it, Ava? You're scaring me."

Ava blinked, the images blurring and fading away. She'd never experienced something like that before—not outside her nightmares. A waking dream. A vision of sorts. And like her dreams, the images melted away, drifting like whispers of smoke through her fingers and leaving behind anxiety and unease in their wake. "I . . . I'm not sure," she said finally. "But something's wrong. Something's happened to Sophie. I'm sure of it."

Caleb had his phone out before she'd finished talking. He dialed Gideon and frowned when he got voice mail. "They must still be in the air. I'll try Tyra." He waited, watching Ava worriedly as it rang.

She heard Tyra's curt voice mail message as well. "What are we going to do?" Ava stood up and wiped at the remaining blood on her lip. "Something's happened. I know it."

Caleb stood as well, pocketed his phone, and pulled her close. "We can't do anything from here," he said. "We need to get to New Elysia."

"But—"

"We'll call every time we stop. Think about it, Ava. We have no idea where they are. We can't go chasing after them until we have more information. And Andreas Petrov has a sensor. He'll have a better chance of tracking Sophie down than we will, right?"

Ava thought back to the man who had helped Tiernan track Caleb. Tiernan had told her he was gifted. He'd actually never heard of a sensor with such strong abilities.

Ava didn't like it, but she nodded. "Okay, let's go." And as she clung to Caleb, she clenched her eyes shut as they shifted through the miles, thinking only of her promise to Sophie that she'd be safe, that Isaiah would be safe, and she prayed that it hadn't been a lie.

CHAPTER EIGHT

The helicopter touched down at the base of the mountain, and Gideon searched the steep incline with a frown. "Sure would have been easier if they would have let us land in the city."

Tiernan grunted and started up the mountain. "Pretty sure the Council wants to keep your visit under wraps. The head of the Guardians walking into New Elysia? Might draw some attention."

Gideon couldn't hold back a grin. "Yeah. I can imagine."

They took their time, and Gideon wondered if the Protector was apprehensive about everything. Or perhaps, like Gideon, he was simply enjoying these last moments of quiet—of peace—a respite from the insanity, if only for a brief time.

He wondered how Madeleine was handling it all.

I haven't seen her since . . .

He couldn't remember, actually.

Too long.

He felt her, the twinge of her power growing stronger with every step he took up the mountain, settling into his bones and relieving the tension in his shoulders. He tried to ignore it. Tried to focus instead on the dirt and rocks beneath his feet, the sunshine overhead, the cool breeze ruffling his hair.

"You okay?" Tiernan asked, shooting a quick look over his shoulder.

The Protector was more perceptive than many suspected, but Gideon didn't want to talk about his feelings. About Madeleine.

"Fine."

"Any word from Foster?"

Gideon frowned, irritated that he'd allowed himself to be so distracted, and reached for his phone. "I should check in with him. And the safe houses. Make sure ev—" He stopped mid stride when he saw the number of missed messages from Caleb and cursed under his breath. He didn't bother listening to the voice mails and was about to dial Caleb directly when the phone vibrated with a call from Tyra. "Everything okay?"

"Not even close."

Gideon's skin chilled. "What happened?"

"Attacked by Rogues." Tyra's hurried words belied her nerves, even in the face of her military bearing. "They came out of nowhere. A pyro took me out. Davis is . . . he's dead. We tried to fight, but they had a blank or a stunner . . . I'm not sure. The cryo and her brother—"

"Sophie?"

Tyra heaved a heavy sigh. "She's alive. At least she was the last time I saw her. They knocked me out—knocked us all out—and when I came to, she and the boy were gone."

Gideon looked up and could tell from Tiernan's concentrated frown that he had heard the entire exchange.

They started up the mountain with a greater sense of urgency.

"Any idea where they went? Direction? Anything?"

They picked up the pace, half jogging, half running, and their booted steps echoed on the rocks.

"I don't know. I don't—" Tyra let out a groan. "Maybe if we had a tracker, but none of us can pick up a trail of any kind. They might have masked it. I just don't know."

"What about the others?"

"Everyone else is all right, except Davis." Her voice caught. "I stayed with him while Adam and the others continued on to the rendezvous point. They should reach the safe house tonight, but there's something else you should know."

Gideon stepped around a large rock. "What is it?"

"The boy—Isaiah? From what I could gather listening in on their conversation, it looks like he's a telepath, perhaps a bit of an empath as well."

"Which way?"

"Looks like he can just read, at least for now, but if he's like Ava, like Emma? Who knows when the block's completely lifted?"

Gideon groaned quietly.

"Exactly," Tyra replied.

If Isaiah could plant thoughts and emotions and influence people like Emma? They definitely needed him on their side.

"Well, we'll just have to get them back," he said, voice firm despite his own doubts. "Are you . . . can you handle things there?" It was a lot to ask, he knew, but the local authorities would have to be dealt with as well as the dead body in an alley.

"I got this," she said in a low, resigned voice. "But Gideon?"

"Yeah?"

"When you figure out where they are? I want in." Her voice was icy, deadly, and Gideon was reminded why Tyra Resick was his second-in-command. She was tough. She was ruthless. She was capable. And she wouldn't rest until these Rogues were dealt with.

"Got it," Gideon said and hung up.

The higher they got, the colder the temperature and the bigger the patches of stubborn snow clustered alongside the path interspersed with spring buds and green. They finally rounded a familiar corner and came to a stop at the cloaked gate to New Elysia.

Gideon started forward, but Tiernan stopped him with a hand. "We need to wait."

He started to argue but swallowed the words. He knew Tiernan was right. They were at the Council's mercy now and couldn't risk causing trouble. There was too much at stake. Still, it didn't keep him from worrying, from pacing back and forth before the invisible barrier, willing someone to emerge.

With barely a shimmer to herald their arrival, Caleb and Ava appeared a few feet away, Ava stumbling a bit as she gained her footing. Caleb sat heavily on a fallen log and reached for the R-cubes in his pocket.

Before Gideon could ask if he was all right, Ava ran unsteadily toward him. "Something's happened to Sophie!"

Gideon grabbed her by the upper arms, steadying her as she swayed slightly. "I know. I talked to Tyra."

"You did?" Her eyes were panicked, wide, and searching. "What did she say? What happened?"

"Wait a minute." Tiernan pushed off the tree he was leaning against and stalked toward them. "You didn't talk to Tyra?"

"We couldn't get through," Caleb said through a mouthful of cubes. "Not to you or her. But Ava . . . Ava felt something happen."

She waved off their talk with a frustrated exhale. "None of that matters now. What did Tyra say?"

Gideon relayed their conversation in quiet tones, distracted by the idea that Ava might sense something happening to her sister. It was definitely something they'd have to explore when the girl wasn't frenzied by concern and fear.

"The Rogues," Ava said, rubbing her hands over her face. "I should have known."

"How could you?" Tiernan asked.

"We need to find them."

"I can send a team with a tracker back to the scene," Gideon said. "Tyra couldn't find a trail, but maybe—"

"I'll go," Tiernan said.

"You should talk to Andreas first." Ava reached out to touch his arm. "Remember the sensor?"

"The one who helped track Caleb?" Gideon recalled them talking about a powerful sensor who had been able to track Caleb from a hundred miles away. He'd never heard of anything like it.

"We figure he's our best shot at finding Sophie and Isaiah," Caleb said, getting to his feet. "As long as he—" Caleb's gaze tracked over Gideon's shoulder, and he turned to see the shimmer of someone emerging from the gate—tall, dark-haired, and intimidating.

Rafael Vinci. It had been a while.

"Took you long enough," Tiernan growled.

"Mind your place, Protector," Rafe said, but there was no real heat behind his words. The Council member greeted Gideon with a slight bow and a handshake, Caleb with a cheeky grin, and Ava with a look that was equal parts trepidation and begrudging respect. "Never thought I'd see you here again," he said.

"That makes two of us," Ava replied.

They followed Rafe through the shimmering warmth of the cloak, walking abreast through the gap in the high, stone wall. The gate clanged shut behind them, and they continued down the red gravel path through the forest.

It hasn't changed.

Gideon expected the same could be said of New Elysia in general—of the Council, of the Race as a whole, actually.

Well, things are certainly about to.

He hoped they were all ready for it.

The ping of water dripping through the trees echoed along with their crunching footsteps, and Gideon realized Caleb was telling Rafe about the Rogue attack.

"I believe Madeleine was hoping the girl and her brother would have accompanied you here," Rafe said pointedly.

Gideon cleared his throat. "This is all new to them," he said. "I thought it best that they be kept safe until we'd come to some sort of agreement."

"Well, apparently *safe* is a relative term," Rafe said, a little acid in his tone.

Gideon stiffened. "That's out of line."

"You know what's out of line? *You*. Coming here for our help, but making it very clear that it has to be on your terms." Rafe ran his hands through his hair, tugging on the ends. "Look, I'm on your side here, but you're going to have to come halfway. Show some trust—"

"You don't think me coming *here*—" Gideon waved his hand to encompass it all—New Elysia, the Council, for all intents and purposes, enemy territory. "Walking into a place where I've been known as a *criminal* for decades—you don't think that's coming halfway?" His lip curled as the anger twisted in his chest. "You don't think putting myself in the Council's hands, hands that have made it very clear they'd like to wrap themselves around my throat, shows enough trust?"

"Oh, for heaven's sake," Ava muttered, shoving the two men apart with her mind. "We do not have *time* for this!" She glared at Gideon. "You need to get off your high horse. We need them. You know it. I know it. And they know it." She pointed at each of them in turn to punctuate her words then turned her fiery eyes on Rafe. "And you need to cut him some slack. You all have been hunting down his people like animals for more than a century. Don't you think trust is a big step for him? Not to mention Caleb. My God, they were ready to lock him up and throw away the key!"

"They understand now he—"

"That's great, but he's hardly in good standing with the Council. None of us are, when you get down to it, so putting ourselves in your hands is about the biggest show of trust we can make. Wouldn't you agree?" When Rafe's eyes fell to the ground, Ava threw up her hands. "Let's move *on*, shall we?"

she asked, stalking away without waiting for them to follow.

The men shared a sheepish glance, but it was Tiernan who spoke, clapping Caleb on the shoulder.

"How do you ever get a word in edgewise?" he asked, smirking.

"I heard that!" Ava shouted without looking back. "Let's go!"

Caleb shoved off Tiernan and shifted to Ava's side, and the other men hurried to catch up.

All Ava's irritation melted away when she crested the hill looking down over New Elysia. Glass, metal, and white stone sparkled in the sunlight as the circular city spread out before them, untouched by the mountain's shadows at this hour. Ava swallowed a choking flood of nerves and . . .

Well, not fear. *Not really.*

She wasn't *afraid* of the Council, at least not for herself. She was worried, though. Worried about Caleb and Tiernan, Gideon and the Guardians. The refugees.

Sophie and Isaiah.

A lot rested on this alliance. It was their only hope, really. Convincing the Council of that was another matter entirely, however. She'd gotten her own firsthand glimpse of the Council and its devotion to the Law. What they were proposing flew in the face of that. It could change everything. Especially once the Council and the people of New Elysia found out that instead of hunting down the Guardians they were working *with* them, that the Half-Breeds weren't the threat any longer, or that the Rogues, so easily handled in the past, now posed a threat greater than any of them had ever imagined.

But first things first.

Ava took a deep breath, letting it out when Caleb took her hand, knitting their fingers together.

"You okay?" he asked.

She nodded. "Yeah. Just . . . you know."

Caleb smiled.

Of course he knows.

He squeezed her hand, and they started down the hill. "It's going to be okay."

"You think?"

"Yeah. Of course."

"How can you be so sure?"

He turned and blinked. "Because it has to be."

She leaned into him and rubbed her cheek against his shoulder. "Am I too pushy?" she asked, thinking about Tiernan's comments. "I mean, do you feel like—"

"You're perfect," he said and kissed the top of her head. "Well, maybe not *perfect*," he amended, "but perfect for me."

She laughed, but when she looked up, she saw he was serious.

"Maybe it's selfish, but I love you. I *need* you exactly the way you are," he said quietly. "You push me to be—no, you make me *want* to be better."

Ava flushed, uncomfortable with the compliment, but she squeezed his hand. "You do the same for me."

He lifted their joined hands and pressed a kiss to the back of hers, starting a little when he spotted the marking under the cuff of her jacket.

"What's this?" he asked, pushing up her sleeve to reveal the tattoo. He ran a finger over the knot, the touch sending heat up her arm.

Ava shrugged. "It's a reminder, I guess. Of what we're fighting for."

Caleb smiled softly and placed another kiss on the tattoo before lowering her sleeve and letting their joined hands dangle between them.

They walked in silence and paused to let the others catch up as they neared the city.

Rafe led them, keeping within the forest but not bothering to avoid sensors and cameras. "We just don't want to make it a public event," he explained. "We're to meet the Council at my house, since it's the most isolated."

Rafe's house was smaller than Ava expected, given his position. It was similar to Caleb's, actually —a two-story white stone home with a modest front yard and a palm scanner next to the front door.

She had barely registered the more modern interior—a vague impression of black leather, metal and glass—before she spotted the familiar figures from her last visit to New Elysia. A large, intimidating, bald man with golden eyes sat in a black armchair—Kaeden Cross—and on the sofa, dressed in a creamy white flowing dress was Naomi Duncan. Her black hair was in uncharacteristically tight braids, but her dark eyes were still kind and compassionate. Andreas Petrov sat reclined on the other end of the sofa, impeccably dressed in a dark suit with not a blond hair out of place.

And standing to the side, but commanding all the attention in the room, was Caleb's mother. Her chin lifted and nostrils flared when they entered the living room. She'd let her hair down, and the brown waves hung flatteringly around her shoulders, but it didn't soften her bearing at all. She was as regal and imposing as ever, and flashes of their last encounter flitted through Ava's mind. When she caught Madeleine's eyes, the woman stiffened.

Apparently, Madeleine remembered it as well.

Ava winced inwardly. She'd hoped to be a help in this mission, but maybe she'd be more of a hindrance. Regardless of Caleb's assurances to the contrary, Ava was pretty sure his mother didn't like her.

Rafe stepped forward and presented the group with a sweep of his hand. "I'd introduce everyone, but I'm relatively certain we're all acquainted. Since this is an informal meeting, perhaps we should get started?"

"Of course," Madeleine said quickly. She laid a hand on the chair next to her.

Is it trembling?

Ava wasn't sure.

The Council leader cleared her throat. "Please, everyone sit down. Make yourselves comfortable. Could I offer you some refreshments?"

Definitely trembling, and her voice is shaking, too.

Ava noticed the older woman kept her gaze rather determinedly away from Gideon as she turned toward a table laid out with coffee, a pitcher of water, and cookies with blue sprinkles. Ava fought to control a hysterical giggle at the thought they would discuss the future of the world over blue-sprinkled cookies.

"Thank you," Gideon said stiffly. "I believe we'd rather get down to business?" He cast a look toward Tiernan, who took up his usual position leaning against a wall and keeping everyone, as well as the front door, in sight.

Caleb led Ava to a low chaise, and they sat down next to each other.

She noticed Madeleine looking at their joined hands and fought the urge to pull away like a guilty schoolgirl caught by her boyfriend's mother.

Gideon waited until Madeleine took a seat before doing the same.

And then . . . nothing. Absolute silence.

Ava had heard the phrase "cut the tension with a knife," but she would have needed a chainsaw in this situation. She glanced at Tiernan, who simply shrugged and rearranged himself in all his looming glory.

Naomi looked decidedly uncomfortable.

Andreas watched it all with an amused smirk on his face.

Ava cleared her throat.

Gideon flinched but covered it with a cough. "Right," he said, slapping his palms lightly on his knees. "I believe Tiernan has explained the situation?"

Madeleine seemed to shake out her nerves, straightened to look him in the eye, and nodded, the imperious leader who Ava remembered reappearing. "Yes. I was under the impression the other—" She glanced at Ava. "Sophie Wright and her brother would be coming with you."

Gideon let out a heavy breath. "Perhaps that would have been best."

Madeleine looked confused until Rafe said, "The Rogues took them."

Madeleine shot to her feet and paced across the room, pressing her fingers to her lips. "You're certain it was Rogues?"

"Who else? It wasn't you, right?" Gideon asked.

"Of course not!"

"So Borré has them," he said, rubbing his eyes.

"Sophie won't help them," Ava said. "She wouldn't. Neither would Isaiah."

"And you're certain these two are . . . like you?" Madeleine asked.

"The DNA testing proved a common father with Ava," Gideon replied. "And that Sophie and Isaiah are full siblings."

"And their power?" Kaeden asked, his gold eyes glittering.

"Sophie's a cryo," Gideon replied. "Isaiah is apparently a telepath. Perhaps an empath as well. Their mother must have been quite powerful."

"An empath? Well, that doesn't seem like such a threat," Naomi interjected, a hopeful look on her face. "It's hardly an offensive gift."

"If he's been genetically altered, there's no telling what he could do," Madeleine replied, sinking to her seat. "If he's able to instill thoughts and emotions as well as read them—"

"Like Emma," Ava murmured.

"Similar, yes," Gideon said, running his hands through his hair. "Emma alters thoughts and memories, most likely through manipulating the frontal lobes or the hippocampus. If Isaiah is able to manipulate emotions as well, it would probably be via a different portion of the brain."

"Manipulate emotions?" Caleb leaned forward, his hand tightening on Ava's. "Is that even possible?"

"I'd say at this point anything is possible," Gideon replied. "Paralyzing fear, uncontrollable anger, even love can be a dangerous emotion."

His words settled in the room. They all knew it was true.

Ava remembered what Emma had almost made her do and imagined what she would do if someone made her believe Caleb was in danger.

Anything.

"We have to get them back," she said. "Both of them."

Tiernan pushed away from the wall to face Andreas. "Can your sensor help?"

Andreas pursed his lips. "Most likely. It's easier if he has a sample from the subject."

"What kind of sample?" Gideon asked. "We drew some blood and brought it with us."

Andreas nodded. "That should do it."

"Wait a minute." Madeleine held up a hand. "Which sensor are you talking about?"

"A young man recently acquired," Andreas said smoothly. "He's proven useful to the Bureau."

At Ava's questioning look, Caleb whispered, "The Protection Bureau. It's the agency that oversees the Protectors and their activities. Andreas is Council liaison to the Bureau."

"We utilize sensors, among other things, to aid Protectors in pursuit of potential threats to the Race," Andreas said.

"You mean Half-Breeds," Ava clarified, and the man inclined his head in acknowledgement.

Madeleine cleared her throat. "In light of these developments, I'd say we need to cut this meeting short. Finding Sophie and Isaiah needs to be our top priority. Are we agreed?" She looked at each Council member in turn, receiving unanimous nods of agreement. "Kaeden, perhaps you can head up the investigation of the site of the Rogue attack. Have our best people comb the area. Maybe they can turn something up that's been missed." The Council member nodded, and Madeleine turned to Rafe and Naomi. "I think we need to have a plan in place to inform the people of the situation when the time comes. We need them behind us if we're going to take on the Rogues."

"Should we have a contingency plan to evacuate the city?" Rafe asked.

"We need a contingency plan for everything," Madeleine said with a sigh. "Until we know more, we need to be ready for anything."

"Perhaps you should accompany me to Bureau headquarters," Andreas said to Tiernan. "Bring these samples you spoke of."

Gideon shot to his feet. "I'll go with you."

Ava had never seen the man look so nervous. She glanced at Madeleine, who'd taken a sudden interest in her folded hands.

"Maybe I should go with you, too," Ava said. "I seem to have some kind of connection to Sophie. I don't know if it'll help, but—"

"Very well," Andreas said with an annoyed sigh. "Anyone else coming along?"

Caleb started to get up, but Madeleine beat him to it. "Caleb, if I might, I'd like to have a word with you."

"But Ava—"

"I'm fine," Ava said quickly. The last thing she wanted was to be the cause of more conflict between the two of them.

"You sure?"

"Of course. I'll catch up with you at your place, okay?" Ava felt her cheeks heat when she realized what Caleb's *mother* had just heard her say. "I mean, uh, to eat something, or we can meet there and then go eat something or—"

Caleb choked on a laugh.

I am going to kill him.

"I'll see you there in a few hours," he said.

She left with the others before her face exploded in flames.

CHAPTER NINE

"Are you sure you know where you're going?" Finn asked, picking a twig out of his curly brown hair.

Emma scowled. "Of course I do. Do I need to remind you that this is *my* mission? You're just along for the ride."

Finn's eyebrows shot up.

He said nothing—nobody dared where Emma was concerned—but she didn't have to be a mind reader to know what he was thinking. She'd begged Father to let her do this on her own, but ever since the incident with Ava, he'd insisted that she be accompanied wherever she went. And always by Finn MacKenzie, the worthless creep. The Rogue didn't even have any useful gifts other than the usual speed and strength, only an annoying immunity to the gifts of others. Including Emma's. Which kind of explained why he'd gone from Father's foot soldier to Emma's babysitter.

He shot her an annoyed glance.

Emma knew he saw it as a demotion. Still, she was Borré's daughter, which brought with it a certain deference, and he dared not speak out about her or against her. It didn't keep him from complaining, though.

"You sure we're not lost?" He kicked at a rock, and it ricocheted, nearly hitting Emma in the knee.

"We're not lost." She reached out with her gift and prodded at his mind. Maybe she could get through enough to shut him up.

"Would have been faster to take the car."

Emma sighed.

No such luck.

"We couldn't risk anyone seeing us driving off with them," she said. "It's smarter to approach from the rear. I'll get them to go with us, and we'll be back at the car before dark." She'd told him this at least a dozen times. If she didn't need him to give a good report to her father, she'd consider leaving him behind.

Or in a ditch, I'm not picky.

She hated him. Hated her father for making her put up with him.

She sighed.

This mission would do it, though. It'd get her back in Father's good graces, and she'd be his second, as she'd always been meant to be. She simply had to do a good job, put up with Finn—the idiot—and get back without killing him.

She could do it. She could do anything if she put her mind to it.

They walked in silence for a few minutes, Finn blessedly distracted by something on his phone, and Emma let her mind wander. As usual, it drifted back to Ava and what she'd done wrong—if there was something she could have done better. She'd been so convinced that once she'd shown Ava what she was missing—that Caleb and the others were holding her back—that she'd join their cause and take her rightful place.

She'd underestimated her sister's loyalty, obviously. Emma had to admit her judgment might have been clouded by her own excitement at having found her sister. She'd met other siblings, of course, but Ava had been the first *sister*, and she'd hoped for that closeness she'd read about in books. She'd hoped that she and Ava would become best friends.

I was so close . . .

Emma shook off her melancholy. There was no use dwelling on the past. She had to look to the future and this new opportunity to draw Ava into the fold.

They skirted the wetlands, Emma frowning as her boots squelched in the spring mud, and came to the edge of the greenbelt.

She peered through the underbrush at the back of the house and smiled when she spotted the woman on her knees in the small garden to the right.

The woman grumbled as she tugged on a stubborn weed and gave a little cheer when it came free. She tossed it into the nearly full wheelbarrow without looking.

"Stay here, out of sight for a minute," Emma whispered to Finn. When he started to argue, she said, "Just for a minute. Let me talk to her first."

He nodded, and she emerged from the trees, crossing the yard on light footsteps.

When the woman looked up, confused, Emma smiled. "Mrs. Michaels?"

"Yes? I'm sorry, can I help you?" She got to her feet and pulled off her gardening gloves.

"I'm Emma. A friend of Ava's. We spoke on a phone a while back?" She was tempted to see if she could do this without using her gift, but overconfidence had been her downfall before, so she reached for it, pushed a little bit.

Yes, you know me. You trust me.

"Oh, yes, of course," Sarah Michaels said, waving dismissively and looking flustered before reaching out to shake Emma's hand. "I'm so sorry. You took me a little off guard."

She looked nothing like Ava with her dark hair and blue eyes, but then she wouldn't, would she? She wasn't really Ava's mother. Merely a human.

"Oh, no, it's fine," Emma said, putting on her best innocent look. "I'm sorry to drop in uninvited like this."

"Don't be ridiculous. Any friend of Ava's is welcome here." Sarah's smile fell slightly. "She's all right, isn't she?"

"Yes. Ava's fine. I just . . ." She looked around the yard. "I needed to speak with you and Mr. Michaels for a moment, if that's all right. Is he here?"

Sarah hesitated, and Emma pushed her a little more.

Everything's fine. You trust me.

Her face smoothed. "Of course. He's in the house. Come on inside, and we'll have something to drink."

Emma followed her, glancing back to see Finn starting out from the shadows of the trees. She raised a hand to still him but knew he'd probably move closer once they were inside.

She and Sarah walked through the sliding glass door, and the older woman called out to her husband as she pulled a few bottles of water out of the refrigerator.

When Ava's dad walked into the room, she introduced them with a smile. "You remember Emma, honey, don't you? Ava's friend?"

He looked a little confused but held out a hand anyway. "Hello, Emma."

"Mr. Michaels."

"Joe, please. Call me Joe."

The three of them stood around the kitchen island, and for a moment, Emma was filled with a sudden nostalgia—or perhaps *longing* was a better word, since she'd never actually experienced having a family like this. Ava was brought up here. Raised by parents who loved her, protected her.

Parents who never hurt her.

A twinge of pain shot through Emma, but she shook it off.

Time to move on.

"What is it you needed to talk to us about, Emma?" Sarah asked kindly, starting at something she spotted in the backyard.

Emma looked over her shoulder.

Finn stood at the back door like a stalker.

Idiot.

With a roll of her eyes, Emma waved Finn in. "This is my friend, Finn. We're here to take you to Ava."

"To Ava?" Joe shook his head slightly. "Why are we going to see Ava?"

Emma drew in a heavy breath and forced a wave of placid acceptance their way. "She needs you to come with us. She's fine. You'll be fine. But you need to get your coats and come with us now."

They both looked a little dazed, and Emma wondered if she'd overdone the compulsion. Sometimes she didn't even know her own power, and humans were so easy.

"Is there someone who'll miss you if you're gone?" she asked gently.

"Um. No, not really," Sarah said slowly. "Mrs. Emerson next door?"

"Why don't you call her?" Emma suggested. "Let her know you're going on a little vacation while your husband gathers your things?"

They both nodded, and with glazed eyes and parted lips, Ava's parents moved in slow, shuffling steps like zombies.

Emma leaned against the counter to wait as they fulfilled her instructions.

"That's really kind of creepy," Finn muttered.

Emma shrugged. "Gets the job done."

After a few minutes, Sarah hung up the phone and Joe helped her into her coat. They approached Emma and stood before her, waiting expectantly.

"So weak," Emma murmured, half to herself.

"Human," Finn said, as though it explained everything. It did, actually.

"Well, let's get going," Emma said brightly as she reached for the sliding door.

For a moment, Sarah's eyes cleared. "Where are we going?"

Emma turned back with a wave of irritation and the glazed look returned. "You don't need to worry about that, do you?"

They nodded in unison. "We don't need to worry about that."

Emma smiled in satisfaction and opened the door.

"How have you been?" Madeleine asked, crumbling a cookie between her fingers. Everyone else had left, and Caleb had been tempted to follow, but he knew he had to speak with his mother. It had been too long.

"Fine," he said. "You know. Busy."

"On assignment," she said wryly.

"Right."

Madeleine put the cookie on a napkin and squared her shoulders. "I want you to know that I understand. About the Guardians."

"Oh?" He didn't know what else to say.

She nodded. "Given your feelings for Miss—for Ava, it makes sen—"

"This isn't about Ava. At least not entirely." He sat back in his seat at the dining room table, spinning the water bottle absently. "Ava may have been the catalyst, but I've felt this way for a while. What we were doing, how we were treating the Half-Breeds, it's wrong." His mother stiffened, and he hastened to say, "I know the Council has the Race's best interests at heart. But hunting these people down—*killing* them in many cases, too many cases. What gives us the right?"

"We need to protect our people."

"From what?" Caleb asked, his voice a near-whisper. "From them? From exposure? I mean, think about it, Mother. What's the worst that could happen?"

Madeleine's blue glare was icy. "You obviously don't remember your history."

"Oh, I remember it fine, Mother, believe me. It was pounded into me from the cradle."

"They're unpredictable. Uncontrollable. There's a reason it's forbidden—"

"I know!" He caught himself and lowered his voice. He wasn't going to argue. That wouldn't do any of them any good. "I understand your concerns, but we can't keep operating out of fear. The Half-Breeds are people, Mother. They deserve to be treated with some respect. They need our help, not our condemnation."

"And what of the Race?" she asked.

"The Race will survive, as it always has," he said gently, reaching out to lay a hand over hers. "But it can't be at the expense of others. We've always prided ourselves on aiding and protecting humanity. Shouldn't that extend to everyone, even if they're not entirely human?"

His mother turned away but she seemed to be contemplating his words. She jumped and pulled her phone from her pocket with an apologetic look. Caleb shrugged, and she answered the phone. "Yes?"

Caleb tried not to eavesdrop on the conversation and got up to look out the kitchen window until his mother hung up.

"I've got to go," she said. "I'm needed back at my office."

"Okay." He picked up his coat and squeezed the fabric between his fingers. "Are you all right? With . . . Gideon here?"

"I will be." His mother looked down and took a deep breath. "I'll do what needs to be done." She squared her shoulders and lifted her chin.

His mother had always done her duty, and Caleb was only now beginning to understand the toll that took.

"Now, I really need to . . ." She waved her hand toward the door.

Caleb nodded. "I'll walk with you."

They left the house, the mountain air cooling as the sun neared the horizon. Madeleine tucked her hands in her coat pockets and Caleb glanced at her out of the corner of his eyes. They used to be so close, but now he wasn't sure what to say to her.

His mother seemed to feel the same way, but she inhaled and let it out slowly. "You're convinced this is our best option? This alliance?"

"It's the only option," he replied. "The Twelve, they're . . . well, you saw what Ava can do, and Mother, what you saw in the Council chamber? That's the tip of the iceberg."

Her eyes widened. "Really?"

He nodded. "Sophie, too. Even with the block not fully removed, her cryokinetic ability is astounding. Think of what she'll be able to do when it's lifted."

"And then there's the boy," she murmured. "Emma Reiko makes four. That means there are still eight more. We need to get Sophie and Isaiah back. And as many more as we can find, although I have no idea how to go about doing that." She let out a frustrated grunt and swept her hair back from her face to secure it with a band at her nape.

"Actually, Ava had an idea," Caleb said, as they rounded a corner and the Council Arena came into view. "The Twelve share DNA, so perhaps a search of our medical records might be helpful. With three samples, our scientists should be able to pinpoint some common markers, I would think."

"It's worth a shot. I'm willing to try anything at this point."

"Anything?" He shot her another sidelong glance. "Even an alliance with the Guardians?"

Madeleine curled her lips into a humorless smile. "If what you're telling me is true, and the Twelve are all that Borré designed them to be? Son, to protect our people, I'd form an alliance with the devil himself."

Her smile fell, and Caleb realized that, to his mother, that's exactly what she was doing. He could only imagine what it was like for her. Even being separated from Ava for such a short time and distance, her absence gnawed at him, like a missing piece waiting anxiously to be filled. And when they were reunited, it was as if everything was right—everything *fit* once again. For his parents, those feelings had to be magnified a hundredfold, and to not be able to act on them . . .

Well, it had to be painful.

Torture.

Wrong.

He got the distinct impression his mother didn't really want to talk about Gideon, however, so he changed tacks. "What do you know about this sensor?"

"Hmm?" His mother turned to him, and he realized she'd been lost in thought.

"This powerful sensor Andreas has? What do you know of him?"

She frowned. "Andreas handles Bureau business. I don't know much about the inner workings."

"Still, this sensor is more powerful than any I'd ever heard of before— Gideon, too, for that matter." Madeleine stiffened at the name, but Caleb pretended not to notice. "He helped Tiernan track me across hundreds of miles, Mother."

"You're joking."

Caleb let out a startled laugh. "You didn't know?"

"No, I had no idea," she said, pulling the collar of her coat up around her ears. "Andreas didn't tell me a thing. I knew, of course, that the Bureau was tracking you, given the situation with Borré's escape, but the details . . ."

"Maybe he was trying to spare you."

"I should still be informed. The whole Council should have been made aware of such a gift."

An idea began to form in Caleb's mind. He almost hesitated to voice it. "There's more."

"More?" She turned to him with an arched brow. "What do you mean?"

"It's possible the sensor is a Half-Breed I was sent to retrieve for the Guardians."

Her eyes widened in shock. "A Half-Breed? Working in the Protection Bureau?"

"I don't know for sure. It seems like too much of a coincidence, for Evan to disappear and Andreas to acquire a sensor shortly after." He shook his head ruefully. "I can't believe I didn't even think to ask Andreas the sensor's name."

His mother stopped in the middle of the sidewalk and grabbed his arm to stop him. "All right, I think you need to start at the beginning and tell me exactly what happened," she said. "Obviously, I've been left out of the loop on a few things. Important things." She looked supremely annoyed at the idea.

Caleb took a deep breath and told his mother about being sent to take the Half-Breed, a sensor named Evan, to the Guardian Colony. He described how'd he'd been intercepted and his mind had been tampered with.

His mother nodded—she knew much of the details concerning the Emma debacle already—but frowned when he explained that Andreas had told Tiernan about an extraordinarily powered sensor who could track over long distances, and that it was only when Caleb had been released from the compulsion that they had put together the possibility that the Half-Breed Evan and Andreas' sensor could be one and the same.

"But now, I'm wondering—"

"If he's not a Half-Breed at all?" Madeleine started to walk again, and Caleb hurried to catch up. "It would fit. Living in the human world, gifts beyond the norm. It makes sense."

"Another one of the Twelve, here this whole time?" Caleb mused.

"It's possible," Madeleine said, quickening her pace as she dialed her phone. "Whatever's going on at my office can wait. We need to get to the Bureau to find out exactly who—and what—this Evan is."

A chill of apprehension shot up Caleb's spine. "And if he's one of the Twelve?"

Madeleine held up a finger as she instructed her assistant to reschedule the rest of the day. "If he is," she said as she hung up, "then we'll discuss, as a group, how to move forward."

Caleb's lips lifted. "It sounds like you're ready to move forward with the alliance."

"As if there were any doubt," Madeleine said, a determined set to her shoulders as they walked through the front doors of the central building. "As if I ever had a choice."

The Protection Bureau occupied two floors below ground in New Elysia's central building. Ava wasn't sure exactly what she'd expected—the stereotypical police headquarters perhaps, with scruffy, puffy-eyed agents poring over case files and guzzling coffee. Maybe something more sci-fi with holographic computer screens and a wall of laser rifles.

Maybe I've seen too many movies.

In reality, the main surveillance room was a little more than the first, and a little less than the second. It was circular, an apparent theme in the city, with a screen in the center of the room that could be seen from any direction. Of course, the word *screen* was a bit of a misnomer. There was no actual screen to be seen, just projections of maps, photographs, and other data that flashed by in layers of text and images.

Ava watched the flickering lights and wondered how anybody was able to keep up.

Surrounding the screen, four rows of white tables—too sleek to be called desks, really, but they apparently functioned as such—radiated out like a bull's-eye, the last row hugging the curved walls, with the chairs on the inside facing out at more projected images flittering along the painted surface. Protectors and surveillance agents sat at some of the desks, examining their own monitors or consulting quietly with one other. Others chairs were empty with papers and computer pads stacked neatly before them.

It was obviously more technologically advanced than anything Ava had seen before—even at the Guardian compound—but at the same time, it seemed somehow normal. Maybe she was getting used to this strange new world after all.

Maybe. Kinda. Sorta.

Enough so she wasn't shocked when someone did something amazing, something that *should* be impossible, or when a creature that looked more angel than human walked into the room.

"This is Le Kwon, head of Bureau Surveillance," Andreas said, holding out a hand as the woman approached.

She was tall, probably six foot or better, Ava guessed, with glowing porcelain skin and long, glossy blue-black hair that hung—flowed, really—down her lower back. Like most Protectors, she was dressed in black from head to toe and her almond-shaped eyes, green and gold and topped by delicately arched brows, took in the scene with calm intent. Even without saying a word, she exuded authority and efficiency. She reminded Ava a bit of Katherine, but even more beautiful, like Talia—something she'd once doubted was even possible.

Ava realized she was staring and blinked, her gaze dropping to the floor. She finally looked up when Andreas said her name, and she realized he was introducing them.

"Nice to meet you," Kwon said, her voice low and husky. "To what do I owe the pleasure?" She looked expectantly at Andreas.

No nonsense. I like her.

"New assignment. We'll need Evan," Andreas said briskly, scanning the room. "Where is he?"

At the mention of the sensor's name, Ava exchanged a significant look with Tiernan.

So we were right. Evan is in New Elysia.

"He took a break," Kwon said. "He was here most of the night tracking a Half-Breed in California—"

"California?" Andreas smiled, obviously pleased. "That's the farthest yet, isn't it?"

Kwon tilted her elegant head in acknowledgement. "His gift is remarkable."

"How did he end up here?" Tiernan asked, beating Ava to it.

"Stroke of luck, actually," Andreas replied. "Protectors had been dispatched to apprehend him, but he was gone. They tracked him to Canada and found him wandering in the forest."

Ava glanced at Tiernan, but Andreas apparently caught the silent exchange.

"What is it?" he asked.

She cleared her throat and faced him head-on. "Caleb was bringing him to the Colony when he was intercepted by the Rogues."

Andreas' eyes widened. "Well, then. It's fortunate he was able to escape—both for him and for us, isn't it?" He turned to Kwon. "We need to find two Race who've been abducted by Rogues. They're both in the database already—Sophie Wright and Isaiah Bennett."

"The Half-Breeds?"

"Apparently not," Andreas said wryly.

Kwon picked up a tablet, fingernails clicking as she tapped and swiped. "When were they taken?"

Andreas relayed the information in clipped tones, turned to Gideon, and extended his hand. "The samples?"

Gideon reached into his pocket, but when Ava stiffened beside him, he hesitated and looked at her.

"Caleb's coming, and he's not alone," she said quietly. "I hope everything's all right."

Sure enough, a moment later, he and Madeleine walked in wearing identical expressions of grim determination.

"Where's Evan?" Madeleine asked.

"The man of the hour," Andreas murmured. "He should be here shortly. Is there a problem?"

Madeleine's eyes narrowed. "I'm not certain. Perhaps you'd care to explain to me how a suspected Half-Breed came to be working in Bureau headquarters."

"I don't believe I like your tone."

"I don't believe I give a damn!" Madeleine turned her withering glare on Kwon. "Did you know about this?"

Kwon paled. "I don't know what you're talking about."

"Clear the room!" Andreas shouted. "Madeleine, calm down," he said, holding up his hands.

Madeleine waited for the other agents to leave before she said through gritted teeth, "Don't tell me to calm down. You violated protocol. This should have been brought before the Council, not to mention Kwon."

"There wasn't time."

"There's *always* time!"

"We needed to find Caleb. The Council made it our top priority!"

"That doesn't mean we blithely throw away centuries of Law—"

"For God's sake, Madeleine, I didn't throw away the Law. I did what I had to do to find. Your. Son." He slapped the table to emphasize his words, ice blue eyes flashing in anger.

Madeleine scowled at him for a long moment before she took a deep breath, her eyes fluttering closed briefly as she let it out. "Is he a Half-Breed?"

"What are you talking about?"

"Did you even have him tested?"

"I made a judgment call. His gift—"

"Judgment call?" Madeleine's voice rose again. "After Ava? After everything we've learned, you found no need to *test* the boy?"

Andreas slumped slightly. "What exactly are you saying? Do you think—" His gaze darted to Ava.

"I don't know what to think," Madeleine snapped. "But you said yourself the boy has an extraordinary gift. It definitely begs the question."

"Excuse me," Kwon interjected, raising a hand. "Begs what question? What is going on here?"

Madeleine's jaw tightened, and it was obvious she was debating how much to reveal.

The room stilled and everyone seemed to hold their breath, waiting for Madeleine to decide.

"If Race security is at risk, I need to know what's happening," Kwon said.

With a curt nod, Madeleine filled her in.

She'd just gotten to Sophie and Isaiah's abduction when the door opened and a teenage boy walked in dressed in baggy jeans and a T-shirt, his blue eyes widening as he took in the scene, focusing quickly on Caleb.

"Hello, Evan," he said.

"Caleb?" His step faltered then he approached them slowly, his eyes flitting around the group. "Are you . . . okay?"

"Yes, thanks in part to you, if I'm not mistaken."

The boy's cheeks flushed, and he shrugged, jamming his hands in his pockets. "It's no big deal."

"It *is* a big deal," Caleb said quietly, laying a hand on the boy's shoulder. "You probably saved my life." He patted him once then stepped back. "I want you to meet some people." He reached out and took Ava's hand to pull her forward. "This is Ava."

His wide blue eyes grew even wider, if that were possible. "*The* Ava?"

This time it was Caleb who reddened. "The one and only."

Ava smiled. "It's nice to meet you, Evan."

Caleb introduced Tiernan, Gideon, and finally, Madeleine.

His mother seemed content to let her son take the lead, which was odd, but Ava wasn't going to question it. Her intuition seemed to be feeding on the tension in the room, although she couldn't tell if it was coming from Kwon's irritation at being left in the dark, Andreas' frustration at being questioned, or maybe even Evan's uncertainty as he tried to figure out why he'd been summoned. She let her mind wander a bit and tried to relax, hoping her gift would do the same. Ava didn't like feeling so on edge.

"First things first," Andreas said, acquiescing enough to glance at Madeleine for approval before he turned to Gideon. "The samples?"

The Guardian leader hesitated for a moment before he reached into his pocket to withdraw two vials of blood and handed them to Andreas.

The Council member gave them to Kwon who tapped the table and a small panel retracted before her.

She withdrew a long needle with a round handle on one end and pierced the cap on one of the vials to withdraw a drop of blood. Kwon held the needle out to Evan.

To Ava's surprise, the boy didn't hesitate to take the needle between his thumb and forefinger, smearing the drop of blood between them. He stared blankly at the redness on his skin, and then shuddered as if he'd been startled. "Not far," he said in a monotone voice, almost as if he was in a trance.

Kwon handed him a computer pad, and he ran his fingers over it quickly.

It took Ava a moment to realize that she and Andreas were looking at the central screen instead of at Evan, and she turned to find a series of maps flashing in the middle of the room.

"North," Evan said in that same almost dead voice. "No . . . west. Northwest. Not sure how far. I can't get a clear read. But northwest. Definitely." He shuddered again, and his blue eyes cleared and focused.

Ava wondered which was real and which was a contact lens, because, yes, she knew. Like she'd known about Sophie, she knew.

"Good," Andreas said, taking the pad from him and setting it down. "Now, Evan, there's a little test we'd like to administer."

They explained the process—just a drop of blood to examine his DNA—but Ava barely heard them, because she already knew Evan was Race. He was her brother. He was one of the Twelve.

Five.

This made five that she knew of. That left seven still to find. And with Evan on their side Ava was beginning to think they might actually have a chance.

CHAPTER TEN

"I'm telling you, we need to go after them," Caleb said, not for the first time.

The Guardian delegation had withdrawn to his mother's office after the DNA testing had proven what they'd all suspected. Evan was one of the Twelve. Kwon had quietly put a couple of Protectors on him, and Andreas was sticking close as he tried to narrow down Sophie's location, but Caleb didn't really believe the boy was a threat. No, Caleb was focused on getting to Sophie and Isaiah now that they had an idea where they were.

"Gotta say I'm with Caleb on this one," Tiernan said. "We can't afford to leave those two in Rogue hands."

Ava sat up, shoulders stiff, and jutted her chin out. "Sophie won't help them, not willingly, at least."

They all knew that didn't really matter, though. Not with Emma on the side of the Rogues.

"I understand the risks," Madeleine said. "But we can't simply send Protectors into a Rogue stronghold. Not until we have a better idea what they'd be walking into."

"So what? We sit on our hands?" Caleb jumped to his feet, his chair rolling back with the force.

"Of course not!" His mother pinched the bridge of her nose and took a breath to collect herself before meeting his gaze again, speaking calmly.

"We follow protocol. We send an advance team and try to gather some intel."

"In the meantime, they could move Sophie and Isaiah, or Emma could manipulate them, lift their blocks, and—"

"No." Ava's voice was quiet, but it still drew the attention of everyone in the room. "No, we can't let that happen."

Caleb could almost feel her fear, her anger. "The Rogues won't use them. We won't let them."

"It's not only that," Ava said, eyeing him with—was it apprehension? "It's not only Emma's compulsion I'm worried about. It's the block."

"What do you mean?" Madeleine asked.

Ava flitted a glance at his mother but focused back on him when she said, "The problems I've been having. The nosebleeds and headaches? They've been getting worse."

A weight settled in Caleb's stomach.

He'd suspected, of course. He'd wanted to believe her when she said she was fine, but he'd known she really wasn't.

"How much worse?" he asked.

Ava cleared her throat and looked away at the wall, the floor, anywhere but at Caleb. "A lot. It's not only when I use my gifts now. And it's not only headaches."

Concern turned to fear turned to outright fury as Ava told them about the nightmares, the increased physical symptoms, and how she'd been managing them with the help of the Guardian healer.

"I can't believe she kept this to herself," Gideon all but snarled.

"Doctor-patient confidentiality," Ava said with a twisted smile. "It's not exclusively for humans, you know?"

"And this Talia," Madeleine said, waiting for Ava's nod, "she thinks these symptoms are a result of lifting the block?"

Ava nodded. "I've been thinking a lot about what Emma said to me about the nosebleeds. She said our . . . father—" She grimaced as she said the word. "She said he would fix things. That when I got to him, it wouldn't hurt anymore. She said he'd help me 'like he helped the others.' "

Tiernan pushed away from the wall to pace slowly across the room. "A booby trap?"

Ava laughed humorlessly. "Yeah. I think so."

"I don't think I'm following," Madeleine said, leaning forward on her desk and rubbing a hand over her forehead.

"Borré manipulated their DNA," Caleb said. His voice shook with underlying fury. "Not only to create the perfect Race, but also to tie them to him. The symptoms, I'm guessing, will only get worse until they get the remedy from Borré himself." He turned angry eyes on Ava. "That's it, right?"

"I think so."

"And you kept this from me."

"I didn't want you to worry—"

"You lied!" Caleb shouted, his damning words echoing off the walls. He clenched his shaking hands into fists and turned and stalked out of the office, ignoring Ava's quiet plea for him to come back.

He raced down the stairs and out the front door, not even realizing he was running until he found himself in the middle of the forest. He stopped, kicked at a stone, and grimaced in satisfaction when it knocked the bark off a tree. He paced around the small clearing, rage and indignation burning through him. He couldn't believe Ava had lied to him. Had looked him right in the eye and lied to him, and then tried to defend herself by saying she didn't want him to worry.

As if he could do anything *but* worry when it came to Ava. As if he didn't worry about her every minute of every day. He knew the real reason, of course. She didn't want to be stopped. She was obsessed with bringing down her father, even if it *killed—*

"Caleb?"

He whirled around to find Ava standing near a tree at the edge of the clearing. He'd been so lost in his own thoughts he hadn't even felt her approach.

"I came out here because I want to be alone." He crossed his arms over his chest, bracing himself against the urge to reach out to her.

"Please, Caleb. I'm sorry." Tears clogged her words and gleamed in her eyes, but he would not be moved.

"For what? For lying to me? For putting yourself in danger every time— *every single time*— you used your gifts?"

"Caleb—"

"Or maybe for pretending that we had something more than just the bond? That this was some kind of partnership? That we could rely on each other—"

"We can!" Ava took a step toward him, but he held out a hand to stop her.

Pine needles and pebbles around his feet stirred with her emotion, hovering and bouncing on the ground. He felt a tug toward her. A *physical* tug.

"Don't even think about it," he snarled.

Ava's eyes widened. "I wouldn't. Caleb, you know I wouldn't."

"Do I? How exactly do I know that, Ava?"

"Will you please just listen to me!" she shouted, the dirt swirling higher around them.

When he clenched his jaw against more angry words, she closed her eyes and took a deep breath. The debris settled, and he sensed the settling of her gift.

She pulled a tissue from her pocket to wipe a small drop of blood from her nose.

Caleb fought not to wince, but his stomach churned again. "Are you all right?" he asked after a long, silent moment.

"Ha." She swiped at the tears glistening on her cheeks. "Not really, no."

He wanted to go to her. Everything in him screamed for him to go to her, but he resisted. "Why didn't you tell me?"

She sighed and looked out through the trees. "You remember that day at the park, after the Rogue attack. After Emma . . ." Her voice was quiet, distant with memory. "I asked you to promise me that if I was needed, you'd let me fight."

"I said I'd try."

She turned the full force of her gaze on him, hot and earnest. "Try isn't enough, Caleb. Not for this. Can't you see? We're not just talking about me here, or you, or the Race. It's not only about Rogues and Guardians and the Council. This is about everyone. The whole world. If the Rogues succeed—"

"They won't succeed."

"They *can't* succeed," she said. "We can't let them, Caleb. No matter the cost. There's too much at risk."

Caleb knew she was right.

Borré and the Rogues wanted power, and if they got it, anyone who stood against them would be destroyed. Humanity would become nothing more than slaves to their whims. There would be no one left to fight for them, to defend them.

"I know that," he said, finally taking a step toward her, then another, until they were close enough to touch, although he still didn't reach out. "You think I don't know what's at stake? I know very well."

"Then you should understand—"

"No," he said firmly as he shook his head. "I mean, yes, I understand why you feel you have to do whatever it takes, including putting yourself at risk. God, Ava, don't you think I feel that way, too? I was raised to help others—to Protect the Race, to aid humanity. It's instilled in us from birth. I get that. How could you think I wouldn't? What I don't understand is why you thought you couldn't trust me."

Ava's face fell, a new round of tears sparkling in her eyes. "I do trust you. Please . . . *please* don't think that."

"You know what else I remember from that day at the park?"

"What?" she whispered.

"I remember saying we'd face this together." His voice caught, and he swallowed down a flood of emotion. "How can we do that if we're not honest with each other?"

"I—" She reached out, her fingers barely touching his, and her pain twisted with his own. Her sorrow and regret pulsed within his chest. "I'm so sorry, Caleb. I should have told you. I should have trusted you."

He pulled her close, wrapping his arms tightly around her as she sobbed against his chest, mumbling, "I'm sorry," over and over again.

He hushed her and pressed kisses into her hair. "It's okay. It's okay. We'll figure it out."

"How?" she asked through her sniffles.

But Caleb didn't have an answer, so he just held her close until her crying stopped and the light faded around them.

It was fully dark by the time Ava and Caleb emerged from the forest, hand in hand. She knew they hadn't resolved everything, but at least they'd cleared the air. Ava had truly believed she was doing the right thing, protecting Caleb, but hadn't fully realized how her actions, her lies, might affect him. When she'd found him in the woods, she felt the pain and betrayal pouring off him in waves.

She hated that she'd been the one to put it there.

Exhausted, they made their way to Caleb's house. He'd paused briefly to text Tiernan and let him know they were calling it a night. She couldn't blame him. The Protector was probably the only one who wouldn't ask endless questions, and neither one of them was up for that at the moment. There was so much to do, but they'd need rest to face what lay ahead. And Ava needed this time with Caleb to try to repair the damage she'd done.

They didn't even make it to the bedroom, collapsing on Caleb's sofa and falling into a dead sleep, wrapped up in a blanket and each other.

Ava rose with the dawn and dragged Caleb with her. They cleaned up and headed for the Council Arena, stopping briefly along the way for coffee and breakfast sandwiches. Madeleine and Gideon met them in the Protection Bureau's lab, a place Ava was quite familiar with after her own testing as a suspected Half-Breed. The Council leader and rebel Guardian stood stilly on opposite sides of an exam table as the Race physician and his assistant bustled about readying their equipment.

"Where's Tiernan?" Caleb asked as he shrugged out of his coat and hung it on a hook by the door.

"He and Andreas are debriefing Evan," Madeleine replied, "as well as trying to get a better read on Sophie and Isaiah's location." At his questioning look, she added, "No luck yet."

"Ms. Michaels?" The doctor smiled, and she realized it was the same man who had conducted some of her other tests. "Are you ready to get started?"

"I didn't realize we'd have an audience."

"We won't be doing or discussing anything too personal," he replied. "But if you'd prefer—" He gestured as though he was going to open the door and usher everybody out, but Ava waved a hand in dismissal.

"No, it's fine," she said as she slipped off her coat and hopped up on the table. "What's the plan?"

He rolled over a low cart carrying some kind of scanner and pulled a small tool out of a clip on the side. When Ava flinched, he held it up so she could examine it. "It's noninvasive," he assured her.

She laughed. "Well, that's good. I'd rather not have my head dissected."

"No, nothing like that. I just need to touch it to your forehead," he murmured, running the cool metal across her skin as he adjusted some dials.

Ava gasped as a three-dimensional rendering of her brain appeared in the air above the scanner. "We didn't do that before."

The doctor grinned. "Well, not where you could see it anyway." He fiddled with the knobs some more and the green and blue lines came into sharper focus.

"What exactly are you looking for?" Ava asked.

He held up a finger and pressed another button.

A second brain appeared next to Ava's, but where the outlines and definition on hers were clear and precise, the second brain appeared almost blurry in places.

"This is your brain," he said, pointing to Ava's, then the second one. "This is your brain on a psychic block." He laughed but sobered when he saw nobody else joined in. The doctor cleared his throat as he focused back on the images. "This is a rendering of Evan Davis' brain," he explained, as he picked up a pen and started to point out the blurry sections. "These areas, I believe, are where the psychic block remains intact."

"Wow," Ava murmured. "I pictured it like more of—I don't know—a wall, I guess?"

"That's understandable," he replied. "But it's actually more of a dampening field, for lack of a better term. It muffles the gifts, like stuffing cotton in your ears. Much stronger, of course."

"So can you lift it?" Madeleine asked, stepping forward to examine Evan's rendering a little more closely.

"I believe so," the doctor replied. "As you can see, there are areas where it's already weakened, others where it's collapsed completely. I'm not certain if that's a flaw or by design. It's possible Borré, or whoever actually put the blocks in place, always intended them to remain intact for a limited time."

"That makes sense," Caleb mused. "If what we suspect is true, and the removal of the block instills these symptoms that only Borré can alleviate—"

"It follows that the blocks are designed to fail, eventually," the doctor said, "forcing the patient to return to him. It's like calling his children home. Rather ingenious"—he caught Ava's black look—"in a sociopathic madman kind of way, of course."

"Of course."

Flustered, the doctor reached into a drawer and withdrew a syringe. "If I might take a blood sample?"

Ava held out her arm and looked away as he drew the blood.

He squeezed a few drops into another machine and tapped at the screen for a few minutes, eyes glued to the output until he nodded emphatically. "It's as we thought."

"What is?" Ava jumped down off the table and joined the little group as they clustered around the computer screen. She recognized the double helix formation of DNA, slowly rotating on the screen. Four actually, lined up side by side.

"This is yours," the doctor replied, pointing to the first image. "These are Sophie's, Isaiah's, and Evan's. As we expected, the common DNA markers indicate you are all siblings. Of course, Isaiah and Sophie show more commonalities since they share a mother as well as a father. These pairs"—he pointed to the bottom of the spiral—"are what we look for in verifying Half-Breeds. In this case, they indicate full Race blood, as you know. But the composition of this pair"—he pointed to the center of Sophie's double-helix—"is common to all four of you, but not to other Race." He laced Ava, watching and apparently waiting for that to sink in.

"Are you saying," Ava said slowly, "that that's what makes us the Twelve?"

"That's exactly what I'm saying," he replied. "But there's more." He tapped at the screen and it fluctuated, morphing into four horizontal rows consisting of dotted lines with dots and dashes of varying widths. "Look at this," he said, running the tip of a pen down the rows. "You see this gap here?"

Ava looked closer, and sure enough, there was an identical gap in each of the four rows. "What does that mean?"

He tapped his pen on the screen once as he spoke. "I think this is what's causing your symptoms. I believe lowering the block itself isn't the problem, but when your Race gifts are released, so is this."

Ava swallowed, feeling lightheaded. "And what exactly is 'this'? What does it do?"

"Essentially, it's a timer," he said.

"Timer? What's that supposed to mean?" Caleb asked.

"It means he's put us on a countdown," Ava said numbly. "That's why the symptoms have been getting worse."

"A countdown? To what?"

Ava feared she already knew, but she looked to the doctor for confirmation. For condemnation.

"I'm afraid the deterioration is cumulative," he said quietly. "If it's not stopped—"

"I'll die."

"Eventually, yes."

"Well, you have to do something." Caleb said, fists clenched at his sides. "Surely there's a treatment."

"I can help alleviate the symptoms, slow the advance, as I believe the Guardian healer has been doing," the doctor replied. "We'll continue searching for an answer, of course."

"Of course we will," Madeleine said briskly. "I want your best on this, Doctor."

"Yes. That goes without saying," he replied. "But I have to warn you. Without knowing exactly how Borré created this, it could take us months, *years* even, to find an answer."

Ava nodded, numb and out of tears. "And that will be too late, won't it?"

"At the rate your symptoms are advancing, I'm afraid so."

Caleb took her hand and squeezed it, gentle but firm. "It won't come to that," he said.

Ava took a deep breath. "Well, there's no use focusing on that right now, is there?" she asked. "You'll keep looking for an answer—not only for me, but for Sophie and the others as well. They don't have any symptoms yet, but if what you're saying is right, it's only a matter of time." Her voice caught.

"Ava—"

"I'm fine, Caleb," she said. Realizing how short she sounded, she turned and placed her palm along his cheek as she looked into his troubled eyes. "I promise you, this is not really news to me. I've kind of suspected it all along. But there's nothing to be done right now other than what we're already doing."

He held her gaze for a long moment then leaned in to kiss her softly. "All right."

"What about tracking the other Twelve?" she asked, breaking the tension in the room.

"Well, at least there I have some good news," he said. "It will be simple enough to cross-check our medical database for the Twelve markers. It'll take some time, but it's definitely possible."

Madeleine cleared her throat, and Ava thought she spotted a sparkle of tears in the woman's eyes. "Bring everyone in," she said briskly. "I want teams working around the clock, both on finding the Twelve, and finding a treatment for them once we do. Work with Kwon and Andreas to coordinate. I want—" Her cell phone buzzed, drawing a soft curse, and she excused herself to leave the room and answer the phone.

They'd just resumed examining the medical data when she burst back in.

"Ava, I think you need to come with me," she said.

"What is it?" Caleb asked, taking her hand as they left the room with Gideon trailing after them.

"Katherine's here."

"Katherine?" Ava quickened her steps as they walked through the surveillance room and down a hall. "What does that have to do with me?"

"She's not alone," Madeleine replied as she unlocked the door to a small conference room and held it open.

Sure enough, Katherine stood inside, and next to her, a familiar figure—tall, blond and beautiful. It took Ava a moment to reconcile seeing someone from her old life in this strange part of her new one.

"Lucy?"

"Ava!" Her voice broke as she raced forward to grab her in a tight hug. "Are you all right?"

"W-what are you doing here?" Ava turned wide eyes on Katherine.

The Protector threw up her hands. "She came to me and said she had to find you. That it was an emergency."

"You told me," Lucy said, "if anything strange happened. If I needed help, I should find her."

"Lucy, what's happened?" Panic kicked up her pulse as Ava gripped her friend's shoulders. "What's going on?"

"It's your parents, Ava," she said, gasping through tears. "They've been kidnapped."

Ava felt her knees buckle, and the floor rose to meet her, cold and hard against her palms as she tried to hold on, her nails scraping on the tile. She was hazily aware of things breaking around her—glass cracking, chairs toppling—although she couldn't be sure with the panic coursing through her.

"Ava, breathe. Please . . . you've got to calm down. Breathe."

Am I not breathing?

No, there was no air. She couldn't draw any in. Something was tightening around her chest, holding her tight.

"Come on, Ava," a voice called to her from a distance, warm fingers trailing down her face. "You have to breathe. Listen to the sound of my voice."

She blinked, the fuzzy colors before her gaining clarity, forming a familiar face. "Caleb?"

"That's right. Now, breathe with me. Come on, you can do it. Nice and slow. In . . . and out."

She matched her breaths to his, slow and steady, in and out, and the blackness at the edge of her vision withdrew as her gift settled. She lifted a trembling hand to lay it over his on her face, seeking his warmth, his power flowing through her to ease her pain. "Caleb?"

"It's all right. We're going to find them. They're going to be fine."

She nodded and took another shaky breath, then another, until she felt steady enough to get to her feet. She noticed the shards of glass and broken furniture littering the floor. "Sorry," she whispered.

To her surprise, Madeleine ran a soothing hand down her arm. "Nothing to apologize for."

"Ava?" Lucy's eyes were wide, shocked. "What the hell is going on?"

"I'll explain it all, I promise," Ava said, crossing the room to take her friend's hands. "But I need to know what happened to my parents. Please, Luce. Just tell me what happened."

She nodded slowly. "A girl came to me and said I had to bring you a message," she said. "I told her I didn't know where you were, but she said I'd have to find a way. She seemed to know that I could find you. I don't know how she knew when I didn't even know . . ."

Ava's hands grew cold and clammy, the edges of panic tingling in her stomach again.

"She made me memorize it. Said she had your parents and that if you wanted them back, you had to meet her 'where you almost met your potential.' She said I had to get that part exactly right—'where you almost met your potential.' What does that even mean, Ava?"

Her voice drifted away, coming to Ava through a tunnel.

"This girl, did she tell you her name?" Ava asked. Her vision was fading again, growing dark and hazy around the edges.

She heard a quiet, "Emma" before a loud crash and a shout, and everything went black.

CHAPTER ELEVEN

The sun shone bright white against the clear, pale blue sky, but Elias Borré saw none of it. His mind moved a mile a minute, as it always did, and plans formed and reformed like Play-Doh in the hands of a three-year-old.

A three-year-old genius.

Elias lifted his lips in amusement. "Are our guests settling in to their new accommodations?" he asked quietly, not turning away from the window.

"Yes, Father," Emma replied. "Mr. and Mrs. Michaels seem to be quite comfortable."

"Excellent." He stroked his chin and frowned at the prickle of a whisker he missed while shaving. "They are to be treated well, Emma. They cared for your sister and kept her safe and protected. That should be rewarded."

"Yes, Father."

He hummed then turned from the window to face her. "How did it go with the roommate?"

Emma smiled hesitantly. "She tried to tell me she couldn't reach Ava, but I knew she was lying. I barely had to push her at all, and she left with Katherine for New Elysia. It all went exactly as you predicted, Father."

He crossed to her and ran a hand over her hair. "Well done, daughter."

Emma preened under his praise, arching into the touch like a cat. "Thank you." She glanced up at him and swallowed. "I think . . . I mean, if you approve, of course, that it would be better if I met with Ava alone." When his eyes narrowed, she hastened to add, "She's sure to be upset. Perhaps she'd find me less threatening?"

"Are you certain you can handle that?" he asked. "Your sister's powers are formidable."

Emma stiffened. "I can calm her down. Reason with her."

"Really? After what happened at the Colony?"

"Please, Father, I can do it. Let me try. I promise. I can do this."

"Don't grovel, Emma. It's beneath you," he said, his fingers tightening on her scalp briefly.

He'd always intended to let her go alone, of course. It was time for her to try to rebuild the relationship she'd destroyed with Ava. Emma would become an ally, someone Ava could trust. It had been his plan all along, before Emma had acted on her own and set things back.

"Father?" Emma said weakly, and he looked down to see her face contorted in pain.

Ah, well.

He hadn't done it intentionally, but it probably couldn't hurt to drive the point home a little more before he sent her on her way. He pulled back his gift and her features eased. He leaned down and pressed a kiss to the top of her head. "You'll go alone," he said quietly. "And you'll do exactly as you're told. Right, daughter?"

"Yes, Father. You know I will."

"It will be difficult to gain her trust again. Are you certain you're up to the challenge?"

"I am," she said quickly. "I can do it."

He nodded and patted her cheek. "Remember, use your gift only as a last resort. She can sense it now."

"Yes, Father."

"Building trust takes time, and a common enemy always helps. Do you understand what I'm saying, Emma?"

She looked up at him, eyes wide—pale green and black.

So beautiful. A masterpiece, really.

"Yes, Father."

"You're to go, and you're to go alone. No cell phone. No trackers."

Lucy's voice echoed in Ava's ears as she made her way through the forest, running as fast as she could. The trees blurred in her vision, her focus on the path before her—the gaps in the trees and firm ground beneath her feet. Caleb had shifted her as far as Red Lake and wanted to take her even closer, but Ava had refused, not wanting to risk putting her parents in any more danger.

It had been a heated but short-lived debate. She'd made him promise not to follow her, and although she could feel his fear, he'd agreed to wait for word if she promised to be careful.

Be careful.

Ava wasn't exactly certain how she was supposed to do that.

Emma has my parents. Emma and Elias Borré.

Ava fought down another swell of panic and tried to focus on the task at hand—one foot in front of the other—setting course for the clearing near the Guardian Colony where she'd last seen Emma.

Where I almost killed Caleb.

Adrenaline coursed through her, mingling with her gift and flaring with an urge to find, to protect. To hurt those who dared to hurt her own. She gritted her teeth and forced herself to move even faster.

Then it hit her, like a punch to the stomach—the familiar twinge of Emma's power—and her step faltered as guilt and memories hit in its wake. Ava slowed, feeling Emma drawing nearer with every step, until she stood just a few feet from the edge of the clearing. The air stilled around her, the forest growing silent as if it too sensed the tension radiating from every inch of Ava's skin. With a trembling hand, she pushed aside a low-hanging branch and stepped into the clearing, heart pounding when she saw Emma standing in almost the same place where she'd last found her.

"What are you doing out here?"

"Waiting for you."

"Waiting for . . . why?"

"To help you, of course."

"Hello, Ava." Present clashed with past as she spoke for the first time.

The air vibrated around them, and Ava fought to keep control of her anger, her power. "Where are my parents?"

"They're not your parents, Ava. You know that."

A rock zinged across the clearing, and Ava took a deep breath. She needed to stay in control. She needed to get to her parents and at this moment, Emma was her sole connection. "Where are they?" she asked. "If you've hurt them—"

"Nobody wants to hurt them. They've done us a great service, after all." Emma smiled softly. "Caring for you all those years until it was time for you to come home. We all owe them a considerable debt."

Ava didn't rise to the bait. "Emma. Where are they? What do you want?"

Emma shook her head slightly. "You know, Ava. It's so simple."

"You want me."

"*Father* wants you. He wants you to come home and take your place at his side." She took a step forward, and it took all Ava's focus not to turn and run, or cause a tree to fall on Emma's head. One or the other was equally possible at that moment.

"And Borré thought kidnapping my parents and blackmailing me was the best way to gain my support?"

Emma sighed and looked through the trees for a moment before she turned back to Ava, brow furrowed with concern. "Father means well, even if it's not always apparent. He sees a great future for our people and that sometimes . . . affects his judgment."

"Was it his idea to make me into a killer?" Ava spat. "Or was that all you?"

Emma actually had the grace to look chagrined. "That was my mistake. I . . . shouldn't have done that to you, Ava. I apologize."

Ava let out a humorless laugh. "You apologize? You twisted my mind, manipulated me, made me create and destroy an innocent animal—tried to get me to *murder* someone I love, and all you've got is 'I'm sorry'?"

"I didn't want to do it," Emma replied, tears glistening in her eyes. "Father . . . he needed you. He can be—" Her voice cracked, and she swallowed, fingers pressed to her lips. "He's a dangerous man, Ava," she said. "I love him, but you don't want to cross him."

Ava's skin chilled. "What will he do to my parents?"

"Nothing," she replied quickly. "If you do what he says, he'll let them go. We'll blur their memories, and they'll go on with their lives none the wiser. Safe and sound."

"And what does he want in exchange for that?" Ava asked. "None of this 'take your rightful place' crap either. I want specifics. What will it take for him to let them go?"

Emma closed the space between them, and Ava felt their connection— like the one to Sophie, Isaiah . . . even, to a lesser degree, Evan. The bond of the Twelve.

"He needs a show of faith," Emma replied. "You do something for him and he'll do something for you."

"Like releasing my parents?"

"Eventually, yes. Once you've proven yourself trustworthy. Once you've bound yourself to him and cut ties to the Council and the Guardians."

Ava's heart pounded in her chest. "And how, exactly, do I do that?"

"One step at a time," Emma said. "First, I take you to meet our father."

It had gone better than Emma had expected. Not that Ava had embraced her with open arms, welcoming back her long-lost sister, but she hadn't picked her up and thrown her across the forest.

It's a start.

She led Ava out of the clearing on the opposite side of where she'd entered, and her sister seemed surprised to find a gravel road a short distance away, Emma's SUV parked and waiting for them.

"Where are we going?" Ava asked.

"It's not far." She rounded to the driver's side and got in, Ava following suit after a brief hesitation.

"I can't believe I'm doing this," she muttered.

"It'll be all right," Emma replied. "I'll be there with you the whole time."

"And that's supposed to make me feel better?"

Emma swallowed her disappointment at Ava's brusque reply. "I know you don't trust me. Not after what I did. But I'd never let him hurt you," she said. She expected Ava to argue the point, but she just turned away to rest her head against the window.

They drove in silence for a while, Emma navigating the narrow, twisting road with halfhearted attention. She was too focused on Ava, the return of her sister—the bond of the Twelve stronger than any mated couple.

She needs to accept her fate, her destiny . . . embrace the place she's going to have in this new world once—

"What happens when I meet him?" Ava asked, still gazing out at the passing scenery.

"He only wants to talk to you." Emma chewed on her lip as she glanced at her. "Ease your pain a bit?"

Ava started at that and turned to face her. "How?"

Emma turned a corner and they emerged onto a paved road. "I don't know everything."

"But you know something."

Emma nodded and tried to sort out her words before speaking. "Each of us, when the block is lifted, is compelled to return home, to return to Father. The longer we wait—"

"The more painful it is."

"Yes."

"And if we don't go to him?"

Emma looked at her but didn't answer when the tension in Ava's jaw made it clear it wasn't necessary. "We need each other," Emma explained. "Our bond, as the Twelve, is extraordinarily strong. You've felt it, right?"

Ava shrugged a shoulder and looked back out the window.

"Our bond to Father is even stronger. When we are near him, we are finally complete. He relieves our pain, and his presence, his influence, solidifies our gifts."

"Kumbaya." Ava wanted to scream.

"It's what we are, Ava," Emma said quietly. "It's what we were created to be."

Ava glared at her, eyes flashing. "He's not God."

"No, I know that," Emma hastened to add. "But he *is* our father, and he wants to help us."

Ava turned away to look out the window again, and Emma let it go. She ignored the impulse to reach out with her gift to soothe her sister and tried to do it with words instead.

"I know it's scary," she said. "I know it's not something you want. But it will be okay, Ava. I promise, it'll be okay."

Ava didn't respond, but she didn't argue either, so Emma claimed that as a victory.

They made their way out of the wilderness, farmland and scattered houses eventually condensing into neighborhoods.

Ava tensed as Emma turned and pulled into the driveway of a brick rambler settled on a narrow strip of grass between two larger homes in the center of a cul-de-sac. "This is a Rogue stronghold?" she asked with a surprised snort.

Emma laughed. "Hardly. It's just a neutral place for you to meet our father."

"Are my parents here?"

Emma shook her head and shot her an apologetic look. "You need to speak to him first."

Weedy flowerbeds bordered the walkway to a faded red front door. Emma didn't knock but glanced at Ava before she turned the knob.

Something drew her in, like invisible fingertips clawing at her gift and pulling her forward. She stumbled over the threshold as she tried to resist.

"It's unsettling if you're not accustomed to it," Emma whispered as she gripped Ava's elbow to steady her. "You'll get used to it. Try not to fight it, and you'll feel much better. I promise."

Ava didn't think she had much choice, actually. The power flowed over her, settling her gift, but not in the same way as Caleb. Where his power seemed to fit with hers, interlinking like pieces of a puzzle, Borré's—if that's what it truly was—stretched over her body, enveloping her like a second skin. It didn't seem to be trying to control her, though, not like Emma. It was more like a layer of warmth that seemed to seep into her, blending with her blood and merging with muscle and bone.

Like it's part of me.

Emma didn't take the lead but watched her, smiling softly as Ava took a few tentative steps toward the back of the house.

He was drawing her closer, calling her without words, her gift reaching toward the relief that he promised. The ache in her muscles eased.

The living room to her left had no furniture but was marred by a mottled brown stain in the middle of the carpet. The house was older, not really run-down, but musty with disuse as if it had been empty for a while.

She shivered as she entered a narrow hallway lit by a bare bulb in a fixture overhead, the glass cover missing.

Fingertips brushed her palm, and Ava's gift surged, taking her breath for a moment. She looked down to see Emma gripping her hand. Ava pulled away, ignoring the hurt look on her sister's face.

"I was only trying to help," Emma whispered.

"I don't need any help."

She emerged into a large room, split into a kitchen on the left, and a family room with a vaulted ceiling on the right. Like the rest of what she'd seen so far, this room was devoid of furniture, but a man stood against an unlit fireplace on the far side of the room.

Ava wasn't sure what she'd expected—someone larger, perhaps, more like Tiernan, or more evil-looking, although she couldn't imagine what that meant, but the man who stood waiting for her with a half smile on his face didn't look overly evil, and he wasn't particularly intimidating.

He looked . . . normal. About six feet tall with wavy brown hair, dressed in a pair of jeans and boots, a black T-shirt and leather jacket.

"Hello, Ava."

She started when she realized he was closer than she'd thought. She kept moving toward him, however, until she could make out the black and hazel-gold of his eyes.

Elias Borré.

He reached out with one hand, and she froze.

He smiled and tilted his head, his hand still extended. "I don't want to hurt you. Quite the opposite, in fact."

"Where—" Her voice cracked, and she shook her head, a little dazed, as she swallowed. "Where are my parents?"

Borré frowned. "They're fine, I assure you. I wish them no harm."

"You could have fooled me."

Borré dropped his hand, a flash of something—irritation, Ava suspected—lighting his eyes as they narrowed slightly.

Ava winced as her headache sharpened, piercing, before it settled back to a low throb.

"I am many things, Ava, but I am no liar," he said in a low voice. "If I tell you I mean them no harm, no harm will come to them." He turned, ran his fingers across the fireplace mantle, and examined them with a frown, smearing his thumb and forefinger together. "Of course, that is as long as no one does anything to change my mind." He wiped his hands off on his jeans and turned back to her.

Ava's fear and anger swelled, her gift growing to respond.

The windows rattled and Borré's smile widened. "Impressive," he said.

A crack formed in the sliding glass door, splintering outward in a web as Ava fought to control her power.

Borré's hand shot out to grip her wrist and the door exploded outward, a shower of broken glass tinkling on the patio.

Then, as quickly as it rose, her gift withdrew, collapsing within her so quickly her knees buckled.

Borré's grip kept her on her feet, his fingers pressing harshly into her skin. He drew her up and laid his other palm on her head.

"What are you—" Ava tried to pull away, but Borré was stronger than he looked. She couldn't move, frozen under his touch and the intensity of his gaze.

A flood of warmth surged up from her feet, as if he pulled it through her, soothing heat skirting along muscle and bone, up her spine, and out her scalp. Her body tingled, muscles contracting and relaxing, her head lolling back on her shoulders as a wave of comfort swept through her. She blinked and realized she was lying on the floor and looking up at Borré and Emma. Her whole body felt heavy, loose-limbed, and it took a moment before she could even sit up.

"What did you do to me?"

"How do you feel?" Borré asked.

Emma was watching her with wide, excited eyes, fingers clenching as if she itched to reach out and touch her.

Ava turned to Borré. "What happened?"

"How do you feel?" he asked again, emphasizing each word a little more.

Ava closed her eyes and tried to take inventory of her still tingling body. "I feel—" Her gift swelled within her, but didn't act out. She was in perfect control. "My headache . . . it's gone," she said quietly as she opened her eyes. "I feel . . . I feel better than I have in months, actually." She hated to admit it, but it was true. No pain. No nausea. If anything she felt stronger, more powerful. Clear and focused.

Borré reached out to help her as she made to stand, but when she stiffened, he backed off.

She walked to the broken window, the cool air refreshing on her cheeks. Everything seemed brighter, sharper, the details of every sight and every sound more defined, even without accessing her Race gifts.

"It's how you were meant to be," Borré said quietly, and she realized he was standing right behind her. "It's the way you were created to be."

And just like that, the awe over her sudden change fell away. "I want to see my parents."

"In time," he said, and she could hear the disappointment in his voice. "First, I need something from you."

She turned to face him and squared her shoulders. "What?"

"A simple task, really," he replied, returning to his spot by the fireplace.

Emma watched them both but stayed in the shadows.

"What task?"

"I assume you are familiar with the Protection Bureau?" When Ava didn't reply, he shrugged slightly. "The Bureau monitors the perimeter of New Elysia, both via cloaks and more conventional methods. I simply require access to those monitors."

"You plan to invade New Elysia?"

"You make it sound like an act of war," Borré said, shaking his head. "I mean to liberate our people. The Council is no longer acting in their best interests."

"And what happens to them?"

"What do you care? From what I understand you're no friend of the Council." Borré crossed the room and looked out the window. "I have no desire to hurt any of them, but I will do what I must to help our people."

"Yeah, you're a real patriot."

He flashed her an irritated look. "You want your parents released unharmed. You bring me the codes to access Bureau surveillance and you get your wish."

"And how exactly am I supposed to do that?" she asked.

"I'm sure you'll find a way," he replied. "From what I understand you have quite a few connections in high places."

She thought of Caleb . . . Madeleine. "But they're not just going to give me the codes."

He slapped a hand against the wall. "Well, you're simply going to have to figure it out, aren't you?" He rolled his shoulders and lowered his voice. "Be convincing. Use the gifts that I gave you. Find a way. Oh, and Ava?" He appeared calm once again and approached her, looking into her eyes. "I will know if you betray me. Make no mistake, if you try to warn Madeleine or the Council or that Protector of yours, I will know. And your parents will suffer for your indiscretion."

"If you hurt them—"

"It's not up to me, Ava," he said, his voice deadly quiet. "This is all up to you. You can save your parents, save yourself, by joining me and taking your rightful place. Or you can choose to turn your back on your birthright and lose everything." He ran a hand through his hair and smiled. "But take some time to think it over, all right? Say, twenty-four hours?" He motioned to Emma, who came to stand at his side. "Your sister will take you to a safe place to . . . contemplate your situation, and she can answer any questions you may have."

He started for the door, and without thinking, Ava reached out with her gift to stop him in place.

A sharp, stabbing pain sliced through her skull, and Ava fell to her knees, gripping her head as she screamed in agony. She curled in on herself, the pain echoing through her body in throbbing waves as her vision blurred. She didn't know how long it was before the pain eased, and Borré's booted feet appeared before her eyes.

"I wouldn't do that again," he said. When she whimpered, he crouched down and tilted his head to look into her eyes. "I don't want to hurt you, Ava. It hurts me, too, don't you see? But discipline is important for a child. You know, spare the rod and all that—" He waved a hand. "Children need to learn, and how can they learn if they've never been taught?" He reached into his inside jacket pocket and pulled out a handkerchief. "You have a little   " He motioned toward his own nose as he handed her the cloth.

She wiped at her upper lip, red staining the white cotton.

Borré stood, and she rolled onto her back to look up at him. "Now you've learned," he said, straightening his jacket with a flick of the wrists. "I'm confident you won't make the same mistake again." He turned on his heel and stalked down the hallway, calling over his shoulder, "Twenty-four hours. Think about what I said," without breaking stride.

Ava heard the front door open and close before Emma fell to her knees beside her.

"Are you all right?" she asked, hands fluttering around Ava's face as though she was afraid to touch her.

"He's insane."

"He's our father."

Ava rolled away from Emma and pulled her knees into her chest. "God help us," she murmured.

CHAPTER TWELVE

"We have to get out of here," Sophie whispered, glancing out the crack in the door at the two huge men standing guard before closing it with a quiet click.

"You should let me try—"

"No!" Sophie belatedly realized she'd answered Isaiah's thought rather than spoken words.

He'd been practicing since they arrived at the mansion, and Sophie had to admit she was surprised by how quickly his gift had grown stronger and evolved beyond simply reading minds to projecting his own thoughts as well. She'd even caught herself getting him a bottle of water out of the refrigerator before she realized he'd planted the idea.

"It's because of him."

"I know."

They'd met the man Ava told them about—their father, Elias Borré—and although Sophie's head had told her not to trust him, her body seemed to innately do just that. She'd relaxed, her gift growing stronger but more under her control somehow, and Isaiah had confirmed he felt the same.

Borré had assured her it wouldn't be long before their blocks were lifted. As soon as they'd proven their loyalty, they could take their places at his side. Sophie, however, didn't plan to stick around for that. The guy was seriously creepy, and she knew Ava had to be out of her mind with worry.

"I think—" Sophie raised her brows in question when Isaiah raised a hand and pointed toward the ceiling.

"They're listening."

"How do you know?"

Isaiah rolled his eyes. *"Duh. I've been eavesdropping on the guys outside."* He reached out to touch her hand. *"Borré will be back soon with the girl—Emma. We need to be gone when they get back."*

Sophie nodded. She knew he was right. Ava had told her a little bit about Emma and what she could do. It wasn't something she wanted to risk. To be used against her will—

"Hey." Isaiah shook her arm gently. *"You have to let me help."*

"No, it's too dangerous."

"All of this is dangerous!" He waved a hand to encapsulate the spacious apartment where they'd been held since their arrival. *"Soph, I know you want to protect me, but this isn't the time. We need to work together if we're going to get out of here."*

Sophie let out a heavy breath. *"What do you know about our guards?"*

"Simple thugs. Strong and fast. One of them can fly a bit, but that's all."

"Fly? Seriously?"

Isaiah shrugged.

"We'll need a car. If we can even get out of the house."

Isaiah grinned. *"Leave that to me."* He approached the door, laid a hand on it, and closed his eyes.

"What are you—" she whispered, swallowing her words when he raised his other hand.

She made out low voices on the other side of the door, the knob turned, and Isaiah backed away as one of the guards walked in—the taller one with blond hair. Sophie wondered if he was the one who could fly.

Flying. My life is ridiculous.

"We need to move you to a more secure location," the guard said, stalking over to peer out the windows. "Gather your things."

Sophie cast a surprised look at Isaiah, who grinned.

They snatched up their coats and bags and followed the man into the hallway.

"What did you do to him?" Sophie whispered.

"Paranoia. He's not sure who to trust."

"But how?"

"I'm not exactly sure," Isaiah replied. *"I'm also not sure how long it'll*

last, so we better move it."

They followed the man down the hallway, pressing against the wall as he drew his gun and peered around the corner down the stairs. He waved them forward, and they descended the winding staircase silently.

Isaiah kept his breathing slow and steady and his eyes focused on the guard's back.

Sophie assumed he was dishing out more of whatever was making the guard help them.

The tiled floor of the entryway shone in the light from the windows alongside the huge double doors. The guard reached for the knob.

"What are you doing?"

They whirled around to find the other guard—shorter and dark-haired— emerging from a hallway leading to the back of the mansion.

"Where are you going?"

The blond guard straightened. "We've got to get them to a more secure location."

"What are you talking about?" The man took a step forward, and Sophie reached out to grip Isaiah's hand.

He remained focused on the blond man, who stepped in front of them.

"Who are you working with?" he asked the dark-haired man, slowly raising the gun to point it at him.

"Hank? What the hell are you doing?" He raised his hands, eyes darting around the foyer.

"You're working with the Council, aren't you?"

"No! What's wrong with you?" In a flash, he dropped to the floor and rolled away as Hank fired, the bullet shattering the tile floor.

Shouts erupted from the back of the house.

"Go!" Hank snarled, jerking his head toward the door.

Sophie reached for the knob but froze in place, unable to move.

"Soph?" Isaiah nudged her.

"Something's happening," she mumbled through numb lips. "I can't move."

Isaiah went to reach for the doorknob, but he, too, stopped with his arm extended. "Me either."

Out of the corner of her eye, Sophie saw five more men pour out from the hallway, four with guns drawn, the other simply watching them intently.

"It's got to be him," she thought, picturing the man in her mind.

Isaiah managed a small nod. *"He's strong. He's not responding to me."*

Sophie took a deep breath and reached for her gift, like Ava had told her. Isaiah gripped her hand, and his power seemed to help hers along.

The temperature dipped, and frost crawled along the edges of the windows, crackling quietly as icicles dripped from the doorways.

The dark-haired guard was walking slowly toward Hank, hands held up. "Come on, buddy, you know me," he said calmly. "You know us all. We're all loyal to the cause, you know this."

Hank's hand trembled, the gun barrel lowering slightly. "I don't—I don't understand."

"I'm losing him." Isaiah winced and stared harder at the guard. *"I can't hold him much longer."*

With a burst of power, the ice from the windows, the ceiling, and the walls converged, compressing into a bowling-ball-sized sphere. It shot out from them and slammed into the man holding them captive.

He flew down the hallway, and Sophie almost collapsed as his hold on her vanished.

She wrenched the door open. "Let's go!"

Gunfire erupted, and Sophie threw up a wall of ice to protect them as they raced out the door and down the front steps. Three cars were parked in the circular drive, and she turned panicked eyes on Isaiah, who in turn looked back at the blond guard, Hank.

"Keys!" he shouted, and the man didn't hesitate to toss them to him.

They ran to the car, pellets of ice shooting back at the house as the Rogues took cover.

Sophie fumbled as she tried to get the key in the ignition, but finally, the SUV started with a low purr. She slammed it into gear and sped out of the circular drive, screeching to a stop as they neared the road.

"What are you doing?" Isaiah shrieked, staring back at the men running out of the mansion.

Sophie grabbed his hand and closed her eyes. She let her gift surge through her, boosted by Isaiah's power, and visualized the water in the air—the air in the tires. After a moment, a series of loud bangs resounded behind them and Sophie smiled in satisfaction.

"What did you do?" Isaiah asked as she pulled out onto the road and stomped on the gas.

She winked at him. "I changed the air in the tires. To ice. Something I learned from our sister."

"Huh." He sat back and let out a little laugh. "I can't believe that worked."

"Yeah, well, we're not out of the woods—"

A loud thump sounded on the roof of the car as if emphasizing her unspoken words.

"What was that?" she asked.

A head appeared at the top of the windshield. The dark-haired guard glared down at them then drew back his gun and pounded at the glass with the handle, a crack splintering along the edge of the window.

"That's the one who can fly," Isaiah said, buckling his seat belt.

"So I noticed," Sophie replied through gritted teeth, swerving in an attempt to dislodge him.

The tires squealed on the wet pavement as the man rolled off the roof. He didn't hit the ground, though.

Sophie gasped as she spotted him in the rearview mirror, hovering a foot above the road and keeping pace with them as she drove.

He reached for the car again, his fingers gripping the roof as she slowed to round a tight corner.

"Crap," she muttered. "Can you do something about him?"

Isaiah closed his eyes for a minute. "It's not working. I think I can only sneak in, you know? He must know what I'm trying to do."

Icy rain beat down on the car, and Sophie grinned when the man cursed and pounded on the side window. She swerved again, and he flipped back up onto the roof.

"Uh-oh," Isaiah said, looking out the rear window. "More on the way."

Sophie grimaced at the sight in the rearview mirror.

The cars may have been disabled, but the Rogues could still run, and where she had to follow the road, she watched them leaping over logs and cutting through the woods in a straight line. They'd be on them in no time. Sophie's mind raced for a solution, but she saw only one.

She slammed on the brakes.

The man on the roof flew forward, flipping through the air before hovering a foot above the ground, breathing heavily.

"What are you doing?" Isaiah shouted.

The guard got to his feet, and Sophie shot a shower of ice balls at him, knocking him to the side of the road. He collapsed and struggled to get up again, but she knew she'd only bought herself a few minutes.

She turned to her brother, opening the driver's side door and unbuckling his seat belt in one motion before dragging him across the seat. "Get to

Ava—"

"What? No!" He tried to pull her back into the car.

"Isaiah, listen to me!" She grabbed him by the shoulders and looked into his eyes. "We can't get away—not together. I can hold them off for a bit, long enough for you to get away."

"Sophie—"

"Get to Ava. You remember where to go?"

He hesitated then nodded. "New Elysia. In the mountains near . . ." His eyes drifted to the rearview mirror.

She didn't look. "Kalispell," she said, shaking him slightly to draw his focus. "Keep going, and you'll hit the city in about a half an hour. Head for the mountains. They'll be looking for us. Tiernan will come after you. Then you'll help them find me. Don't forget."

"I won't." His eyes filled with tears. "Sophie—"

"It's the only way. Just go in that direction, and he'll find you eventually. You have to keep moving. I won't be able to hold them off for long." She looked back at the guard, who was struggling to regain his feet. She shot another ice ball his way then glanced nervously down the road. "Go now!" she said, slamming the door.

Her brother looked up at her with tears running down his cheeks.

She fought her own emotion and pressed a hand against the glass. "Go," she mouthed.

He nodded and hit the gas, tires squealing as he sped down the road.

Sophie turned to face their pursuers, gathering her power around her.

Snow began to fall, wind whipping it into a near blizzard. It was about to get very, very cold.

Sophie smiled.

Caleb paced across the well-worn orange carpet in the cheap motel in Red Lake, his anxiety at an all-time high. It had been hours since Ava had left. The sun was low in the sky, and each minute seemed to tick by even slower than the last. She'd said she would call. She had promised she'd be careful.

What was I thinking? How could I let her go alone?

He peered out the window, scrolling distractedly through the contacts on his cell phone and willing her to call. Text. Send a smoke signal to say she was okay.

C'mon, give me something. I'm not picky.

The phone buzzed, and he jumped, frowning when he saw it wasn't Ava calling, but his mother.

"Hello? What's happened?"

He heard his mother sigh. "The Council has approved the alliance. The Guardians and their charges are welcome in New Elysia."

"That's good."

"It's a PR nightmare," she said with a wry laugh. "But public opinion seems to be on our side, at least at this point."

"How'd you manage that?"

"We told the truth," she replied. "There are rumblings of discontent that we didn't share the information sooner, but the polls show that most see the alliance as the best and only solution."

"And the Half-Breeds?"

"Will be safe for the time being. I gave Gideon my word." Her voice trembled a little and she cleared her throat. "It's a temporary amnesty for those currently with the Guardians. Those we have in custody will remain there. Once the threat has passed, we will readdress the situation and the Half-Breed policies."

Caleb was grateful that was a discussion he would have no part in. If he had his way, once this was all over, he and Ava would be far away from New Elysia, and the Council, and politics in any and all forms.

"Have you heard from Ava?" Madeleine asked.

"Not yet."

"I'm sure she's fine. The girl is quite resourceful."

Caleb snorted. "That she is. The problem is, so is Elias Borré."

"Do you need backup? I could send Katherine—"

"Isn't she taking Ava's roommate home?"

"I promised Ava I'd keep Lucy here. Keep her safe until this is all over."

"What about Tiernan?"

"Evan got a lead on Isaiah," she replied. "Tiernan's following up on it."

"A lead? What kind o—" His call waiting beeped, and Caleb's pulse quickened when he saw Ava's name. "I need to call you back. Ava's on the other line." He hung up without waiting for a response. "Ava? Are you okay?"

"I'm fine." Her voice was quiet, almost a whisper. "I can't talk long."

"Where are you?"

"I'm not exactly sure. Somewhere near North Dakota, I think."

"North Dakota? Ava—"

"I'm fine. I have to meet with Borré tomorrow to find out about my parents."

"Tomorrow?"

"Caleb, listen." He heard her moving around, her voice slightly muffled. "I know you're worried, but I'm all right. I promise you I am. I need to do this."

Caleb took a deep breath. "I don't like it."

"I know you don't," she said quietly. "But I don't have a choice. Not right now. You should go back to New Elysia, and I'll meet you—"

"Absolutely not!"

"Borré doesn't want to hurt me," she said. "In his mind, he wants to help me. I really don't think I'm in any danger."

"You've got to be kidding me," he said, tightening his fingers on the phone until it creaked. "Have you forgotten what Emma did to you?"

"Of course not," she said, but it sounded tired, lacking any heat. "But I don't have a choice, Caleb. I have to get my parents away from him and find out what's happened to Sophie and Isaiah. This is the only way."

"It's not," he said. "I got word that they have a lead on Isaiah. Tiernan's on the way to find him right now."

"Really? Is he okay? Where is he? What about Sophie?"

"I don't know. But—"

"You should go with Tiernan. If they've gotten away, the Rogues will be after them. They might need you to shift them to safety."

Caleb went back to the window and looked out over the all but deserted parking lot. "But what if you need me?"

"I always need you. You know that." She sighed, and he pictured her rubbing her forehead. "But there's nothing you can do for me right now. And if there's a chance to get Sophie and Isaiah back to safety, we need to help them."

He tugged at his hair, torn by his desire to be there for her and his understanding that he might be of more use elsewhere. "Are you really all right? Please, tell me the truth."

"I'm fine, Caleb. Better than I have been in months, actually."

He heard her moving around, possibly settling on a bed.

"We were right about Borré. He can relieve our symptoms."

"I don't like it."

She laughed, but there was no humor in it. "I don't either, but I really believe he doesn't want to keep me here against my will. He wants me to come to him willingly, even if he has to use the people I love to do it."

"But what does he want from you?"

He heard her hesitation, even over the phone.

"I'll know more tomorrow," she said. "After I meet with him, I'll call you to come get me, okay?"

"Are you sure?"

"I'm sure." He thought she was going to hang up, but she said, "Trust me, please?"

Caleb let out a breath and leaned his forehead against the window. "You know I do. Just be careful, okay?"

"I promise."

Caleb hung up and allowed himself a few minutes to worry about his decision before grabbing his backpack and dialing Tiernan.

"Yeah?"

"Heard you got a lead."

"Maybe."

"Thought you could use some backup."

"Definitely."

"Text me the coordinates, and I'm on my way." He hung up and chewed on a couple of R-cubes, washing them down with a gulp of water from the bathroom sink. When his phone buzzed, he glanced at Tiernan's text, shouldered his backpack, and shifted south, the motel room blurring into a mess of orange and brown before vanishing completely.

"Everything all right?" Emma asked as she closed the hotel room door.

"Dandy."

Emma sighed and climbed up to sit cross-legged on one of the beds. "I know you don't believe this, but I really do want to help you."

Ava couldn't even bring herself to answer. Instead, she flopped back on her own bed and threw an arm across her eyes.

After a few minutes, Emma asked, "Are you going to do it?"

Ava huffed. "I don't have much choice, do I?" She rolled onto her side and propped her head on her bent arm. "What I don't get is why? With the resources at his disposal, Borré shouldn't even need those codes. Not to mention the fact he has a mole in New Elysia."

"A mole?" Emma actually looked surprised.

Ava wasn't sure if that meant they were wrong about Borré having someone near the Council, or if Emma was merely unaware of it. "So why ask for the codes? Is it just to see what kind of hoops I'll jump through, because—"

"It's not that," Emma said quietly. "Although Father demands obedience, obviously."

"Why, then?"

Emma chewed on her lip, looking away as she thought about her answer. "It's a show of faith. Father is big on those. He wants you to cut any ties you have to the Council or to the Guardians. By giving him the codes, you'll become an enemy to the Race. A Rogue. He wants you to rely on him and him alone. It's the only way he can be certain of your loyalty."

Ava scoffed. "And how does he know I won't turn on him?"

"You saw what happens when you do."

"Just because I can't attack him doesn't mean I have to serve him."

"You can't betray him—"

"I can do a lot of things."

"No, you don't understand," Emma said shifting on the bed to face her. "Father will know if you lie."

Ava couldn't resist the opportunity to learn a little more about Borré. "Is that his gift? He's a human lie detector?"

"He's a lot more than that."

Ava sighed in frustration. "More than what? What is he?"

"He's a genius. A scientist. He created us."

"I know that, but he's Race, right? So what's his gift? What qualifies him to lead the Rogues, anyway?"

Emma looked away, and for a moment, Ava doubted she would answer, but she squared her shoulders and turned back, licking her lips before she said quietly, "He uses gifts."

Ava blinked. "What? What do you mean?"

"Like the Twelve, Father can boost our gifts, make us stronger. But he also can access any gift and use it himself," she said, the words falling over each other as if she wanted to get them out as quickly as possible. "Not against your will—not ours anyway, the Twelve are too strong. Other Race, though, he can use. And if we allow it—"

Ava digested that for a moment. "So you mean back there at the house, when he hurt me. That was . . . that was you?"

Emma's cheeks colored as she dropped her gaze to the floor. "Not me . . . I would never hurt you, Ava. But he used my gift, yes. To supplement the protection around himself."

"Protection?"

"It's part of our makeup," Emma said. "It's not in our design to be able to turn on our creator. If we try to move against him, it's bad, but he used my gift to make it worse. To make a point." She swallowed and glanced up before focusing on the carpet. "I'm sorry. I know it's painful. I know—"

Ava's mouth dropped open. "He's done it to you, too, hasn't he?" When Emma was silent, Ava shook her head. "But how could you let him? Why would you let him do that to you?"

"Because I deserved it!" she shouted. "I was stubborn and disobedient, and I put the whole plan at risk!"

"Emma, no!"

"Stop," she said, sliding off the bed and grabbing her coat. "You don't understand. You can't understand because you're new to all this."

"Where are you going?"

She shrugged into her coat. "I'm going to check the perimeter."

"Emma, wait." Ava jumped up and grabbed her arm. "You don't have to do this. We could fight him. You and me. It doesn't—"

"No, I can't," Emma said, yanking her arm away. "And neither can you. The sooner you can face that, the better for us all." She locked eyes with Ava and reached for the doorknob.

"You should know, Sophie tried to escape," Emma said, turning to face the door. "She's being punished, and I can promise you it isn't pleasant. Not even a little bit." She looked over her shoulder with tears in her eyes. "That's what waits for you if you disobey, Ava. That's what waits for all of us. Can't you see? None of us has a choice. Not if we want to survive. It's just the way it is." She took a deep breath and walked out the door, closing it quietly behind her.

Ava stared at the wood for a long time before she finally stumbled back to the bed and crawled under the covers. It was even longer before she was able to close her eyes and fall asleep.

CHAPTER THIRTEEN

Borré's eyes, so similar to her own, gleamed in the dim light of the room. He sat reclined on a low, tufted settee, his legs crossed, and fingers stroking his lower lip.

This house was newer, furnished, but still not lived in as far as Ava could tell. They'd left the hotel at the break of dawn and driven a few hundred miles to cross the border into Montana, Emma uncharacteristically quiet as she watched Ava when she didn't think she was paying attention.

Ava *was* paying attention. She just didn't want to acknowledge her sister, unsure if she should hate her for what she'd done or feel sorry for her. In a lot of ways, Emma was a victim, twisted by Borré's influence, and a pawn to be used at his whim, and yet, she defended him, loved him, excusing his abuse with heartfelt words and teary eyes. In the end, what choice did she have, really? His hold on her was too great, too strong.

Borré's gaze flicked subtly to Emma on the other side of the room in a silent signal.

His daughter crossed to slip gracefully to her knees on the plush rug at his feet, her nerves only evident through the slight tremble of her fingertips.

"Have you thought about my offer?" Borré asked with an almost imperceptible arch of his brow.

His offer—interesting way to put it.

"You say that like I have other options," Ava replied, trying to swallow the contempt in her voice.

"You always have a choice, my dear."

"Don't call me that."

Borré's lips twitched. "So stubborn," he said, shaking his head. "But regardless of your protests, I have a feeling you've realized the opportunity before you. It is our time, Ava. You can be a part of it. You're *meant* to be a part of it."

A quiet knock sounded at the door, and Emma jumped up to answer it.

A man walked into the room, sallow and faded from head to toe—pale red hair, pale skin, pale green eyes—as though the color saturation on his entire body had been turned down a few notches.

Something about him . . .

Ava realized he'd been there for the Rogue attack at the Colony, but it was more than that. Not his face, but his presence. Something ominous and dark, like a figure from a—

"It was you," she murmured. "You killed him. I saw you in my dream."

The man arched a nearly invisible eyebrow but said nothing.

"What is this?" she demanded, a surge of panic and fear forcing her gift to the surface, as she turned on Borré.

The table legs thumped on the floor.

"What's he doing here?"

"I see you recognize Mr. Bartok. I suspected as much." Borré smiled and admired his fingernails. "As for his presence, think of it as a show of good faith."

Ava held back her gift but turned her body to put the wall at her back as she kept her eyes focused on the man. "What do you mean?"

"There's something you should know, something I suspect you already know," Borré said as he picked a nonexistent piece of lint from his trouser leg. "Your police friend? What was his name . . . Simpson?"

"Simmons. Nick Simmons." Saying the name sent a chill down Ava's spine. She still saw him lying in a pool of blood as if an image from her dream, but, as it turned out, it hadn't been a dream at all.

"Simmons. Yes, that's it exactly." Borré laid a palm on Emma's head—almost like a benediction—and she got to her feet and approached Bartok.

Her pupils dilated, the green swallowed up by darkness, and she stood facing the red-haired man with her head tipped slightly to one side.

"What's going on?" Bartok asked, his words beginning to slur.

"What *is* going on?" Ava asked, her gift flaring again with her anger, causing the window to rattle. Ava knew what he was feeling. She was very familiar with Emma's influence. "Stop playing games. What is he doing here, and what is this all about?"

Borré's lips quirked. "I'm proposing an exchange."

"What kind of exchange?" Ava glanced at Bartok, who was now staring into Emma's eyes, his mouth hanging open slightly.

"You stand accused of a crime—"

"Which I didn't commit," Ava said, scowling.

"No, of course not," Borré said with a condescending smile. "Anyone could look at you and see you're no murderer. Sadly, though, the evidence says otherwise." When Ava opened her mouth to respond, he held up a finger. "True. It was manipulated. My bad, as the kids say these days. However, what's done is done and all that."

"Do you intend to *ever* get to the point?"

Borré's eyes sharpened, his tone grew icy, and for the first time, Ava saw the killer behind the calm façade. "The *point*, my dear, is that I have something you want, and you have something I want. I believe I have a solution that will prove mutually beneficial."

She fought to keep her voice steady. "What solution?"

"Him," he replied, with a glance toward Bartok.

"He's fighting me," Emma said quietly, and Ava noticed the tension in Bartok's shoulders, the clench of his jaw, and the spray of perspiration on his upper lip.

Borré rose and approached the pair to lay a gentle hand on Emma's shoulder.

Immediately, Bartok relaxed, his mouth falling open once again.

"As I was saying." Borré turned back to Ava but kept his touch on Emma. "I have the true killer of Officer Simmons, as well as the murder weapon. With the aid of your sister, Mr. Bartok here will surrender to the proper authorities and confess to the crime, effectively clearing your name."

"What makes you think I need your help?"

"You're trapped, for lack of a better word," he replied. "You can't go out into the human world while you're a wanted fugitive. Human law enforcement may be inept, but it's not *that* inept. How long do you think it will take for someone to spot your picture on TV and call in a tip to one of those horrible police reality shows? Then where will you be?"

"I'm offering you freedom," he said, shrugging his shoulders as if it was as simple as that. "Freedom to come and go as you please. Have a life again. Finish school, if that's what you want. Get a job. Though the appeal of *that* is lost on me." His mouth curled in distaste.

Ava sensed the twinge of Emma's gift, but it wasn't targeting her. She wasn't being influenced. Bartok stood stock-still, however, clearly under her spell. A string of drool hung from the corner of his open mouth, and Ava swallowed, her own mouth dry. "And what do you want in exchange?" she asked, looking away from the spectacle.

"Oh, I think you know the answer to that question."

"Me."

"You."

"The security codes."

"For a start." Borré smiled, stroking Emma's head gently. "But even more, for you to take your rightful place at my side. It's time we all take our rightful places. The Council has made a mess of things for our people. We're hiding in dark corners instead of taking on the mantle of leadership."

"With you at the top, of course."

Borré laughed. "It's not about me, Ava. Can't you see that? It's about making the world a better place, not only for me and you, but also for all Race."

"And the humans?"

His jaw twitched, the only hint at his annoyance at the question. "Humans, as a rule, are irrelevant." Ava stiffened, and he hurried to add, "But they will benefit by this new world order as well. Think about it. If we're able to share our knowledge without fear, imagine all the good we can do. Diseases will be eradicated. Hunger will be nonexistent."

"In return, all you ask is for their loyalty."

Surrender.

He smiled. "A small price to pay."

Ava could imagine the price. With Borré in charge, humans would become nothing more than slaves. He would start with big promises, but once he gained control, those promises would crumble, and before they even realized what was happening, the humans would be dependent on him for everything.

Dependence. The very opposite of freedom.

But she couldn't think about that now. Now, she had more immediate concerns—her own freedom, her parents, and Sophie and Isaiah.

"You really think he'll confess?" she asked.

Borré raised a brow and turned to Bartok. "Who killed Officer Nick

Simmons?"

Without hesitation, Bartok replied, "I did."

"You will go to Allenmore, to the police department, and confess to the crime."

"Yes, sir."

"You will describe in detail how you killed Officer Simmons and surrender the knife you used to do it."

"Yes, sir." He reached into his coat pocket and pulled out a plastic bag.

It crinkled, and Ava spotted the blade inside. When bits of dried blood broke free of the knife and collected in the bottom of the bag, bile rose in Ava's throat, but she swallowed it down with determination.

No time for weakness.

"You will tell them you are a hypnotist and used your skills to trick the witnesses into their testimony."

Ava gave him a skeptical look. "You really think they're going to buy that?"

Borré rolled his eyes. "Humans believe what they want to believe. Especially when they've been given a little push." He turned back to Bartok. "Do you understand your mission?"

"Yes, sir." He turned toward the door, and Borré stopped him with a word. He looked at Ava, waiting.

She knew what she had to do. So she took a deep breath and looked her father dead in the eyes. "Done."

Emma's face broke into a wide smile, and she bounced on her toes in excitement.

Borré simply turned to Bartok and said, "Go."

The assassin left the room, and Borré smiled at Ava.

"Welcome to the family," he said. "Emma will see you back to Kalispell. I assume you can find your way to New Elysia from there."

Ava nodded.

"Retrieve the codes, contact Emma, and we will rendezvous at our headquarters. Once the codes have been verified, your parents will be released. No harm done."

"How do I know they'll be safe?" she asked.

"You have my word."

"Pardon me if that doesn't hold much weight at the moment."

To her surprise, Borré laughed. "Oh, you're a lot like me, you know?" He crossed his arms, his fingers plucking at his lip. "So put yourself in my shoes, Ava. I have no reason to harm your parents as long as you are working with me. It's very simple, isn't it?" His smile belied the obvious underlying threat in his words. "Don't cross me, daughter, and Joe and Sarah Michaels will be fine."

"How do I know you haven't already done something to them?" she asked, lifting her chin. "I want to talk to them."

"Oh, I wouldn't advise that," he said, tutting slightly as he waved to Emma.

She retrieved a small laptop from the kitchen counter and brought it to them.

"However, I can show you they are absolutely fine at the moment." He set the laptop on a low table and clicked a few keys before turning the screen to face her.

Ava blinked in surprise when she recognized the image. "I don't understand."

There were her parents, sitting at the table—her father reading the paper as her mother slathered jelly on toast.

"That's our kitchen at home," Ava murmured.

"Not exactly," Borré replied. "It's a replica. Emma could do the same thing with her mind, of course. Your sister is quite talented." He glanced at Emma, who blushed and smiled. "But her gifts were needed elsewhere, so constructing a reasonable facsimile of your childhood home was a relatively simple alternative. We only needed a few rooms, actually. Humans are quite simple, and as I said, they believe what they want to believe."

"So, they think they're at home? They don't know about any of this?"

" 'Ignorance is bliss,' as they say." Borré closed the laptop and tucked it under his arm. "They are in no danger at the moment, and as long as you fulfill your promise, they never will be."

"Father demands obedience."

"I understand."

"I believe you do," Borré said softly. He turned and left the room.

Ava didn't hear the front door close, but his gift slipped away like fingers trailing over her skin.

"We should go," Emma said.

"Will he do what he says?" Ava asked when they finally got back to the car. "Will he let them go?"

"Father doesn't lie."

They turned west heading out of the neighborhood and away from the small town Ava could see in the rearview mirror.

"Can I ask you something?"

"Of course."

"What about the rest of us? How many have come back to Borré already?"

Emma shot her a glance and worried at her lip. "A few."

"You're not supposed to tell me?"

She shrugged. "Father hasn't forbidden it. I don't suppose it matters, really. It's not like you could tell anyone where they are, and Father will know if you do."

"How?"

"He always knows."

Her voice was dead, quiet, and it sent a shiver down Ava's back. "So?" she asked, clearing her throat as she picked at her jeans. "How many?"

"We've all been accounted for."

Ava slumped on the seat. All but Ava and Evan—possibly Isaiah if he really had managed to get away. Three against nine.

Not great odds.

"Can you tell me about them?" Ava tried to keep the fear from her voice, tried to sound curious about her newfound family.

Emma smiled. "They're all great," she said. "Only one other girl, besides you and Sophie. She came to us a couple of weeks ago. Her name's Mara. She's kind of quiet. Likes computers more than people, really."

"What's her gift?"

"Electrical field manipulation. Everything from shooting lightning bolts to controlling power grids and manipulating technology."

Ava chuckled a shaky laugh. "More proof Borré doesn't need the codes at all."

Emma shrugged. "Maybe there are limits to what she can do. I don't know. Like I said, she's kind of quiet."

The conversation continued in the same vein, and Emma seemed more than eager to answer Ava's questions. Unfortunately, the more she found out about the Twelve, the more she worried about how they would ever stop Borré.

Jae was a shifter but could also move large objects or even groups of people. Max was, in Emma's words, virtually invulnerable—able to absorb kinetic energy and use it himself. Lucien's Veil rendered him invisible, and he could use it to envelop others. Amrit was able to manipulate nature, even affecting the weather or stimulating plant growth. Christopher, the pyrokinetic Ava had encountered on several occasions, was part of the group. Even Sloan Bartok was one of the Twelve and able to control bodily functions—paralysis, stopping a heart midbeat, exploding internal organs. It was no surprise he was an assassin.

"But Borré sacrificed Sloan," Ava said, unable to imagine the damage he could do. "How could he let him go to Allenmore and turn himself in if he's one of the Twelve?"

Emma sighed long and hard. "Father is upset with Sloan. He's been a bit too quick to question Father's methods lately. He's simply using this as a disciplinary measure."

"Confessing to murder? How is he supposed to aid in this grand plan if he's in prison?"

Emma laughed. "Oh, Sloan won't go to prison. They can't hold him if he doesn't allow it." She shifted and took an exit off the freeway. "No, Sloan will sit in a jail cell for a few days to prove himself trustworthy, then he'll walk out and come back to us."

Ava absorbed that for a moment. "So . . . he let you do what you did to him?"

"Well, technically he couldn't resist both Father and me, but yes. In this case, he did." She shrugged. "It isn't discipline if he knows it's not real. In time, his memories will come back and he'll know it's time to leave." She glanced at Ava. "And you'll be cleared of the murder charges. Problem solved."

"I can't imagine Borré will ever let me go back to my life, regardless of what he says."

Emma reached across the seat to pat the back of Ava's hand, and she could feel the girl's gift zing through her. "It'll be fine, Ava. You'll see. Do what Father asks, and it'll all be over soon."

Ava nodded, unsure of how to respond. She knew what she had to do, but there were a lot of lives hanging in the balance. She prayed she was doing the right thing.

Andreas was anxious, jittery, and that was a feeling he was utterly unaccustomed to. Something was happening, and he didn't need the gift of precognition to see it coming.

He got up from his bed, unable to sleep anymore, and pulled on a pair of pants before crossing the room to pour himself a drink. He sipped the bourbon but didn't really taste it, the warmth settling into his stomach as he gazed out his living room windows over New Elysia.

He gulped down the rest of the alcohol, swishing it around his mouth before swallowing, then left his glass on the windowsill before heading into his office. He didn't bother turning on the lights but flipped on the security projections that covered one wall. Images flickered over the painted surface from every camera throughout the city.

He sat down and leaned back in his plush, leather chair, crossing his bare feet on the desk. He flicked a finger, idly scrolling through the projections. The city perimeter was quiet, New Elysia sleeping for the most part. He switched to the cameras inside the central building and nodded in approval at the young man slumped over a desk in his office.

Evan.

He had to admit the boy was dedicated. Sleeping on the job was not something Andreas usually encouraged, but Evan had been going nonstop trying to track down Sophie and Isaiah. When he'd locked on to Isaiah, it had been a victory for them all, and he had refused to go home until he'd heard whether or not Tiernan had tracked the boy down.

They were still waiting.

The surveillance room was empty save one agent seated along the outer ring of desks, monitoring the cameras like Andreas was. The man yawned—a new recruit, hence the night shift, but reliable.

What's his name? James? Justin?

Andreas shrugged. He couldn't be expected to keep them all straight. He had a lot on his plate, especially lately.

James—*or Justin*—straightened and looked toward the door suddenly, and Andreas switched cameras to see what he was looking at.

Ava Michaels walked into the room, her step faltering a little before a bright smile lit her face. She approached Justin—*or James*—and spoke with him for a moment then the man flew through the air and slammed up against the wall.

Andreas shot to his feet as a red light started to flash next to his bank of monitors. He was reaching for his shoes when his phone rang.

"Petrov."

"It's Kwon. We have a breach."

"I know. I'm on my way." He tugged on a shirt and grabbed his coat. "Has the hall been locked down?"

"As we speak. Security's on it." She paused, and Andreas heard a rumple of fabric, the slam of a door. "It's the girl. Ava."

"Yes."

"Why would she do this?"

Andreas pulled the front door closed behind him and quickened his steps. "I have no idea. But tell security to be careful. The girl has a lot of power."

"I'm aware."

"Do we have a dampener in the city?"

"All out on assignment," Kwon replied. "I'll mobilize more Protectors. We'll get to the bottom of this."

Andreas doubted it, but he didn't say so. Instead, he told Kwon he'd see her soon and dialed another number. "We have a situation," he said, starting to run. "The girl has been caught trying to access the Bureau surveillance system."

"Has she been apprehended?"

"Not yet," Andreas replied, "but Protectors are closing in. Even if she gets out of New Elysia, she won't get far."

"Understood."

"Do you want me to—"

"The situation is under control."

The call disconnected, and Andreas frowned at his phone before cramming it back into his pocket.

He rounded a corner and spotted Protectors closing in on the Central building. He sped up and took the steps two at a time, sliding through the door before it closed. They raced toward the stairs, but Andreas opted for the elevator.

The doors opened, and he pressed his back against the front wall, peering around the corner when he heard nothing but quiet voices. He slipped into the outer office and nodded at the Protectors who flanked the doors to the surveillance room.

Le Kwon approached him, head bowed.

"We've muffled the room. She shouldn't be able to hear or sense us, at least not right away," Kwon said. "She's still in there with the overnight tech. He's been stalling."

"Good man."

Kwon nodded. "He won't be able to keep it up much longer. We need to move quickly if we're going to have the element of surprise."

The door to the stairway opened, and Tiernan Ross and Caleb Foster came running in.

"What's going on? Where's Ava?" Caleb demanded.

Andreas held up a hand. "She's inside."

"Well, what are we doing out here? I don't know what you people think is going on, but Ava is no threat." He started toward the doors with Tiernan close behind him.

Kwon called out for them to stop, but neither listened, pushing through the line of Protectors and into the surveillance room. Kwon and Andreas followed, the Protectors coming in behind them.

So much for being careful.

Ava looked up as they came into the room, the tech still against the wall with a computer pad clutched in his fingers.

"Stay back!" she warned, throwing up a hand.

The Protectors flew back through the doors, the clatter of them landing on the floor muffled in the outer room.

Caleb approached her, hands held up. "Ava, what are you doing?"

"I'm sorry, Caleb," she said, drawing in a shaky breath. "I have to do this." She turned back toward the tech, and he whimpered in pain before sliding to the floor, unconscious. She whirled around and started to edge toward the door. "I have to go."

"We can't let you do that," Kwon said, stepping in front of her.

"I don't want to hurt you."

"Ava—" Tiernan started toward her, but froze midstep, his muscles taut as he tried to move. He cursed.

Ava shrugged. "Sorry, big guy."

Andreas watched in awe as once again, the girl called on her gift, pushing everyone away from her and away from the door. She swiped at a drop of blood on her upper lip, but her power didn't falter. He couldn't move a muscle. She walked toward the door, her eyes darting around for any sign of movement before she rested her gaze on Caleb.

"I'm sorry," she whispered before she turned and ran.

It was a full minute before the paralyzing effect of Ava's gift wore off, and the Protectors in the outer room took off in pursuit.

Andreas stopped Caleb and Tiernan before they could follow suit. "I'll get Evan on this right away," he said. "Keep your phones on."

The Protectors were out the door before he'd even finished speaking.

CHAPTER
FOURTEEN

Caleb wanted to shift, to go faster, but there was no point when they didn't have a clear trail for Ava.

Tiernan had to stop periodically to touch the ground and sniff the air—commune with nature or whatever. Caleb never pretended to understand Tiernan's gift. It worked, but it was frustrating when it meant they had to slow their pace and keep quiet—all the things Caleb did not want to do.

He wanted to scream. He wanted to run. He wanted to shift.

He wanted to get to Ava.

"Listen, can we just—" His phone buzzed and Caleb fumbled for it, answering without even looking at the caller ID. "Yeah?"

"It's Andreas. Evan says south-southwest about three miles."

"How is she moving so fast?"

"She obviously knows where she's going. You don't. I'll be in touch." Andreas hung up, and Tiernan looked at Caleb expectantly.

"Three miles south-southwest," he said, stuffing his phone back in his pocket. "I think we better go my way." He held out his arms, and Tiernan's eyes widened.

"No way. You know I hate shifting."

"Come on, we don't have time for this." Caleb waved him forward with both hands. "It's perfectly safe."

"Yeah, spreading my atoms all over God's creation is safe. Right." Tiernan backed away and turned to run.

Caleb beat him to it, shifting to stand right in front of him.

Tiernan stopped short but not before bumping right into Caleb, who grabbed him and held on tight.

"You might want to close your eyes."

"No!"

But it was too late.

Caleb shifted them not quite three miles but close enough. They materialized on a heavily wooded hill, and through the trees, he could make out a lake to the west.

"Damn it, Foster." Tiernan stumbled out of his hold and bent over, placing his hands on his knees as he retched onto the damp earth.

"I told you to close your eyes." Caleb popped an R-cube into his mouth and started toward the lake. "Come on. We need to get going. I can feel her. She isn't far."

Tiernan wiped his mouth and started after him. "Wai—"

A fireball shot over their heads and slammed into a tree, and the dry pine needles erupted in flames.

Tiernan cursed and ducked down to run toward Caleb, who was hunkered behind a large rock. "Looks like we've got company."

"Yeah." Caleb peered over the top of the rock.

"You see Ava?"

Caleb dropped back toward the rock as another fireball shot past, closer than the last. "No. There are two of them, though. Christopher—"

"The pyro?"

Another fireball hit the rock in response.

"Yeah. The pyro," Caleb said wryly. "I can't see the other one."

Tiernan scanned the area and seemed to focus on the lake in the distance. "I have an idea."

"I'm listening."

"Fire and water don't mix, right?" He glanced significantly toward the lake.

Caleb grinned.

The next time Christopher emerged to launch a fireball in their direction, Caleb held Tiernan tightly and shifted them as close as they could get to his position.

Christopher froze, his eyes wide, but before he could recover, Caleb dropped Tiernan and grabbed Christopher.

"Remember me?" Caleb asked.

Tiernan kept his feet under him and took off after the other man standing a few feet away.

Max.

"Tiernan, wait!" Caleb shouted. "Whatever you do, don't hit him!"

"What?"

Christopher was heating up, ready to attack again, so Caleb didn't get a chance to reply. He sucked in a deep breath and shifted them away again.

They materialized at the bottom of the lake.

Try and light up now, buddy.

Christopher struggled in the water, disoriented, and unable to detect which way was up.

Caleb didn't waste any more time and shifted back to Tiernan, hoping he wasn't too late. He appeared in the same spot he'd just left, spun, and ducked behind a tree to try to figure out what was happening.

Tiernan's body flew by, landing a few feet away, and rolled to a stop in a crumpled heap.

Caleb shifted to his side. "You hit him, didn't you?"

Tiernan's moan was his only response for several seconds. He rolled onto his back. "That guy is strong."

"He's a kinetic absorber," Caleb replied, dragging Tiernan back behind the tree as he scanned the area for Max. "Any energy you throw at him, he absorbs and sends right back at you."

"You might have mentioned that," Tiernan growled, rising to a sitting position.

"I tried."

Max was coming toward them, cracking his neck as he stretched his arms over his head.

"So how do we beat him?"

"No idea." Caleb got into a crouch and inched away, keeping in the shadow of the trees as Tiernan followed. "I can't let him catch sight of me, though."

"Why not?"

"Well, look who the cat dragged in." Max's looming figure appeared over them, a rather sick smile on his face. "Hello, traitor."

Tiernan grabbed Caleb's arm. "I think now would be a good time to get us out of here."

Caleb winced. "Not gonna happen. Max here is sucking on my power like the parasite he is."

Max leaned against a tree and grinned. "Not very filling, actually. Maybe the big guy can punch me again. Now, that was fun."

"Where's Ava?"

Max's eyebrows shot up. "Oh, she's long gone by now, I'm sure. Word to the wise, if you know what's good for you, you'll stay away from her." He leaned in, grin widening. "I hear she's got some overprotective brothers." He winked.

Tiernan cursed, and the thought echoed in Caleb's gut. "You're one of them," he said. "The Twelve."

Max laughed. "Which should tell you that you have no idea what I'm capable of." He sobered. "What we are all capable of."

Christopher shouted for help from somewhere in the middle of the lake, and Max jerked his head up. "Looks like you two have a bit of a reprieve this time," he said, looking over his shoulder. "Next time, though . . ." He took off at a run toward the lake.

"Yeah. I kind of hate that guy," Tiernan muttered as he leaned back against a tree, exhausted.

"Yeah."

"So what now?"

Caleb checked his phone and took out the battery in the hopes the water hadn't damaged it permanently. He sat down on the ground and braced himself against another tree. "Now we wait."

Emma was waiting exactly where she said she'd be. When she spotted Ava running toward her she waved frantically, bouncing on her toes.

Sometimes, it was easy to see how young she really was.

"How did it go?" she asked when Ava came to a stop before her.

"Exactly as planned."

"You got the codes?"

"I got caught. Which, I'm assuming, was kind of the point," Ava said drily, following her sister to the SUV parked a few feet away. She glanced over her shoulder, wondering why Caleb and Tiernan were no longer chasing her.

"Don't worry about them. Christopher and Max were supposed to delay them, not hurt them." Ava shot her a questioning look, and Emma said,

"Father knows they're important to you. He would never harm someone important to you unless he had no other choice."

Ava hunkered down in the seat and buckled her seat belt. "Where are we going? Another empty house?"

Emma smiled. "Not this time. I am going to have to ask you wear this, though." She reached between the seats to pull out a silky black scarf. She bit her lip and shrugged slightly. "You can't know where our base is until Father's convinced you're on our side. Sorry."

"I've got nowhere else to go now." Ava shrugged and wrapped the scarf around her head, covering her eyes. "Is this okay?"

Emma didn't say anything for a minute, and Ava imagined her waving a hand before her face. "Fine," she said finally.

Ava wasn't sure if this was more about trying to keep the location a secret, or if Emma was just in a hurry, but the engine roared as their speed increased, and Ava planted her feet in the floorboards at the first hard curve. The silence was heavy. Ava could almost feel Emma's unspoken words, unasked questions.

"Is something wrong?" she asked.

"What are you going to do?" Emma blurted out.

"About what specifically?"

"About all of this. About us. About Father." She turned a corner, and Ava braced herself on the center console.

Ava sighed heavily. "I don't want to hurt anyone."

"None of us do," Emma said quickly. "That's why Father has a plan. He wants to take control with as few casualties as possible."

"I guess . . . I'll do what I have to do." Ava rested her head against the seat. She was so tired. Her head ached, and she felt fuzzy—off. She couldn't remember if she'd gotten any sleep the night before or how long ago that really was. She'd returned to the city, had something to eat—

It's still morning, isn't it?

She'd asked some questions to try to figure out how to get the codes. She'd seen Caleb and Tiernan. They must have just returned with Isaiah and then . . .

Ava sighed. Caleb had been worried about her. He had known something was wrong, and once again, despite all her promises, she'd hidden even more from him. She hadn't wanted to and tried to find a way around it, but until her parents were safe, she didn't see any other option.

Her head hurt. Her stomach ached. She felt lost. It was hard to know what was right and wrong anymore.

Emma didn't respond, and the rest of the ride was in silence.

Eventually, the pavement below the tires turned to gravel then, from what Ava could tell from the bumpy ride, pot-holed dirt. The darkness of the blindfold focused her other senses, and she listened to the purr of the engine, the rattle of the tires, and was almost lulled to sleep by the rhythm. She startled when the car slowed to a stop, all senses on high alert as Emma got out and the car door slammed behind her. She heard voices.

"Any problems?"

"Not at all."

"He's waiting for you inside." A scrape of shoes on the ground and the passenger door opened. "Do you need any help with her?"

"No, we've got it under control. Thanks."

Ava recognized Emma when she leaned across her to unbuckle the seat belt and tugged lightly on Ava's arm.

"Come on. It's okay," she said quietly.

Ava stumbled out of the car, steadying herself on Emma's arm and ignoring the surge of Emma's gift. She shuffled forward and tripped over some kind of threshold, the ground turning solid beneath her feet.

"Sorry," Emma said, her words echoing faintly. "I should have warned you."

They continued down what appeared to be some kind of hall or tunnel—if the reverberation of their footsteps was any indication—and turned a corner before Emma stopped.

Ava heard a whir, a clack of metal, and they moved forward a few steps. The floor dropped beneath her, and Ava's stomach swooped.

"You can take the blindfold off now," Emma said.

Ava swept the scarf away, blinking a few times to adjust her eyes.

They were in an elevator—kind of old, but well maintained—and they were going down.

"Where are we?" she asked.

"Well, I can't say specifically," Emma replied. "Not yet, at least. But we're in a bunker. It was abandoned years ago, and Father took it upon himself to do some renovations."

The elevator came to a stop and the doors opened on another dim hallway. The walls, ceiling, and floor were all metal, broken by doors every few feet along the way. A door opened at the end of the hall as they walked out of the elevator, and Ava spotted what looked like a control room—

computers, monitors, lots of people moving around—before it slammed shut with a metallic thud.

"This way," Emma said, indicating one of the doors to the left.

Fluorescent lights flickered on overhead as they walked into a small conference room with a table in the middle surrounded by four plastic chairs. Bookshelves lined two walls, every space crammed full of thick volumes, and Ava spotted atlases and history books in her brief perusal. The other two walls were covered with overlapping maps, red circles, and pushpins forming a pattern she couldn't discern.

Borré's imprint announced his arrival before the door opened, and Ava's muscles tensed as he walked in, accompanied by a thin, young woman with blond hair she tucked nervously behind her ear.

"Welcome home," he said, pulling Emma into a hug and kissing both her cheeks. He turned to Ava. "I trust everything went well?"

"As well as could be expected," she replied.

His lips lifted as he nodded once. "This is Eve," he said, indicating the blonde.

She fidgeted with the ends of her hair and came to stand beside him.

"Not one of your sisters, but useful to the cause in her own way, aren't you dear?" He laid his hand on her head, and she tucked her chin to her chest, her gaze dropping deferentially to the floor. "So," he said, turning to Ava. "Did you bring the codes?"

Ava fumbled in her pocket for the drive he'd supplied and held it out to him. "It worked just as you said."

He took the drive and handed it to Emma. "Take it to Mara. Let me know what she says."

Emma nodded and left the room quietly.

"What now?" Ava asked, her gaze flicking from the closed door to Borré to the meek girl at his side.

"Now, dear daughter, it's time to see where your loyalties lie."

"You said you'd release my parents."

Borré smiled. "That I did. The question is, Ava, if I do, what will you do?"

What will I do?

"Will you take your place by my side? With your brothers and sisters? Assure your parents safety, the safety of those you love?"

Do I have choice?

"Will you fight the Council? Let a government for the people—for the

Race—take its place?"

The Council sees me as an enemy now. I've got no choice.

Ava swallowed, her head pounding.

Borré seemed to understand and reached out to touch her head, although his other hand stayed on Eve.

The pain eased.

"What will you do, Ava?" he asked quietly.

"I . . ." She shook her head and rubbed her hands over her face. "If I join you, you'll make sure my parents are safe?"

"Yes."

"Lucy? My other human friends? They won't be harmed?"

"Of course not."

"Caleb?"

Caleb. Tiernan. Gideon. Sophie. The others. What am I doing? Isaiah. Something about Isaiah.

"I'll do all I can to minimize the casualties, Ava. My greatest wish is a peaceful transition."

Ava nodded.

It's all I can hope for, isn't it? What choice do I have?

"Ava?" She looked up to find Borré watching her closely. "Will you stand with me against the Council?"

What choice do I have?

"Yes."

"You'll fight by my side?"

No choice. No other choice.

"If I have to. Yes."

"And you'll never betray me?"

Ava hesitated, but only for a second. "No."

I have no choice.

"I won't betray you."

She realized Borré had closed his eyes, his head tilted back with a slight smile on his face. A smile that widened when he opened his eyes to look at her. "Excellent. That's exactly what I hoped for." He turned to Eve. "You've done well. You may go."

She nodded and left the room as Emma walked in.

"The codes have been verified."

Borré nodded. "Of course they have. You'll be happy to know your sister has agreed to join us."

Emma glanced at Ava doubtfully. "She has?"

"Eve confirmed it." Ava looked confused, and he reached for her, patting her on the shoulder. "Eve is able to detect truth and deception with startling accuracy."

Ava had suspected it. "So that's how you know if someone lies."

"Eve is never wrong, and she's gracious enough to share her gift with me," he said. "You'll be happy to know you passed with flying colors."

Ava straightened. "So what happens now?"

"Now," he said, "I show you around, and you meet your brothers and sisters."

"I want to see my parents first."

"Of course." Borré tilted his head in invitation and led her down the hallway, around a corner, then another, and finally down a long, curving walkway that seemed to be cut into sheer rock.

Lights embedded in the stone cast shadows along the way, and they came to a stop at a thick steel door to what appeared to be a vault.

"Remember, they think they're at home," Borré told her. "It's best for them if you keep the façade alive."

Ava nodded.

Borré pressed a palm to a glass panel and the vault door swung open, revealing a wooden door behind it. He lifted his fist to knock, and Ava heard the tread of footsteps approaching.

"How am I supposed to explain you two?" she asked quietly.

Borré laughed, nodding at Emma. "Oh, they won't notice us." He moved to Emma's side. "Take your time. When you're finished, we'll see about returning them home."

Ava held her breath and waited as the door opened.

"Ava?" Sarah Michaels gaped for a moment before pulling her into a tight hug. "What are you doing here?"

Her mother didn't seem to notice as Emma leaned forward to whisper in Ava's ear, "They don't remember anything about the murder or the police. As far as they're concerned, you're at school and everything's normal."

"Ava?" Her mom pulled back, holding her shoulders as she looked into her eyes. "Are you okay?"

"Yeah . . . yeah, sure, Mom," she said. She inhaled her mother's familiar scent, relaxing but suddenly on the verge of tears. "I was on a break and thought I'd surprise you."

"Break?" Sarah pulled back, her eyes glassy and confused for a moment.

"Spring break?" She turned around to head into the kitchen and ran a finger down the calendar stuck to the door.

"No, spring break's over," Ava replied. "Just a . . . long weekend. Grading period, you know?"

Sarah's face cleared. "Oh, sure." She nodded, smiling widely. "Well, come on in. Are you hungry? I was about to make some tea."

She went about filling a kettle, and Ava glanced back at Emma and Borré before she closed the door behind her and took a moment to examine her surroundings. It really was a remarkable facsimile of her childhood home, right down to the dishtowels and the dented teakettle her mom never wanted to replace. The kitchen table was a little off, missing the scratch she'd put in it building a catapult for science class in junior high. Through the arched doorway she saw the living room, complete with the collection of photographs on the mantle, and the crocheted afghan on the couch.

Her dad walked in, a folded newspaper under his arm.

"I thought I heard your voice," he said, bending to kiss the top of her head. "What are you doing here?"

"Just visiting."

"From Missouri? That's a long way for a weekend," Sarah said.

"I got a deal on a plane ticket."

"Oh yeah? What kind of deal?" her dad asked, taking a seat at the table.

Ava couldn't believe the conversation they were having and tried to rein in her impatience. "You know, a student discount. No biggie." She leaned across the table and touched her dad's hand. "Are you okay?"

"Me? Sure, I'm fine."

"No one has . . . I mean, you're sure?" The tears were back, and Ava swallowed to keep them at bay.

"Ava?" Her mom hurried across the room. "What's wrong?"

Ava swiped at her eyes. "Nothing. I guess I'm just really glad to see you guys."

Her mom sat down next to her and pulled her into a hug while her dad held her hand across the table. For a few minutes, Ava forgot that it wasn't real. She forgot about everything but the comfort of her mom and dad holding her in the kitchen of the house where she grew up.

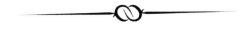

As promised, Borré released her parents, and after a brief session with Emma, they got into a car driven by a Rogue lackey, destined for the airport in Kalispell. They waved gleefully at Ava as the car pulled away. She wasn't exactly sure what they saw—what Emma led them to *believe* they saw—but she was glad they were out of the fake home. It gave her the creeps.

As the car disappeared down the dirt road, she turned to Borré. "No blindfold?"

"For you or them?"

"Either." She shrugged. "Both."

"They won't need it. They won't remember where they've been once they get home," he replied turning back to the entry. "And there's no need to hide anything from you anymore." He smiled and pushed aside the brush covering the heavy doors to the bunker.

Ava took one more look down the road as the dust settled before following him down the tunnel and into the elevator. "Can I ask you something?"

"Of course."

"The DNA time bomb you engineered in us. Is there a cure?"

Borré frowned, and the glance he shot at her seemed more than a little irritated. "It's not a time bomb. It's more of a homing beacon," he said, putting a key in the elevator and turning it before it began to descend. "Something to bring you back to me."

"Or kill us."

Her father slid a palm over her hair. Instantly, her anxiety dissipated, and the low thrum of her gift settled. "See? It's easily remedied," he said.

"But not permanently."

"No, unfortunately not," he said. "But as long as you receive regular treatments the symptoms will be virtually nonexistent."

"Treatment from you."

"Yes."

The elevator doors opened, and Ava realized they were on a different floor than before. Where the hall leading to her parents' quarters had been sparse and industrial, this looked more like a hotel with gleaming wood floors and warmly painted walls. A series of dark wooden doors lined the hall interspersed with bronze sconces casting the ceiling in a golden glow.

Ava gaped openly, following slowly behind her father. Her gift pulsed more intensely than before.

"These are our personal quarters," he explained. "I must be excused for indulging my family a bit. It's a father's prerogative, I think." He smiled at Ava and ducked his head.

They made their way to the end of the hall and a set of double doors.

Ava's gift reached out for the door—*through* the door.

"You feel them, don't you?" he murmured.

Ava nodded, unable to speak.

"I've asked the others to meet us here," he said. "It's not everybody—not yet, but soon." He swung the doors open to a lavish sitting room, resplendent with thick oriental rugs and three plush sofas set around a central fireplace on the far wall. Instead of windows, large paintings of outdoor scenes hung on the walls—a snowy forest, a spring meadow, and one that looked surprisingly familiar.

"New Elysia," she murmured.

"Our home, yes. Or it will be soon."

"So you—*we*—are going to take New Elysia?"

Borré laughed lightly. "First the Council, then the Race, then the world, as they say."

She pulled her eyes away from the painting, drawn into the room by her gift's demands.

"It's intense, isn't it?" Borré asked, his eyes fluttering closed. "So many in the same room." He inhaled deeply, as if enjoying the scent surrounding him, and let it out slowly.

"I believe you've met Christopher," Borré said, indicating a lean, shorter man with dark hair.

"We've not been formally introduced, but yes." Ava nodded stiffly as she recognized the fireball thrower she'd encountered before.

Christopher tipped his head and flopped down on one of the sofas.

"Your brother, Jae," Borré extended a hand toward a larger man with blond hair and almond-shaped green and brown eyes. "He's a shifter, like your Caleb, but with considerably more skill."

Jae smirked and shot her a mock salute.

"The lovely redhead by the fireplace is your sister, Mara, and of course you know Emma." Borré crossed the room to kiss them each on the cheek. "The brooding one in the armchair is Max." His smile swept the room. "Everyone, this is your sister, Ava."

Ava ticked off numbers in her head.

Evan and Isaiah were back in New Elysia. Sloan was gone, for now. That left—

"This isn't everyone."

Borré's face darkened. "No. A few of your siblings have had to be contained as they have yet to have their blocks fully lifted. They have not fully committed to the cause, but they'll come around."

"Sophie?"

He tilted his head in acknowledgement. "Has been a bit of a problem. I'm sure she'll come around soon, though."

"I want—I'd like to see her." She swallowed, her gaze landing on each of her siblings before coming to settle on Borré. "Please . . . Father."

That was wrong. Was that wrong?

A delighted smile lit his face, and he strode toward her and took her shoulders in his hands. "Of course, daughter. Perhaps you can convince Sophie of our mission."

Ava mirrored his smile. "I can try."

She felt warm, safe. Her gift wrapped with all the others.

Sophie's will make it almost complete.

Borré led her back down the hall and pressed his palm to a glass panel next to one of the doors. A blast of cold air swept out at them, stealing Ava's breath.

"Don't worry, her gift's been neutralized, at least a bit," Borré explained. "She can't harm us beyond giving us some goose bumps."

"Neutralized?"

"Until she's proven her loyalty. It's a temporary measure, I assure you, and she's perfectly fine."

Ava nodded and walked into the room, her breath frosting before her. "Sophie?" She looked around the empty room—a small living room with a kitchen off to one side and a doorway opposite.

Sophie appeared in that doorway, eyes wide. "Ava? What are you doing here?"

Blinding pain sliced through Ava's head, and she doubled over from the impact. Memories flooded her mind, and she fought through them, pushing them aside, one mission breaking through.

"I have to go back."

"No way, it's not safe!" Caleb turned away.

"I have to get my parents away from him. We need intel. I need to find Sophie—"

"And how are you going to do that? You said yourself Borré would know

if you were lying."

"Ava? Are you all right?" Borré asked, concern furrowing his brow as he reached for her.

She backed away, hoping it looked more like she was hurrying to Sophie and less like she didn't want him to touch her.

She knew Caleb wouldn't love the idea, so she put it to Gideon instead. "What if I wasn't lying?" She glanced at Isaiah, who was watching with wide eyes.

"No way—"

"Caleb!" She threw up her hands in frustration. "Someone has to figure this out, and I'm the best option." When he pressed his lips together, gaze dropping to the floor, she turned to Isaiah. "Could you do it, you think? Make me believe I'm on Borré's side?"

"I don't know." He looked scared, nervous. "I'm pretty new to all this. I'm not sure it'll stick."

"Even Emma couldn't get it to stick," Caleb said. "You fought through it."

"But if I wanted to believe it," Ava said slowly, her eyes locking with her brother's. "If we worked together?"

Isaiah plucked at his sleeves, too long and stretched wide from the habit, then he nodded. "Yeah. I think I can do it. I can try."

"I just . . . could I have a moment with Sophie, sister to sister?" Ava asked, forcing a hopeful look. "Please, Father?"

His featured softened. "Of course. I'll check on you later." He stepped out of the room and closed it quietly.

Ava whirled on Sophie. "Are you all right?"

"I'm fine, but—" She held a finger to her lips, grabbed Ava's wrist, dragged her through the bedroom and into a small bathroom, and turned on the water. "They monitor every room but this one," she whispered.

"How do you know this one's safe?"

"I don't. Not for sure, but I've gone over every inch, opened up the faucets and looked in the toilet. If there's a mic or a transmitter, I think I would have found it." Sophie squeezed Ava's wrist tightly, her voice a quiet hiss. "Is Isaiah all right?"

"He's fine. He's safe."

Sophie let out a relieved breath and let her go. "Thank God." She leaned against the counter for a moment, her gaze calculating. "So what are you doing here? You and that whack job seemed pretty buddy-buddy."

"It's not what you think."

"I was hoping not."

"You'll need a trigger," Gideon said quietly. *"Something to break through the planted thoughts."*

"When she sees her parents," Caleb suggested.

"No, it has to be Sophie."

Ava and Isaiah exchanged a small smile.

"It could be days before you see Sophie, Ava," Caleb said, glancing apologetically at the boy. *"You have no idea if you can pull this off for that long."*

"I can do it. I'll do it," Ava replied with a firm nod. *"It has to be Sophie."*

"I don't have a lot of time," Ava said, pulling Sophie closer in case someone *was* listening. "I'm going to get you out of here, but we have to be careful."

"Don't worry about me. I'm fine. I can take whatever that sick bastard deals out."

"For now," Ava whispered. "But Emma hasn't gotten her claws into you yet. If Borré decides he's tired of waiting for you to come around, there's no telling what he'll do to you."

"So what do I do?"

"Sit tight," Ava said, squeezing her hand. "I have to get outside, but I'll be back for you. I promise."

"How are you going to get outside without Borré noticing?"

Ava thought about that for a minute. "I guess I could use a diversion?"

"I can't do much in here. The rooms have an effect on my power. I can cool things down, but I can't form a snowflake, let alone anything more."

Ava frowned. "So it's the room? He didn't do anything to you directly?"

"Not that I know of."

"So we need to get you out of here," Ava said. "I think I can handle that."

CHAPTER FIFTEEN

"Ready?" Ava asked.

Sophie nodded. "I don't want to hurt you."

"Don't worry about that. I can take it. Just make it look good."

"Okay."

Ava reached for her gift and concentrated on unlocking the door. When it clicked and swung open, she stepped through, spotting the open doors of the sitting room at the end of the hall.

Her father had evidently been waiting for her and stood up to head for the door when he saw her.

"I'm sorry," Ava said. "I didn't know if I was supposed to wait for someone to let me out."

"Don't ever apologize for using your gifts," he replied. "There's nothing—"

Sophie shoved Ava through the door and into the far wall, whirling around and gathering her power.

Ava wanted to give her a boost, but wasn't sure if Borré would feel it, so instead, she let herself slump to the floor as Sophie hurled a barrage of ice balls toward him.

He retreated behind the double doors, but Ava knew the element of surprise wouldn't last.

Sophie jerked her head in a silent signal and shouted, "You're nothing but his puppet!" as she shot another ice chunk toward Ava.

Ava scrambled to her feet and ran down the hallway as a shower of ice flew her way. She threw herself into the elevator and heard the fight continuing as the doors slid closed. She prayed Sophie would be all right as the elevator shot toward the surface. Ava pulled off her shoe, prying loose the tiny transmitter hidden under the sole before she shoved it back on. When the elevator doors opened, she raced down the hall toward the entrance, listening for any sign she'd been followed, or for someone guarding the entrance. She paused when she reached the door and pressed her ear against it. Hearing nothing, she threw it open and ran across the dirt road to hide behind a cluster of trees.

She dialed her cell phone and pressed the button on the transmitter, cursing when nothing happened. "The red light. Where's the red light?" she murmured, trying not to panic as she shook it a little before pressing the button again.

"Ava?"

She nearly dropped her phone, fumbling it between her shoulder and ear. "Caleb? This damned thing isn't working!"

"Calm down. Check the contacts like I told you," he said. "Are you all right?"

"I'm fine. Don't know how long I have before Borré realizes I've gone, though." She flipped the transmitter open and slid open the little panel on the bottom. "Are my parents okay?"

"We intercepted the car. They're on the way to New Elysia. It's a good thing Lucy was with us, or I don't think we would have gotten them to leave. She's with them now, trying to explain all this."

Some of the tension left Ava's body.

They're safe.

"Thank you." She fiddled with the wires in the transmitter and slid the panel closed. "I found Sophie. We need—"

"What are you doing, Ava?"

She whirled around, Borré's voice chilling her, although not as much as the fact she hadn't sensed him coming. She pressed the button repeatedly and almost collapsing with relief when the red light finally flicked on.

"Ava?" Caleb's voice was frantic on the phone.

Instinctually, she ended the call when Borré's eyes flicked to it. "You can't do this," she said, one last plea. Maybe she could get through to him. "There's got to be a better way."

"There is no other way." Borré took a step toward her. "I don't understand. You lied to me. How did you lie to me?" He looked genuinely confused.

"It's not a lie if you believe it," she said, unable to help herself.

Caleb materialized next to her, and she launched herself into his arms.

"Ava, no!" Borré flung out a hand, and his power reached for her.

She pushed back with her own. "We will stop you," she promised, locking eyes with Borré as the ground fell away beneath her feet.

Isaiah and Tiernan were waiting when they landed, although Ava had no idea where exactly they were.

"Hurry," she said, reaching for Isaiah's hand as Tiernan walked a slow circle around them, keeping watch.

Isaiah held her tightly and closed his eyes, focusing on her thoughts.

She imagined the layout of the bunker, every hallway, every door. She heard Isaiah gasp when she visualized Sophie in her room, and she shook his arm to get his attention. "Now," she said urgently, pulling Caleb toward them until they were linked in a circle. She waited, pushing her own gift toward Isaiah, and Caleb closed his eyes as Isaiah transferred her thoughts to him—her memories.

After a moment, Caleb opened his eyes.

"Got it?" she asked.

Caleb nodded and popped a couple of R-cubes before he disappeared.

"Are you sure this is going to work?" Isaiah asked nervously.

"It'll work."

"It better work fast." Tiernan glowered, on alert as he looked out through the trees. "We need to get out of here."

"It'll work!"

It has to work.

Ava felt the shimmer of Caleb's power an instant before he appeared in front of her, Sophie clutched in his arms.

They both stumbled, and Caleb fell to a knee.

"I don't know how you do that," Sophie mumbled.

Isaiah barreled into her, nearly knocking her off her feet.

"I'm fine. Shhh . . ." she whispered, hugging him tightly.

"I hate to break up the family reunion," Tiernan said. "But we need to get the hell out of here."

Caleb was already swallowing another set of R-cubes and waving Sophie forward.

"No, take Isaiah first," she said, pushing her brother toward him.

Caleb grabbed the boy and disappeared.

"We've got to run," Tiernan said, reaching for Sophie.

"Whoa!" She stepped back. "What are you doing?"

Ava moved between them. "You can't run as fast as us. Not yet, at least. Let Tiernan carry you. When Caleb's dropped Isaiah, he'll come back for you."

Sophie looked skeptical, but she let the Protector throw her over his shoulder.

"Which way!" Ava asked.

Tiernan didn't say a word but started to run.

Ava spared only a quick glance over her shoulder before she took off after him.

It was almost too easy.

Caleb had managed to shift into and out of Sophie's rooms in the Rogue compound, and it seemed like no one was the wiser. She said she'd surrendered not long after Ava's escape and withdrawn to her apartment-slash-prison to wait for him. They'd made it out and back to the car without anyone in pursuit.

Of course, Borré would know where they were headed, but Caleb knew there was no way he'd let Sophie and Ava get away without a fight. He had, from what Ava'd told him, an army at his disposal, so why hadn't he even tried to bring them back?

Caleb didn't like it.

Tiernan had told him not to look a gift horse in the mouth, but Caleb could tell the Protector was on edge as well. His eyes were all but riveted to the rearview mirror of the SUV, and it wasn't until the helicopter left the ground that he seemed to relax.

Caleb still hadn't. And only part of the reason was how much he hated to fly.

They got back to New Elysia long after the sun had set, but once assured that Lucy and her parents were settled and sleeping, Ava couldn't wait to fill Gideon and Madeleine in on what she'd learned.

They met at Madeleine's house, and Caleb noticed that the atmosphere had warmed a bit where his parents were concerned. Perhaps the alliance and their common threat had helped them move beyond their differences, at least a little bit.

"So what did you find out?" Madeleine asked.

Ava filled them in about the Rogue stronghold, Borré's plan, and the Twelve.

"You say he had two others contained? Besides Sophie?" Gideon asked.

"Yes. Borré said they had yet to 'commit to the cause.' "

"So they could still be turned to our side," Madeleine mused.

Tiernan scoffed, leaning on the wall with a clear view of the door. "Unless that sister of yours gets to them first."

Ava shook her head. "I know it's weird, but I don't think Borré will do that. He really wants us to come to him of our own free will—helped along by the little 'homing beacon' he put in our DNA, of course." She paced the floor slowly. "Emma acted on her own with me, and from what she told me, Borré punished her for it.

"When I let him in," she said, seemingly lost in the memory. "When our gifts merged, he didn't just see me. I saw him, too. And he really wants us—all the Twelve—to stand with him willingly. He sees us as the future. A royal family in his new world."

"It's true," Sophie said. "He's big on all that 'take your place at my side' garbage."

"He sees us as the Race perfected." Ava wrinkled her nose in distaste.

Madeleine groaned, clearly aggravated. "And what of the rest of the Race?"

"His loyal subjects. Humans, little more than slaves, chattel." Ava drew in a shaky breath. "Despite his claims that he wants a peaceful transition of power, in the end, they're all expendable."

Caleb cleared his throat. "So what's his plan? How is he going to go about instilling this new world order?"

Ava's small laugh sounded forced. "That's the thing. After all this plotting and planning, it's pretty simple. He's going to stage a coup and overthrow the Council."

"But how?"

"Don't you see? He's bred the Twelve especially for this. With this shifter—" Madeleine waved a beckoning hand toward Ava.

"Jae."

"Jae." Madeleine nodded. "With Jae, he can shift them all into the city without us knowing. Their abilities are stronger than any Race before. They can overpower the Council and lock us away, if not kill us outright."

"If they can access the computer network, they'll control financial transactions . . . food and other supplies," Gideon said.

"The codes," Ava said, stricken. "I gave them the security codes."

"Those codes were reset as soon as you left New Elysia," Madeleine told her, gazing unseeingly out the window at the darkness. "Which he undoubtedly knew would happen. He was testing you. Toying with you. With all of us."

Tiernan pushed away from the wall and crossed his arms over his chest. "So he sneaks his people in, imprisons the Council, basically gains control of the technology, the economy, then the infrastructure of New Elysia, then what?"

"New Elysia is the center of everything Race," Madeleine replied. "If they gain control here, it's a small step to controlling Race cities around the world."

"First the Council, then the Race, then the world," Ava said quietly.

Tiernan clapped his hands together loudly, making everyone jump. "Right. So how do we stop him?"

"First thing is to step up security," Caleb said, his mind whirling with plans. "Put Protectors on the perimeter. We can't rely simply on the surveillance cameras and cloaks."

"Beef up the firewalls, or whatever the techies call them," Tiernan said. "Make it tougher for them to access the system if they do get through."

"The Council should be put in protective custody," Caleb said.

His mother and Gideon exchanged a heavy look.

"What?" he asked.

"We're not sure where Kaeden and Rafe are," she replied. "They were following up on a lead, but haven't been heard from for several hours."

"What about Naomi?"

"With Andreas at Bureau headquarters."

"I think that's where we all should be," Caleb said.

"Agreed." Madeleine reached for her coat. "We need to talk about lifting the blocks as well."

"No," Ava said shortly.

"She's right, Ava." Sophie got to her feet and pulled Isaiah with her. "We need to be ready."

"It's dangerous."

"We don't have a choice," Sophie said, lifting her chin. "Isaiah and I are in this now. You need us, and by my count it's three against nine."

"Four," Ava said stubbornly.

"Evan doesn't count. He's not a fighter," Tiernan said, wincing when Ava looked at him as though he'd stabbed her in the back.

"With his block lifted, he'll be as strong as you, right?" Sophie asked. When Ava shrugged, she said, "Either way, we need all the help we can get."

"We don't even know if they *can* lift the blocks, let alone do it safely."

"We can," Madeleine said. "Our scientists have been studying the block, and the Guardian healer has been quite helpful."

"Talia's here?" Ava asked.

"She arrived with the first wave of Guardian refugees. She seems to think she can help alleviate the symptoms—"

"Alleviate, not cure," Ava snapped.

Caleb sensed her frustration, her fear.

Sophie crossed the room, one hand still holding Isaiah's as she reached out for Ava with the other. "We have to do this," she said quietly. "You know we do."

"I don't want to see you hurt," she whispered.

"We're going to be hurt either way," Sophie replied. "You know it. There's no getting around it. The block will come down eventually, and if we don't join Borré . . ." She glanced at Isaiah, who nodded, and they exchanged a smile before Sophie turned back to Ava. "We know what we're getting into. We have to do this."

Ava's shoulders fell, and she nodded.

Her fear was still there, Caleb could practically taste it, but there was strength as well. The presence of her siblings seemed to intensify her power, solidify it.

"All right then, if that's settled, shall we go?" Madeleine asked as she opened the front door. The group shuffled out in silence, and his mother stopped him with a touch on the arm. "Do you think we can trust them?" she asked.

"Who? Sophie and Isaiah?" At his mother's continued silence, he bristled. "Ava?"

"All of them," she said quietly. "They've been under Borré's influence. How do we know what he's done to them?"

"I would know. If Ava had been affected, I would know," he replied.

watching her walk with her sister and brother down the street. "And I trust her judgment."

"Are you sure we can? There's a lot at stake here, Caleb."

"You think I don't know what's at stake?" he asked with more than a touch of irritation. Seeing his mother's stricken look, the lines along her mouth, her eyes, he realized the toll this was taking on her. As always, her concern was for her people. He forced himself to speak calmly. "Look at it this way, we have to trust someone. We know that we can't take on Borré and the Twelve without them. Do we really have any other options?"

Madeleine pulled the door shut and set off down the walkway next to him. "Even with them, our chances aren't good. Borré has been planning this for years, and we're simply trying to guess when he's going to act, what he's going to do." She yanked her coat closed and jammed her hands in her pockets, her mouth turning down in an angry line. "I hate being at a disadvantage."

They walked in silence for a few minutes, Caleb's eyes drifting over the backs of the people in front of him—Tiernan, Gideon, Ava, and her siblings—a Protector, a rebel, and three people who were turning against their birthright, against their very DNA, to fight for what was right.

"We'll do what we have to do," he said finally. "We've been fighting Rogues for centuries. They're all the same, really."

Madeleine's eyes narrowed. "Selfish."

"Power hungry."

"Prideful."

Caleb grinned and threw an arm over his mother's shoulders. "And you know what they say pride goeth before."

Madeleine's lips twitched. "That's a human saying."

"Doesn't mean it isn't valid," Caleb said. "Sure, Borré has a lot of strength on his side, but our job is to figure out his weakness. And from what Ava's said, I'd say his children are a big one."

Madeleine nodded then looked away, deep in thought. "You think we can use that to our advantage?"

Caleb wasn't sure, but he shrugged and said, "It's a place to start."

"Father? You wanted to see me?"

Elias didn't slow his pace but acknowledged Emma with a nod. "We need to move up the timetable again," he said, turning the corner to head to the control room. "Your sister has forced my hand, unfortunately."

"What do you want me to do?"

He didn't want to ask, but he had to. There was no more time. "I need to know if you can help Amrit and Lucien see the error of their ways."

Emma's step faltered. "You want me to push them?"

"Of course I don't *want* it. But I don't have a choice. We need them." He paused at the door and looked down at his daughter. "Can you do it? And lift their blocks."

Emma chewed on her lip but nodded. "How soon?"

"Now," he replied as he took her by the shoulders, squeezing gently. "Can you do this, Emma? Ava resisted—"

"Ava had help," Emma said quickly. "Caleb was a complication I wasn't prepared for. I can do it, Father. If you need me to, I can do it."

He smiled and ran the backs of his fingers down her cheek. "I believe in you," he said, reaching for the door. "Go now and let me know when it's finished."

Emma turned on her heel and hurried down the hall, almost running.

Such a good girl. So eager to please.

Elias shook off his smile, all business as he burst through the door to find a flurry of activity. He saw Max across the room and recognized the tension in his shoulders, in the set of his jaw.

Hmm. Not good.

"Are you all right?" he asked, laying a hand on the boy's back.

Max shrugged. "Bit of a headache. It's nothing."

"It's not nothing. Let me." He touched his son's forehead, drawing out the pain with a dose of his gift. "Better?"

Max nodded. "Thanks."

"I want you to get another dose before we leave. The others, too. See to it."

"All right."

"How are the preparations going?"

Max turned to a computer screen and skimmed his finger across it, bringing up a checklist. "Weapons have been stocked and loaded. Not that we'll need them."

"A last resort," Elias said, examining the list. "Always have a backup plan, son."

"The forward team has already been dispatched. They should arrive near the gate to New Elysia"—he checked his watch—"within the next hour."

"They know not to get too close and disrupt the cloak. The sensors will be able to detect them, too."

"Sloan's on the way," Max replied. "He'll meet the team at the base of the mountain. He should be able to mask them."

"Good." Elias nodded. "Your sister is working on Amrit and Lucien. Once they're on boa—"

Max stiffened. "What do you mean 'working on'?"

"Your brothers need a little encouragement."

"You said it was our *choice*." Max's jaw tensed, the color high on his cheeks, and Elias knew he needed to tread carefully.

The last thing he needed was another of his offspring to rebel. Children, he was learning, were sometimes more trouble than they were worth. And sometimes, they needed to be reminded of their place. Without Emma, it was a bit more work, but Elias could still discipline his children when the situation called for it.

He felt for Max's gift, the spaces his own filled in, the twining flow of father and son, and pulled his gift back, just a little.

Max winced.

Elias pulled back some more. "Your brothers simply need a little convincing. They need to understand exactly what is at stake here, not only for themselves, but for all our people." He pulled a little more, and Max jerked, obviously fighting the pain, a little drop of blood bubbling at one nostril. Elias leaned closer, until he was eye to eye with his son, determined to make his point. "Sometime we *all* need a little reminder, don't we?"

Max nodded jerkily. "Yes. Yes, of course."

Elias smiled and allowed his gift to flow once again, and Max's whole body loosened as the pain eased.

"Good. Glad we understand each other." He patted his son on the shoulder and turned away when his phone buzzed. "Yes?"

"I thought you'd want to know that your errant daughter has returned to the fold."

Elias grinned. Ava was a handful, he had to give her that. "I trust everything is under control on your end?"

"Protectors are being diverted to the perimeter. We are increasing security measures as we speak. New security codes and firewalls are almost ready."

"Of course, you are privy to the new codes?"

"They won't be a problem."

"Excellent." Borré eyed the checklist on the computer screen idly. "What about the civilians?"

"Encouraged to remain in their homes, at this point. A curfew has been instigated."

Elias huffed out a laugh. "Perfect. And the Council?"

"Madeleine has rebuffed protective custody."

"Of course she has." Elias walked slowly through the room, watching the bustling activity with satisfaction. "It won't be long now. When we have everyone in position, I'll be in touch."

"Understood."

Elias hung up and stood quietly, indulging in a moment of satisfaction. It wasn't over yet—not nearly—but everything seemed to be coming together perfectly.

He turned on his heel and headed out to check on Emma. Using her gift to manipulate her brothers would take a toll, and she'd probably need a little reenergizing. He'd give her a boost, and soon they'd be on the way to New Elysia.

Within twenty-four hours, it would all be over, and a new era would begin.

CHAPTER SIXTEEN

It was after midnight by the time they'd put the extra security measures in play, rousing Protectors out of bed to stand patrol—something that hadn't been necessary for generations, according to Madeleine—and Caleb and Tiernan were overseeing the assignments with Katherine's help. They'd also added cloaks to the protective barrier surrounding the city, and Evan and the other sensors had been brought in as well, set up in an around-the-clock surveillance schedule to add yet another safeguard against invasion.

Ava had been assured that the humans were safe, far from the central building, where they anticipated the attack, but heavily cloaked in a secure facility, and while she thought everything sounded good, she doubted it would be enough. In actuality, she *knew* it wouldn't be. Her instincts whirled around in a confused vortex, bumping against her skin and alerting her to the fact that something wasn't right.

Yeah. Like I need the reminder.

But Ava was at a loss about what else they could do. Once they had all the beefed up security in place, the patrols were patrolling, the sensors were sensing, and the cloaks were as thick as they could make them, in the end, all they could do was wait.

"Are you sure you want to do this now?" she asked Sophie as they sat in one of the medical examining rooms.

Sophie was up on the table, and Isaiah stood in the corner chewing on his thumb knuckle.

"No point putting it off," she replied, touching the back of Ava's hand. "It'll be fine. You'll see."

Ava wasn't sure about that, but the truth was, Sophie was right when she said they didn't really have any other options and that their fate would most likely be the same, whether the block was lifted or not. Without Borré, their destiny was to die, and they all knew it. But Ava didn't have the right to tell Sophie and Isaiah that they couldn't fight, that they couldn't try to take Borré with them.

Talia walked in, along with two Race doctors and Evan.

The sensor had agreed to help and have what remained of his block removed as well. Ava was banking on the power of the Twelve working together. She hoped that the simple presence of a sibling helping ground and strengthen a gift, along with Talia's treatments, would be enough to hold off the worst of the symptoms Borré had planted in them.

The three of them—Evan, Isaiah, and Ava—joined hands with Sophie, and immediately, Ava felt the surge of power, of electricity, running through them like a completed circuit.

Talia took a position behind Sophie and laid her hands gently on the sides of her head.

One of the Race doctors monitored a scanner, while the other approached her, holding some kind of tool. "This will help us locate the weak spots of the block," he explained. "We'll focus our efforts there."

Sophie nodded, casting a quick and nervous glance at Ava.

Ava squeezed her sister's hand and focused on keeping herself calm and sending peaceful thoughts Sophie's way as the doctor touched the tool to her head in several places.

"All right," the doctor said. "I think we've got it. Ready?"

"You can help them," Ava said quietly. "Close your eyes and try to feel what they're doing. Your instinct will be to fight them off, but try and stay calm. I'll help if I can."

Sophie's eyes fluttered shut, and Talia's fingers tightened, flexing in her hair. "I can see it, I think," Talia murmured. "I've never—"

Sophie tensed.

"What is it?" Isaiah's hand tightened on Sophie's, his knuckles turning white as he leaned closer. "Is she okay? Sophie?"

"It's okay," Ava said quietly. She felt them all—Sophie, Talia, the doctor, and the muffling force of the block. "It's okay," she whispered, lending her gift to the rest, feeling the block resist and cling to Sophie like remnants of sticky taffy.

"Little bit more," the doctor said, half to himself.

Then, with a silent *whoosh*, it gave, pulling away and disintegrating.

Sophie gasped, and her gift flashed through her, the echo tingling through them all.

Ava remembered that feeling—the first time, the warmth, the fullness—the feeling of *finally* when her power seemed ready to burst out of her skin.

The temperature in the room dropped as frost crept up the walls.

"Try to pull it back," Ava said, shivering as snowflakes started to fall. "You're not fighting it. It's part of you, like a hand or a foot."

Icy wind began to swirl in the room, a twisting cyclone centered on Sophie.

Her head fell back as the snow whirled around, stinging Ava's cheeks. "It wants to do what you want," Ava shouted over the increasing wind. "It's like letting a rock drop out of your hand or stepping back from the edge of a cliff. You can control it." She leaned closer. "Sophie!"

Sophie's eyes flew open and locked on Ava's. Her nose started to bleed, a ruby-red drop caught on her upper lip.

"Sophie?" Isaiah's worried plea was lost on the wind.

"I know you want to let it go," Ava said. "I know it's overwhelming. But you need to take control. You can do it."

Sophie sniffed, the blood dripping down her chin, and closed her eyes. She shuddered and the wind slowed, then stopped altogether.

Gradually, the temperature rose until the only sound in the room was the quiet drip of melting ice and their own harsh breaths.

Sophie opened her eyes, and the doctor handed her a clump of tissues. She pressed them to her nose.

One by one, they let go until only Isaiah was holding her hand.

"Well, that was weird," she mumbled, her voice muffled by the tissues.

Ava stared at her sister for a minute, stunned, then burst out laughing.

It took another hour before they were able to lift the blocks on Evan and Isaiah. No more indoor snow storms, thankfully, but they had all been treated to a stream of intense emotions as Isaiah worked his way through controlling his gift.

Ava finally understood why Madeleine had been so concerned about him. Fear really was a powerful weapon.

Talia and the Race doctors worked together and dosed them with enough painkillers, along with Talia's mojo, to ward off the headaches. Although nobody said it out loud, everyone knew when the Rogue attack came the four of them would not be enough—even unblocked.

They wandered out of the medical wing, exhausted but also exhilarated, but Ava hung back, dialing Caleb's number to check in.

"Hey." He sounded tired.

"How's everything going?"

Caleb yawned. "We've set up a rotating patrol. Finally. Took some doing. Protectors aren't used to pulling guard duty."

"You coming back soon?"

"I have another couple of hours. I'm on 'til dawn." She heard him adjust his phone, saying something in a muffled voice. "Sorry," he said. "How'd it go on your end? Any problems lifting the blocks?"

"About what we expected," she replied, following the group down a hall to the temporary quarters. She waved to Sophie as she walked into one of the rooms and closed the door quietly behind her. "Everyone's tired, though. Heading to bed."

"I know the feeling." He yawned again. "They get you all set up with somewhere to sleep?"

"Yeah, Madeleine didn't want us to leave the Council Arena until this is all over."

"I know. It's safer having you all together. It's the most protected—" Ava heard a shout on his end. "Caleb?" Her heart stopped as he cursed under his breath. "What's happening?"

"I've gotta go," he said. It sounded like he was running. "Stay with the others."

"Caleb?"

"Tell them someone's gotten through the cloak. Watch out!"

The phone went dead in her hand. She stared at the picture of Caleb smiling at her before it switched to her home screen. "Caleb?" She redialed, holding her breath and exhaling in a panicked whine as it went straight to voice mail.

She crossed the hallway to Sophie's room and pounded on the door.

It flew open a second later. "Ava? What's wrong?"

"Something's happening. Get everyone and meet me in the surveillance room," she called out over her shoulder, already running and dialing again, even though she knew she wouldn't get through.

She burst through the doors to a flurry of activity, a tall man she'd never seen before nearly knocking her over as he raced through the door. A group stood clustered around the central screen, others shouting into phones or across the room.

"How many?"

"At least a dozen, I can't get a clear read!"

"Dispatch everyone we've got—"

"—reports of gunfire—"

"Why aren't the cameras working? I need to see what's happening!" Madeleine's voice rang out above the others, and Ava zeroed in on her, pushing her way through the crowd.

"I have Tiernan Ross on the phone."

Madeleine whirled. "Put it on speaker." Her jaw tensed. "Ross. Report."

"We need reinforcements," Tiernan said through gasping breaths. "They keep coming."

"Divert the rest of the Protectors to their location," Andreas ordered. "Sensors, monitor the rest of the perimeter. I want to know if there's another breach!"

"What about Caleb?" Ava's heart pounded in her chest, her gift yearning to be let loose, to get to Caleb.

"I . . . I don't know," Tiernan ground out. "I haven't seen him since—"

More shouts, and the phone went dead.

Sophie and Isaiah hurried into the room followed closely by Evan.

The sensor took a spot near the central screen, nodding as Andreas started firing questions and commands at him.

Ava fought down her panic, fought to think clearly, fought against her intuition screaming for her to take action because something was wrong, so *wrong*. "We should go, too," she said finally. "We need to help them."

Madeleine stared at her for a moment, and Ava wondered what she was thinking.

Does she think this is exactly what Borré wanted, too? That we don't have any other choice but to play his game by his rules?

The Council leader finally nodded. "The sensors will monitor you from here," she said, grabbing Ava's arm when she turned to leave. "If we can't reestablish communications, it will be up to you," she said quietly. "If you can't fight them off, retreat and regroup until you can come up with a plan of attack. I'm afraid you . . . you may be our only hope."

Ava pulled away, but the words echoed in her ears as she, Sophie, and Isaiah took off running.

Caleb chomped on an R-cube angrily as he huddled behind a tree next to Tiernan.

"Did you have any idea they had so many?" Tiernan asked, reloading his gun.

"No." Caleb cursed under his breath as another wave headed toward them.

The Rogues kept coming. Darting in for an attack then withdrawing before they took any casualties, only to hit again from another direction. None of the Twelve, though, and still no sign of Elias Borré. It was as if he was taunting them, making them exhaust their resources before the real attack.

Tiernan wiped his mouth with the back of his hand, frowned, and wiped blood on his fatigues.

"You okay?" Caleb asked.

"It's nothing. Already healing." Tiernan snuck a look around the tree and cocked his gun. "Ready?"

Without another word, they came out from their hiding place, Caleb shifting to cause a distraction as Tiernan attacked from the other side. Grunts, punches, and sporadic gunfire filled the air, although the presence of a telekinetic on each side made the bullets all but useless. They were forced to resort to hand-to-hand combat, and Caleb had to admit he was exhausted.

"Watch out!" Tiernan shouted, and Caleb whirled, diving to avoid a large rock flying at his head.

"Where are the damned reinforcements?" Caleb shouted back, but nobody answered.

They were all asking the same question. Fifteen Protectors holding off wave after wave of Rogue attacks, coordinated to wear them out, distract them—

Caleb's head snapped up, his body reacting before he could fully process the impact on his gift. He sensed Ava's approach, her power reaching for his.

No. She can't be here.

He ducked a punch, spun, and shifted to avoid another when all the air in his lungs left him in a rush. The weight that had tackled him to the ground rolled off, and Caleb grunted, trying to regain his breath as well as his footing.

Before he could shift again, the Rogue floated into the air and flew through a gap in the trees with a surprised shout, arms and legs flailing.

Ava ran to Caleb's side and reached down to help him up.

"What are you doing here?" he growled, pulling her behind the cover of a large tree.

She rolled her eyes. "You're welcome."

"Ava, I'm serious. I thought you were staying back at Bureau headquarters." He heard a scream and peeked around the tree to see a group of Rogues diving for cover to avoid a couple of Sophie's more impressive ice balls.

Isaiah was staring straight at another Rogue, who finally turned tail and ran off.

"Look," Ava said, knocking a Rogue away from Tiernan, and then another trying to sneak up behind Sophie. "We can argue the point later, okay? We're here to help, so let's make the best of it."

A Rogue staggered to his feet, and a few rocks shot in Ava's direction.

"Looks like they have a telekinetic," she muttered. She stopped the rocks and fired them back at the Rogue, nailing him in the arm with one, despite his attempt at dodging. "Where are they all coming from?" she asked, as two more Rogues appeared in the distance.

"I don't know. I can't even tell how many there are. They keep coming in waves and then retreating."

"Well, what do you guys usually do to beat them?" she asked, using a large tree branch to swat at a couple of advancing Rogues.

Sophie threw ice balls and hit them both in the forehead.

They crumpled to the ground.

"Usually, the odds are a little more in our favor," Caleb replied. "We've never had to take on a group of them."

Ava whirled around and threw a hand out in front of her.

"What is it?" he asked, searching through the trees until he saw a familiar man—tall, thin and more than a little shocked because he was hovering midair. Caleb reached out and touched Ava's arm. "It's okay," he said. "He's one of ours."

Ava released him, and he dropped to the ground, running toward them in a crouch.

"James. It's about time you guys showed up," Caleb said.

"Sorry to keep you waiting," he said with a wry grin, glancing at Ava. "You must be Ava. We never formally met."

"James was part of the rescue mission when you were kidnapped," Caleb explained. "He's a telekinetic like you."

"Well, a telekinetic, anyway," James said, shrugging.

Ava smiled. "Well, it's nice to meet you." There was loud crash overhead, and she ducked as a shower of splintered wood covered them. "Wish it was under better circumstances."

James sobered and turned to Caleb. "What's the situation?"

Caleb filled him in as Ava covered them, diverting any Rogues who got too close. Caleb knew she thought she was hiding the little trickles of blood she'd wiped from her nose, but she wasn't as covert as she thought.

"Does anyone else think this is weird?" Ava asked when another Rogue took off running back the way he came. "They don't actually seem to be trying to get through."

Tiernan ducked behind a neighboring tree and scowled at the three of them. "Having a little vacation?" he asked, his chest heaving as he caught his breath. "Look, I love a good fight as much as the next guy, but this is getting old. We need a plan."

"Oh, a plan? Yes, that's an excellent idea," Ava said with an exaggerated roll of her eyes. "You got one, Mr. Obvious?"

Tiernan spat out a mouthful of blood and grinned. "As a matter of fact, Miss Pain-In-My-Ass, I do."

Ava had to admit it wasn't a bad plan. It wasn't necessarily a *good* plan, but it was the best they had at the moment. Caleb hated it, of course. He hated anything that put Ava in danger, and this even had her a bit nervous.

She took her place on higher ground, a slight rise in the forest with a good view of the action so she was able to keep track of their allies. She hated not being in the thick of things, to leave Caleb and the others, but this was the best use of her abilities.

She saw James on another rise a few hundred feet away—across the valley, if you could call it that, lying on his stomach like her. He had a better vantage point for the Rogue approach, so he would give the signal.

The Rogues had retreated, all but two who kept darting in and attacking to keep them on their toes.

Tiernan suspected it wouldn't be long before there was another full-fledged attack—the true diversion for whatever Borré had planned. They all recognized the strategy, keep the Protectors busy while he launched his coup and hit the Council Arena, but they couldn't leave the perimeter unguarded either. There were civilians to consider, and Ava believed Tiernan when he said Rogues would not hesitate to turn on them if they needed to.

Many of the civilians had no extraordinary gifts—well, beyond the Race norm, at least—but that didn't count for much against trained soldiers, especially when the Rogues had some gifted among them—a telekinetic, a couple of shifters, and a few others, including the guy who could fly.

Despite everything she'd been through, flying still kind of blew Ava's mind.

She shifted against the rocks cutting into her stomach and picked out the others down below. She couldn't see Tiernan, but she knew he was there. Sophie and Isaiah were together behind a cluster of trees, Caleb about twenty feet from them, and the rest of the Protectors were scattered everywhere, waiting.

I really hate waiting.

The hairs on the back of her neck stood at attention, a tingle of awareness sparking her intuition. She didn't question it anymore but reached out with her gift to bounce a few pebbles around near James to get his attention instead.

He nodded in her direction and rose up on his elbows to get a better look.

Ava closed her eyes and focused her gift on the approaching group.

More than a dozen. Twenty-five, thirty, maybe. Could be a few more.

With James and the other new arrivals, they'd be evenly matched. The problem was getting them all together. Ava was coming to realize that fighting a group of Rogues was a lot like herding cats.

Her head pounded. She tried to ignore it.

James lifted his head a little more and waved a hand.

She knew Caleb was watching.

They were ready. As one, half a dozen Protectors, including Tiernan and Caleb, stepped out into the clearing.

Bait.

The Rogues burst out of the trees, their telekinetic sending a shower of rocks to herald the arrival.

The Protectors dodged them easily and pushed forward to meet them in the center of the clearing. Between one breath and the next, the rest of the Protectors joined the fray, arms and legs blurring as they ran and fought, dodged, and parried. Moving the Rogues along . . . corralling them all the way.

Not yet.

It wouldn't be noticeable to anyone on the ground, but Ava saw the method to the madness. The way the Protectors pushed the Rogues together into a loose circle—Protectors on the outside, Rogues in the middle, facing out.

Not long now.

One Rogue broke away and started to retreat through the forest but came to an abrupt stop. He staggered backward, falling and crab walking away from something.

Ava wondered what thought Isaiah had planted in his mind, and she smiled at the possibilities.

Isaiah had said he could handle it, that he could keep the shifters from shifting, the flyer from flying, and still help with a few others if needed. Ava had doubted him because he was so new to his powers, but her brother was proving to be a quick study.

He stepped out from behind a tree just as Sophie did on the other side of the melee.

The wind whipped up below, whirling around in a spiral of ice and snow.

Ava couldn't feel the cold. She zeroed in on Sophie's gift, Isaiah's, too, and added her own to the mix. Not a lot, because she needed to conserve it, but Sophie seemed to be holding her own.

The Rogues struggled against the wind but couldn't make any headway, one step forward leading to two, three steps back.

Ava gathered her gift around her, feeling it swell.

Almost.

With one last glance in Ava's direction, Tiernan bellowed, "Now!" and the Protectors all took cover.

The Rogues didn't move, Isaiah planting the thought that they were surrounded and the fear that they would soon be defeated.

The wind picked up speed, pushing them closer together.

Showtime.

It had been a long time since Ava had let her power loose in such a way—back when she all but destroyed the training field at the Guardian Colony. She ignored the ache in her muscles, the sharp stabbing in her head, and let her gift flow out and down, digging into the frost-covered ground and cracking it apart. A fissure formed beneath the Rogues, splitting the earth open with a deafening crack.

They tried to run, to escape, but Sophie and Isaiah pushed them back. They toppled into the hole—now fifty feet across and growing . . . deeper and wider.

Ava had no idea how deep or wide it would go, but she let her gift guide her, digging and clawing at the rocky soil until the last Rogue toppled in.

Sophie and Isaiah stepped back, and Ava turned her attention to the trees. It was up to her now, but she felt Sophie and Isaiah aiming their power toward her. A hand clasped hers, and she realized Caleb was next to her, doing the same thing. The Protectors were helping, too. She saw Tiernan putting his shoulder into a tall pine, and she aimed her gift that way, the tree giving way and falling across the open hole. One after another, she felled the trees, weaving a roof to the Rogue prison. It wouldn't kill them. It wouldn't even hold them forever, but it was enough to buy them some time.

Ava shivered, a burst of familiar power flowing over her skin. "Can you feel that?"

"Feel what?" Caleb squeezed her hand, but she was watching Sophie. The way she stiffened and looked up at her.

She feels it, too.

"It's Borré," Ava said, wiping the blood from her lip as she pulled a packet of pain pills out of her pocket and swallowed them dry. "It's all of them. They're nearby. They're close."

Caleb shouted for the Protectors, and Tiernan was at his side in an instant. "Borré's making his move," Caleb said. "Take the rest and meet us at the Council Arena. Tell them to be careful. Don't make a move until we know what we're walking into." He handed Ava a couple of R-cubes and pulled her into his arms. "Ready?"

She held on tight and closed her eyes. "Let's go."

CHAPTER
SEVENTEEN

"I don't understand it!" Caleb twisted his fingers in his hair in aggravation.

Ava swayed on her feet, still trying to get her strength back. "Where are we?"

Caleb turned in a slow circle. "Eastern perimeter. I don't get it." He knew the city like the back of his hand. Had shifted through it dozens—hundreds of times. Yet he'd tried three times to get them to the center of the city only to end up somewhere else entirely. He pulled out his phone and called Tiernan, thumbing on the speaker.

"Where are you?" the Protector growled into the phone.

"Near the museum," Caleb replied. "Something's throwing my shifts off."

"You're not alone," Tiernan said with a mixture of frustration and fury in his voice. "I can't even keep everyone together. Everybody thinks they know the way, but we keep going in circles."

"You think it's Borré?"

"It's gotta be."

"No," Ava said slowly. "Not Borré but . . ." She paced away a few steps, speaking half to herself. "I knew something was wrong . . . I thought it was just the situation, you know? My intuition tried to warn me, but I misread it."

"What is it?" Tiernan asked.

"I'm not sure," Caleb replied. He watched Ava as she tried to work it out in her own head. "What are you thinking?"

She stopped and faced him. "When you were taken by the Rogues, we thought Evan escaped. That he was rescued."

"Yeah. That's how he ended up in New Elysia."

Ava chewed on her lip as she contemplated her words. "What if he wasn't? Rescued, I mean."

Caleb ignored Tiernan's irritated grumbling on the phone as he tried to follow her train of thought. "What are you saying?"

Ava's eyes were wide with understanding and with shock. "What if he was taken by Borré, and then *sent* to New Elysia?"

"You think Evan's a Rogue spy?"

"Of course he is," Tiernan grumbled. "This is just great."

"I knew something was off," Ava said. "I felt it when we were together, but I wrote it off. Ignored my instincts. Think about it, though. It makes sense. Who else could be doing this? It has to be Evan."

"But how?" Caleb asked.

"We all have gifts beyond what's normal for Race," she replied. "We knew he was a powerful sensor, but what if he has powers beyond that?"

"Like what?" Tiernan asked. "Some kind of shield?"

"Or an ability to throw off your internal GPS," she said. "Kind of the opposite of tracking someone. If Borré did get to Evan before we did, it's very possible that all this is part of his grand plan."

Tiernan cursed lowly. "So how do we fight it?"

Ava closed her eyes and breathed in and out a few times. "You probably can't," she said. "But I know Evan's power. I think I can get past it." She turned to Caleb. "We'll have to go on foot. Tiernan, where are you?"

"A little north of you, near as I can tell," he replied.

"Is Sophie with you?"

"Yeah, she's right here."

"Good," Ava took off at a slow jog, and Caleb followed close behind her, holding the phone up so they both could talk.

"Sophie's the most familiar with my gift," Ava said. "Tell her to try to zone in on it, and you guys follow her—even if it goes against your instincts. Hopefully, she'll lead you right to us. Once we meet up, we can figure out what to do next."

"Got it." Tiernan hung up, and Caleb pocketed his phone.

Even though everything in him told him they should be going left when Ava turned right, he stuck to her heels. "I think we need to get to the house where we've stashed your parents and Lucy."

Ava's step faltered. "Why there?"

"It's where we set up the secondary surveillance."

She stopped abruptly. "Secondary?"

Caleb grinned. "You don't think we left everything to chance knowing Borré was going to attack the central building, do you? Especially since there is most likely a mole on the Council?" He ran past Ava, feeling pretty self-satisfied, until she grabbed his arm and pulled him in the opposite direction. "Thanks," he said.

"Don't mention it."

Sure enough, Tiernan and the others joined them at the next corner, Sophie in the lead, and they reached the house about five minutes later.

It was cloaked, giving the illusion of a closed restaurant, but once they penetrated the cloak, it revealed a simple one-story house. Caleb and Tiernan led the way into the building, the rest of the Protectors setting up a discreet perimeter outside, melting into the shadows and behind the corners of buildings.

The lights came on as they walked in, and after a moment, Lucy emerged from one of the bedrooms, rubbing the sleep from her eyes.

"What's going on? Is everything okay?" she asked.

"No, not really," Ava said, lowering her voice. "Let's try not to wake my parents."

They followed Caleb down a set of stairs to a small basement that had been converted into a makeshift control room. Three computer screens were set up along one wall—old school, no projections—and Caleb turned them on with the flip of a switch, and a series of video feeds flickered on after a moment.

"Best we could with such short notice," he said distractedly.

"Who knows about this?" Ava asked.

"Only Madeleine. And us, of course. She wasn't sure who she could trust." He adjusted the focus. "We've accessed the security cameras inside the central building."

"Are they all still working? The ones outside were down. Nobody could see what was happening on the perimeter."

"What *was* happening?" Lucy threw up her hands in exasperation. "Is anyone going to tell me what's going on?"

"The Rogues are attacking the city," Ava replied, watching as Caleb cycled through the video feed. "We stopped a group of them near the edge of the city, but we think Borré and the Twelve are making their move against the Council."

Lucy wrapped her arms around her waist. "How are you going to stop them?"

"That's what we're trying to figure out."

Tiernan let out a low curse. "They got the Council."

Caleb clenched his jaw as he looked at the image of a familiar room. He saw his mother standing near the door. He couldn't see everything because of the angle of the camera, but he could make out Naomi and Rafe sitting on a small sofa to Madeleine's right.

"Where is that?" Ava asked.

"Half-Breed holding facility," he replied. "Looks like we're a little late."

He changed cameras again until they were looking at Bureau surveillance headquarters. Sure enough, Borré stood near the center of the room looking over Evan's shoulder at one of the screens. To his left—

"Andreas Petrov," Tiernan spat. "There's your mole."

"You were right, Ava," Caleb said, staring at the screen as the pieces fell into place. "When Evan turned up here, I should have figured it out. It was Andreas and Borré who took him in the first place. He was with the Rogues the whole time, right under our noses."

Ava crossed the room and laid her hands on his shoulders, squeezing softly. "So what do we do now?"

He leaned back in his chair, her warmth along his back soothing him a little. "First thing is to get Evan out of the equation, and then shut down those cameras so we have half a fighting chance."

Tiernan's eyes narrowed on the screen as he thought. "What about Adam?"

"Who's Adam?" Sophie asked.

"Guardian dampener," he replied. She opened her mouth to ask more, but he said, "He can block Race gifts."

"Is he even here?" Ava asked.

"He came in with the first wave of refugees," Caleb replied. "They were put in temporary housing a few blocks from here until something more permanent could be arranged. My mother wouldn't allow them to fight with us."

"I'd think we could use all the help we could get."

"I was working on it," Caleb replied. "But until the Half-Breeds among them were identified, she wouldn't hear of it."

"Speaking of the Guardians, where is Gideon?" Ava asked. "Has anyone heard from him?"

They all exchanged clueless looks until Caleb pulled out his phone and dialed.

"Caleb?" His father whispered. "I heard there was fighting on the perimeter. Are you all right?"

"I'm fine. We're all fine. Where are you? Are you okay?"

"We're in the central building, hiding in some service tunnels." Caleb heard another low voice on the other end of the phone. "We're safe for now, trying to figure out our next move. Borré's got the surveillance room sealed up tight with his soldiers on patrol."

"Evan's one of them," Caleb said. "We need to neutralize him. We were thinking Adam might be able to help."

"Adam's with me," Gideon replied, grunting slightly. "Tyra, too. But we have to get closer for Adam to be able to do anything."

"We need a distraction," Caleb said slowly, his gaze drifting to Ava. "Lucky for us, I happen to know someone who's great at distractions." He swiveled on his chair, his mind racing. "Stay where you are for a few minutes, and let us figure this out on our end. I'll be in touch."

"Got it."

Caleb hung up and turned to the group. "I'm open to suggestions," he said.

Ava moved to stand by Sophie, catching her eye then Isaiah's before turning back to Caleb. "It makes sense that we're the distraction. If we can draw Evan's attention enough, maybe Adam can get close to him."

"Borré will send his goons after you," Tiernan said.

Ava shrugged and reached out for Sophie's hand. "We can handle them."

"Well, you won't handle them alone," Caleb said. "I'm coming with you."

"Me, too." Tiernan started for the door.

"Wait a second," Lucy said quietly. "You're talking about, what, three people on the inside? Against Borré and his super kids?"

"It's all we've got," Caleb replied.

"Not really," she said. "The rest of the Council is in there, too, right?"

"Yeah, but they're locked up. Not really of much use to us." Tiernan headed for the stairs again.

"But . . ." Lucy tugged on her lip, deep in thought. "This guy—*Evan*—you said he zeroes in on Race imprints, right?"

"Which means we can't get anywhere near that building until he's out of the picture," Tiernan said, growling with irritation.

"So what if you send someone in who doesn't have a Race imprint?" Lucy waved her hands with a dramatic flourish.

"Oh, no way," Ava said. "There's no way we're sending you in there alone."

"She won't be alone," a voice said from the top of the stairs, his footsteps echoing on the wood as he descended.

"Dad?" Ava hurried toward him, trying to usher him back upstairs. "Sorry, we didn't mean to wake you." She glanced up the stairs and her face fell. "Mom? You guys should go back to bed. We'll be out of your hair in a minute."

"Don't try to push us out of this," her mother said, straightening her hair as she got to the bottom of the stairs. "You're our daughter, and there's no way we're letting you face this crazy man alone. Even if he is related to you."

"It actually explains a lot," muttered Tiernan.

Ava smacked him.

Her dad took her by the shoulders. "We won't do anything dangerous, but it sounds to me like you need every advantage you can get in there. Madeleine and the others need to be released, and from what I just heard, we're the only ones who can do it."

"It might work," Caleb said quietly. "There are some old access tunnels on the north side of the building. They were used to bring supplies down when they were building but haven't been used in years. They're sealed off, but we should be able to get you in."

Ava was shaking her head before she even spoke. "No way."

"Those tunnels wouldn't be linked to Bureau surveillance either," Tiernan said. "Not with the recent upgrades."

"We'll need a map," Ava's father said, pushing his way past his daughter to Caleb's side. "I need to know exactly where we're going, and how to get them out."

"But—" Ava said.

"Nearest we can tell, they're in the room at the far end of the Half-Breed holding facility." Caleb grabbed a piece of paper to draw a rough sketch. "There are occupants in three of the other holding cells."

"We should get them out, too," Sarah said. When Caleb turned to her in surprise, she shrugged. "You said we need as much help as we can get."

"This is a really bad idea," Ava grumbled, crossing her arms over her chest.

"I don't know if Half-Breeds would be that big on helping the Council," Caleb said. "They haven't exactly been treated well."

Joe patted him on the shoulder. "Leave that to Sarah," he said. "She can be very convincing."

"So how do we open the doors?" Lucy asked, crowding between Ava's parents. "Explosives might draw too much attention."

"You think?" Ava's voice neared shriek level as she turned on Caleb and Tiernan. "Are you *insane*? We're going up against some of the most powerful people in the world, and you want to send my *mom and dad* into the middle of it? This is dangerous. This is crazy. It's—"

"It's our best chance," her dad said quietly. He stepped around his wife to face Ava and gripped her upper arms. "We're only going to get one shot at this, and it makes sense. We need a coordinated attack to create the element of surprise. You and your—" He gestured toward the others. "You all create a diversion. Keep them busy while we sneak in and set the Council and the Half-Breeds loose. With any luck, they won't even know we were there. Meanwhile, Gideon gets this dampener close enough to get Evan out of the picture so the other Protectors can actually get inside the building."

Ava slumped. "Then what?"

"Then—" He frowned. "Then you take them out. Do the whole—" He waved a hand around her head. "You know, superhero thing and save the world."

Ava's lips quirked, and Caleb knew she was trying not to smile. "Not a very well-thought-out plan, Dad."

Her father grinned. "Sometimes, you've got to play it by ear." His smile fell as Ava threw herself at him and buried her face in his chest. "Hey now," he said. "It'll be okay. We may be human, but we're not totally useless, you know?"

"I know."

He pushed her back gently and tipped her chin up to meet his gaze. "You made the choice to fight, Ava. Even though it could cost you everything, you decided it was worth it. Don't we have that same right?"

Caleb watched as Ava looked from her father, to her mother, to Lucy—and finally to her siblings and Tiernan before her gaze rested on him.

"Okay," she said. "But somebody better get my dad a really big gun."

"Follow *me*. How many times do I have to tell you?" Ava grabbed Tiernan as he tried—again—to go in the wrong direction.

Tiernan scowled. "This guy Evan is really getting on my nerves."

"Yeah, well, get in line," Ava muttered. She checked over her shoulder to make sure everyone else was following.

They'd left the rest of the Protectors waiting on the west side of the city, ready for the signal once Evan had been neutralized. Sophie, Isaiah, Caleb, Tiernan, and Ava were nearing the central building from the opposite direction, hopefully drawing Evan's attention enough that the others wouldn't be noticed.

Ava felt them before she spotted them—

Three—no, four of the Twelve.

She couldn't tell exactly who, not yet at least. She didn't know the others' gifts well enough to differentiate exactly what they'd be coming up against. Ava could, however, recognize who *wasn't* there.

No Emma.

That made sense. Borré would want to have her close by.

Sophie took Isaiah and broke off, moving to the left so they could attack from the other side.

Ava stopped at the corner of a building and pressed her back against the cool stone, taking a moment to center herself as Caleb and Tiernan assumed the same position beside her. Tension radiated between them, zinging along an invisible cord from one to the other and back again.

"Ready?" she asked.

Caleb nodded.

Tiernan glowered, and she took that as a yes.

She spotted Sophie a block away and jerked her chin up in a silent signal. Her sister raised a hand in acknowledgement, and Ava turned to peer around the corner, spotting her siblings moving toward them at a slow—almost mocking—pace.

"Come out, come out, wherever you are!" one called out.

"Whatever you do, don't hit that one," Tiernan said.

So that's Max. The other is Jae, the shifter, and—

A fireball hit the building above Ava's head, and they jumped back.

Ah, yes. Christopher.

"That's weird," Ava murmured.

"That's an understatement," Caleb said, eyeing the burning tree branch overhead.

"No, I mean I felt four," Ava said. "I only see three."

"Make that two—no one," Tiernan said, peeking around the building. "Now they're all gone."

"But how?" Ava ducked around to see for herself. "Shifting?"

"Maybe, or—"

Max appeared in front of Tiernan, smirking as he reached out to take him by the throat.

Christopher appeared next, his hand raised with a ball of fire in his palm.

"Watch out!" Caleb shouted.

A chunk of ice knocked Christopher to his knees, the melting water sizzling against his skin as he disappeared.

Max released Tiernan suddenly and vanished as well.

"Jae—the blond—is a shifter, but those two aren't shifting," Ava said finally. "It's got to be the one with the super Veil."

Caleb's eyes widened. "A super Veil?"

"Yeah. What was his name?" Ava thought for a moment. "*Lucien*. Emma told me he could cover more than one person." Ava replied. "But if it's a Veil, I should be able to see through it."

If I can figure out where to look.

She closed her eyes and reached out with her gift.

One to the right. One straight ahead. Two right there.

She opened her eyes and looked in the direction she had sensed them, narrowing her eyes to focus . . . *deeper* to see through the shimmering Veil. "Hello there," she murmured right before she reached out to pluck them up off the ground, smiling at the resulting shout as she threw them down the street and they both blinked into view.

"Nice," Tiernan said, cracking his neck as he caught his breath.

"We need to stop the shifter," Ava said, watching as Jae vanished then appeared next to Christopher.

Max stood and dusted off his jeans, a satisfied smile on his face.

"Uh-oh," Caleb said.

"I told you not to hit him." Tiernan braced himself against the wall.

"What do you—"

An invisible force blasted them, throwing Ava into the middle of the street.

She rolled to a stop, only to find Caleb lying next to her.

"Kinetic absorption," Caleb said. "Whatever power is thrown at him, he can throw right back."

Ava got to her feet and ducked another fireball. "Perfect."

They ran in a crouch to the other side of the street and ducked into the protective shield of a covered patio.

Sophie and Isaiah joined them a moment later.

"So this is going well," Sophie said.

Ava let out a shaky laugh and grabbed Isaiah's arm. "You need to take out Max—the big one," she said. "Caleb, will he be able to turn that around?"

"I don't think so. It's only physical power, not mental."

"Okay, good." Ava nodded, turning back to her brother. "So you take out Max. Make him run away, freeze in terror, whatever you can."

"Be careful," Caleb warned. "He might try to feed on your gift. You might want to make him scared to do that, too."

Isaiah nodded, his eyes wide.

"Sophie, you've got the fireball guy." Ava glanced back across the street at Tiernan. "I'll take the Veil. That leaves the shifter. We don't want him running back to Borré for reinforcements."

Caleb peeled off his jacket and threw it to the ground. "I've got the shifter," he said then disappeared.

"I guess that's means go," Ava said before joining the fray.

Madeleine Foster paced back and forth from the bed to the sofa and back again, ignoring Kaeden's irritated huff.

They'd been unceremoniously dumped in the Half-Breed cell and left to fend for themselves. She had no idea what Borré was doing—how her people were faring—and the not knowing was driving her crazy.

Is Gideon all right? Caleb?

She chewed on her thumbnail and turned on another circuit to the bed and back again.

"I'm going to kill that bastard Andreas with my bare hands," Kaeden said for the hundredth time. "We were so close."

"Not close enough," Rafe said with a sigh.

They had come to Madeleine with their suspicions about Andreas—the unexplained phone calls out of the city, the holes in his story about Evan—but she'd been too late to react. They'd confronted him moments before Borré launched his attack, and Andreas had smiled as his minions escorted them to their new accommodations, his laugh echoing behind them all the way down the hall.

"I'm going to kill him," Kaeden muttered again.

"I'll hold your jacket." Rafe stood up from the sofa to stretch. "But I'd say getting out of this room should be first on the agenda."

"There is no getting out of this room," Madeleine said shortly. "You as well as I know that they're designed to be escape proof."

"They'll have to open that door sometime," Kaeden said through gritted teeth.

Madeleine resisted an urge to tear at her hair. "Do they? It would be just like Borré to leave us here to starve to—"

The tumbler scraping in the lock caused them all to start, and Kaeden shot across the room, behind the door, ready to attack. Madeleine stood in plain sight to draw their captor's attention as Rafe and Naomi got to their feet, braced for a fight.

With a loud click, the door swung open, and the tension thickened in the room, hot and electric.

Kaeden drew back a fist, letting it fly as someone walked through the doorway and stopping just short of punching a young, blond woman in the face.

The girl stumbled back against the wall and threw her hands up to protect her face, a cluster of wires clutched in her fist.

Kaeden stepped forward to wrap his fingers around the woman's throat.

"No wait!" Madeleine grabbed his arm. "I know her."

Kaeden froze, his arm still extended and fingers twitching a hairsbreadth from her neck.

"She's Ava's friend. The human."

"Human?" Kaeden turned in surprise, his hand slowly lowering to his side. "What are you doing here?"

The girl straightened, her chin jutting out as she waved the wires at him. "We're here to rescue you, actually."

"We?"

She pushed the door open a little wider, and Madeleine gaped at the group in the hallway. Ava Michaels' parents stood smiling at her with a half dozen angry Half-Breeds behind them.

"Come on, then," Joe Michaels said with a nod. "We need to get moving."

Madeleine was still a little stunned. "Moving?"

"We need to rendezvous with Gideon. Ava's got a plan."

Madeleine's heart quickened. "Gideon? Is he all right?"

"For now," Joe said, leading them down a hallway and checking a hand-drawn map. "But we need to get into position."

Madeleine glanced nervously back at the Half-Breeds. "What about them?"

"They're here to help."

"Why would they help us?" Madeleine blurted out.

Joe stopped and turned to face her. "Because it's the right thing to do." He tilted his head, a slight smile on his face. "Humans and Half-Breeds coming together to help you out. I bet this is blowing your mind, isn't it?"

Madeleine let out a shaky laugh. "You have no idea."

Sarah stepped forward. "Can we focus on the problem at hand, please? There will be time enough for revelations and epiphanies when this is all over."

Madeleine was pretty sure she heard Rafe snort somewhere behind her, but she ignored it and followed the human, Joe, and hoped for the best.

Gideon checked his watch, his phone, and then his watch again. "Where are they?" he hissed.

"They'll be here," Tyra whispered. "It's only been a few minutes."

Gideon checked his watch once more and adjusted his stance.

They were waiting behind a door in the service tunnel, and he wasn't sure Madeleine and the others were even coming.

Maybe they've been caught trying to escape. Maybe they were hurt or—

"I hear something," Tyra said.

Sure enough, there was a knock on the door, and he opened it to find the Council and a ragtag group of humans and Half-Breeds waiting expectantly. "Stay behind me," he said, pushing his way through the group and pausing only long enough to brush his fingers against Madeleine's as he passed. It helped. Maybe it was selfish, but it helped.

They took the stairs and climbed quickly but quietly.

He paused at the door at the landing and peered through the little window, spotting two of the Twelve stationed outside the surveillance room, and smiled when they took off toward the elevator.

It's working.

"Can you block him yet?" he asked Adam.

The dampener tensed beside him. "Not enough to do any good. He's pretty powerful. I need to be closer. Even then, I don't know if I'll be able to dampen his gift completely."

"Well, you'll just have to try," Gideon said, reaching for the door. "Let's go."

CHAPTER EIGHTEEN

Ava took the R-cube Caleb offered her and wiped her nose with the back of her hand as she chewed and swallowed, the metallic taste of blood sliding down her throat. "Here come two more."

Night melted into day as the sun appeared low in the sky and cast the city in a warm glow. It would have been beautiful if she hadn't been so tired.

"Sloan Bartok. Great," Caleb muttered. "Do you know the other one?"

Ava searched the man's features, his dark skin, black hair, and short but bulky build. "No. Never seen him before. He must be Amrit, the weather manipulator." She gathered her gift. The pendant Caleb gave her so long ago vibrated against her skin. While her body ached and her head pounded, her power still responded eagerly. She tried not to think about the fact that she was made for this. Made to fight.

To kill.

She caught Sophie's eye a few feet away, Isaiah slumped at her feet, her back against a low wall.

They were just as tired as she was. Isaiah let the blood drip from his nose, not even bothering to wipe it away. He got up as Sophie stiffened.

Ava felt it, too.

They're coming.

Max—she recognized him now—and Jae, no longer shifting, thanks to Isaiah, but still a good fighter. Same could be said for the super Veil,

Lucien, as well as Christopher. He had recovered from the last bout and was ready to fight again.

Ava rubbed at the healing burn on her forearm, wincing a little at the reminder that she needed to keep him in her sights.

And now the dark newcomer and the killer—Amrit and Sloan.

Six of the Twelve against three, plus two Protectors.

Ava didn't like the odds, but she had to remind herself that their purpose wasn't really to win the fight. Not that they could.

Not yet, at least.

"Ready?" Caleb looked worried as he searched her face. "Are you okay?"

She nodded. "Yeah. I'm ready. I still don't like the idea of leaving them out here, though."

"Yeah, well I don't like the idea of bringing you in there, so—"

A fireball exploded overhead, and all hell broke loose.

Sophie released a series of ice balls, each bigger than the last, then a slab of ice the size of a refrigerator.

Christopher met a few with fireballs of his own and easily dodged the rest.

Ava took advantage of his distraction to throw him against Jae and slam them both into the side of a house as hard as she could.

Tiernan darted out from the nearby restaurant he'd been using as cover and launched himself at Lucien, and the two exchanged jarring blows in the middle of the street.

The wind picked up suddenly. A flash of lightning crackled across the sky.

A swell of power licked at Ava's skin, and she followed it back, tracking it to the newcomer standing a few feet from Tiernan and Jae, arms lifted and head thrown back.

Before she could do anything, Sophie launched a bowling ball-sized piece of ice toward him.

Ava added her gift to the mix, giving the ball an extra push. It hit Amrit in the stomach and knocked him off his feet.

He flew through the air and landed in the street with a loud grunt.

The lightning stopped and the wind quieted, but picked up again as he got to his feet.

"Is it time yet?" Ava grumbled, bracing herself against the dust stabbing her cheeks as she zeroed in on the stone wall Isaiah had been resting against.

They were trying to cause as little damage to the city as possible, but there wasn't much to work with in a city so neat and clean.

What I wouldn't give for garbage cans or some discarded lumber.

Ava pushed her gift at the wall, hefting two large stones that broke free and hurling them toward the weather guy.

He dodged one, but the other caught him in the leg, causing another pause in the inclement weather.

She was about to throw a couple more pieces of the wall when Caleb barreled down the street, tackling the weather manipulator while he tried to catch his breath.

Sophie turned her attention to Sloan, who was standing calmly in the midst of it all, looking in Ava's direction.

As soon as their eyes locked, Ava doubled over with a gasp, clutching at her stomach and dropping to a knee as a sharp pain shot through her belly. She heard Sloan snicker quietly, and the pain intensified, radiating into her chest and making it hard to breathe. Her lungs were wrapped in iron bands, tightening with every exhale, and black spots swam at the edge of her vision as she fell to all fours. Her body wanted to retch, but she couldn't catch her breath enough to complete the task. Instead, bile climbed into her throat and saliva dripped from her slack jaw to the ground. She was so dizzy, so panicked, that her gift clawed to the surface, and she let it go.

The impact knocked Sloan almost two blocks, but he tucked and rolled and was back on his feet in a second.

Ava tried to catch her breath, blinking when a hand closed on her arm.

Isaiah.

"Are you all right?" he asked, his eyes wide and frightened.

She nodded, still unable to speak.

Isaiah set his jaw and turned toward Sloan.

The killer froze in the middle of the street for several seconds. He visibly shook it off just in time to get coldcocked by Tiernan and drop like a brick.

Caleb appeared beside her. "It's time," he said and spat a mouthful of blood onto the ground. "You ready?"

She wasn't sure who he was asking, but it was Isaiah who replied. "We'll keep them here as long as we can."

Caleb pulled Ava close, and she indulged in the moment of their mingling gifts before the wind picked up again. Isaiah turned back to join the fight, and the world spun, whirling into a blended mass of color before it disappeared around them.

They rematerialized inside the central building, and Caleb yanked her back into an empty doorway before he looked up and down the hall to make sure it was clear. Satisfied, he grabbed her hand, popping a couple of R-cubes and handing her one as he led her silently down the hall.

She wiped saliva and blood from her face with her sleeve and tried to catch her breath. She felt him—Borré drew nearer with every step, and she knew he felt it, too. They had known it would be a risk, but her only hope was that the remaining Twelve—Emma, Evan, and the one with the technology gift, Mara—would be close enough to him that they masked her approach.

They rounded a corner, and Ava stopped abruptly, her instincts finally clearing enough to detect a mass of Race nearby.

"It's okay," Caleb whispered. "It's them."

Sure enough, Gideon and Madeleine appeared at the far end of the hall, followed by the rest of the Council, Tyra, Adam, the dampener, and a handful of others Ava assumed were the Half-Breeds.

"Are my parents okay?" she asked without prelude. "Lucy?"

Gideon nodded. "They're safe. We sent them out the way they came. Joe said he'd get them back to the house, and they'd hole up there until this is all over."

Ava let out a relieved breath and turned her attention to the task at hand as they headed toward the surveillance room. "We need to move quickly. Only three of the Twelve are with Borré right now, but the others will figure out what we're up to at any minute."

Gideon deferred to Madeleine to lead the way.

"We'll shift in," Caleb said quietly, pulling Ava close. "Catch them by surprise."

Gideon nodded, and Caleb and Ava disappeared, reappearing a second later inside the surveillance room.

They were clustered around Evan—Borré, Emma, Andreas, and Mara—but none looked surprised to see the couple.

"Ah, daughter," Borré said with a smile. "We've been expe—"

Ava threw a chair at him, but Borré sidestepped it easily. Emma's gift prodded at her brain, and she turned against her sister, shoving Emma toward the wall with her gift while throwing another chair at Borré.

Caleb vanished and reappeared next to Andreas. He punched the man twice, knocking him to the floor just as the others poured through the doors.

She held Emma against the wall, pushing her a little higher with each step as she approached Borré. A light flared out of the wall and an electric shock hit her and knocked her to her knees.

Mara.

They had them outnumbered, though, and in a moment Mara was down, Adam keeping her gift under control now that Evan was no longer a threat.

His vision cleared, and the boy yelled out that Protectors were on the way.

Ava grinned.

Gideon and Tyra had Emma by the arms. The Protectors would be there any moment, and Borré would be taken into custody. Once he was gone, they'd go about securing the rest of the Twelve and then—

"You can't think I didn't see this coming," Borré said, smiling creepily at her. "You remember I told you your brother Jae was a shifter like your Caleb?" He didn't wait for her to answer. "Well, he's not *exactly* like him. You're all a bit . . . *more,* aren't you?" His gaze drifted to the surveillance room door, where Ava could hear the distinct sounds of fighting coming from the other side.

How did he call them back so quickly?

"Your brothers should be along any moment," he said with slow wink. "Once they've cleaned up the mess outside."

Ava turned panicked eyes toward Caleb, trusting he could read her as well as she hoped.

He disappeared.

"Seems your boy didn't want to stick around for the fun," Borré said as Sloan Bartok walked through the doors and turned his gaze on Gideon and Madeleine.

They both clutched their stomachs and fell to the floor, writhing in pain, and Emma walked sedately to Borré's side.

"Yes, you're all so very gifted," Borré said, stroking Emma's hair lovingly. "Sloan here can control bodily functions, muscle function, respiration . . ."

Gideon gasped for breath as if in demonstration.

"Jae can shift large groups of people for unheard distances. Comes in quite handy, as I'm sure you can imagine. The lovely Mara will provide much needed financial support, thanks to her rather unusual gift." Borré moved toward Ava, Emma close at his side. "Such power is what's needed to lead people like ours, you see. It's the only way."

Ava glared at him. "*Our* power. You use our power to make yourself some kind of king."

Borré tipped his head. "But we share," he said. "It's what family does. You share your power with me. I share my power with you."

"Share?" Ava spat. "What about our mothers? Did you share with them, too? Are they fighting for you now?" She glanced toward the doors.

Borré laughed. "Sadly, your mothers gave their lives for the cause," he said, although he didn't seem sad at all. "They didn't truly see their place in this new world."

"What?" Emma whispered, shock clearly written on her face. "You told me my mother left me. She gave me to you."

Borré touched her cheek. "She did give you to me, but she was nothing truly special. Not like you. Not like your brothers and sisters." He turned his attention back to Ava. "No, your mother and the others were simply a means to an end. *This* end."

Ava looked at Andreas fighting to get to his feet. "And what about him? Did you promise to share with him, too?"

Borré laughed. "Don't be ridiculous. He's not one of us."

Andreas bristled. "But you said—you promised . . ."

"I promised a place for you," Borré said, dismissing him offhand. "You *assumed* it would be a place of importance."

"But—" Andreas shook his head, his face growing red. "But I helped you. You couldn't have done this without me!"

"And you will be rewarded," Borré said as though talking to a child. "Unlike the rest of the Council, you'll be allowed to remain free." He turned away and started toward the door.

"But you said I'd be rich! You promised me power!" Andreas shouted. "You can't do this to me. You need me!"

Borré froze then spun on his heel to face Andreas.

Ava watched wide-eyed, trying to listen to the sounds in the hall at the same time.

A thud.

A shout.

A whimper.

Andreas threw himself at Borré, fists clenched, but fell to the floor, clutching his stomach. Sloan stood over him, watching impassively as the Council member curled into himself. Borré held up a hand, and Sloan tipped his head in acknowledgement. He stepped back, and Andreas drew a deep breath, rolling onto his back as the pain eased. Borré looked down a the panting man then slowly lifted his hand to rest it on Emma's head. Emma closed her eyes, shivering slightly.

"I don't *need* you," Borré said quietly. "As a matter of fact, you've become more of a liability than an asset with your whining and your greed." His fingers tightened in her hair as he accessed her gift, taking her power to use against Andreas.

He cried out, curling up again and pressing his hands to his head. "What are you doing? Stop!" he groaned.

"It's not all about you, you know," Borré said mockingly. "This is about so much more than you. But then the Council always was more concerned about securing its position than about the Race."

Ava's stomach turned, and she finally found her voice. "Emma, stop this," she pleaded. "He's using you. He's going to kill him. *You're* going to kill him."

Emma's eyes flickered open and she focused on Ava. "I can't," she whispered.

"You *can*. You have to fight him."

Emma closed her eyes once more and tears trickled down her cheeks.

Borré simply continued his assault until blood began to drip from Andreas' nose, and then his mouth.

Ava reached out to stop him, but Sloan brought her to her knees with a blast of excruciating pain. Her vision swam as she struggled to maintain consciousness.

Andreas gurgled and spat, gasping for breath against the torment. "Stop," he whimpered. "Please."

"Stop! Please!" Borré mimicked. "When it comes down to it, you've got nothing. No real power. None but what the people give you. You're useless."

As if to emphasize Borré's last word, Andreas let out an agonized scream. The blood poured from his nose and mouth and puddled on the floor beneath his cheek. His eyes popped open, the whites turned red and inflamed, and his pupils blown wide. Finally, with a grisly shudder and one last rasping sigh, he stilled.

Borré stared down at him for a moment longer before he relaxed his fingers and smoothed his hand over Emma's hair. He kissed her cheek. "Thank you, daughter," he murmured against her skin, ignoring Emma's shudder. "Now then," he said, rubbing his hands together as he stepped over Andreas' lifeless body. "Where were we before we were so rudely interrupted?" He seemed to notice Ava again and nodded at Sloan.

Ava drew a shaky breath as the pain eased.

Borré smiled widely. "Ah, yes. You were about to decide where your fate lies, dear daughter," he said. "Will you follow in the footsteps of the illustrious Andreas?" He waved his hand toward the man's body, grimacing distastefully. "Or will you join your family and claim your birthright?" His smile fell, his eyes hardened, and he turned his tone cold and unforgiving. "Last chance, Ava. I suggest you choose wisely."

"Please, Ava," Emma said, her voice shaky and pleading. "Please."

Ava couldn't tell what was happening in the hall, but she knew her time was up. There was only one choice. One solution. Bracing herself, she got to her feet and reached for her gift.

"Ava, no!" Emma whispered.

She knew what she had to do, and taking a deep fortifying breath, Ava unleashed the full force of her power toward Borré, binding him in shackles, his arms pressed tightly to his side, and slamming him up against the curved wall. She envisioned his internal organs, his heart pounding slow and steady in his chest. She pictured it slowing—

Pain slashed through her stomach, through her head, and fired every nerve ending as Sloan launched another barrage. She pushed her gift to the limit and kept her focus steadfastly locked on her father. Ava's pendant burned against her skin as blood flowed from her nose, falling in constant drips to the toes of her shoes.

Sloan moved to her lungs, and she gasped for air and fought to keep her hold on Borré.

The door burst open and an ice ball flew across the room, smashing into Sloan's skull.

Ava filled her lungs with a gulp of precious air as Sophie ran into the room, followed quickly by Isaiah.

"They're coming!" he shouted, taking in the scene with wide eyes.

Ava fought but felt her gift slipping as she resisted the instinct to protect her father, her creator. Hurting him was hurting herself, but she had to keep going and battle through the agonizing pain cutting through her head, through her entire body.

"Don't just stand there like an idiot," Borré snarled at Emma through gritted teeth. "Stop her!"

Emma turned wide, tearful eyes on Ava then looked back at Borré.

"Emma," Ava said, spitting out a mouthful of blood, "you don't have to do this. We can stop him together."

"Don't listen to her," Borré snarled. "End this, *now!*"

Ava was weakening, the pain in her head nearly unbearable. She couldn't keep it up much longer. "He's using you, Emma. Using us all. Think of what he's done to Andreas, to our mothers, to so many . . . others." She choked on blood and spat again. "We need to stop him."

Borré slipped a few inches down the wall.

"Help me, please."

A hand took hers, the familiar swell of Sophie's power giving hers a boost.

Ava didn't look away from Borré, but her hold tightened just a fraction, not a lot, but enough to buy her a few more seconds. She heard Sophie gasp from the pain.

"Emma, this isn't you. You're not a killer," Ava pleaded. "I know you. You're my sister—*our* sister. You don't want to hurt anyone. Not really."

"But—" Emma took a step toward her and hesitated, glancing at her father.

"I know he's your father—the only father you've ever known," Ava said. "But he's wrong. I know you see it. He only wants power for himself."

"Don't listen to her!" Borré shouted.

Ava was vaguely aware of others in the room—Sloan struggling to his feet but standing frozen under Isaiah's influence, Caleb and Tiernan, a band of Half-Breeds and Protectors, fireballs, wind, and fighting all around her—but she braced herself against the wind and lightning and focused on Borré, on Sophie's hold keeping her together, on Emma.

"He won't stop until he kills everyone who stands in his way." Ava's voice was weak so she cleared her throat, fighting to speak clearly. "He wouldn't hesitate to turn on any of us. You've seen it." She caught a flash of movement as Emma looked at Andreas. "I need you, Emma," she whispered. "Help me."

"Take her out!" Borré shrieked.

She winced at the heat of the fireball that came so close to her face only to be deflected at the last minute by a chunk of Sophie's ice.

Emma swallowed hard and latched on to her hand, her gift flowing through Ava and lashing out toward Borré.

Ava almost sobbed at the brief respite Emma's support afforded her. She was vaguely aware of her sister's frantic voice.

"Help us!" Emma shouted over the din in the room. "You know she's right. You know he doesn't care about us!"

"Shut up, you ungrateful brat!" Borré staggered under the onslaught but fought to stand upright as he slid against the wall. "You were nothing until I brought you together. You *are* nothing without me!"

Even with Emma and Sophie's support, Ava's power slipped once more as the effort it took to keep him pinned became too much. The wind buffeted her, and she struggled against its power, her legs shaking with the effort it took to stay upright. She saw Evan out of the corner of her eye as he glanced at Borré and took a step toward her.

"Don't you dare!" Borré snarled, his arms rigid, veins popping out along the tops of his hands as he fought Ava's hold.

Evan swallowed but took another tentative step. "You said nobody would get hurt."

"Don't be an idiot! There is a risk of casualties in every revolution."

"We'll be next," Ava said, and she almost didn't recognize her own voice, dry and cracked. Her head swam. "He won't stop."

"You know he won't, Evan." Emma nudged closer to Ava, urging her to lean on her. "You've seen it."

Evan took another step toward them, and Borré growled in frustration.

"Mara, stop your idiot brother before he ruins everything!"

But Mara was already on her feet and crossing the room.

Ava drew a deep, relieved breath at the vibrating energy, the power that flowed into her—*through* her—as Evan took Emma's hand, and Mara took Sophie's.

"Damn it! You are my children, and you *will* obey me!"

Ava's knees buckled, but Sophie and Emma drew closer and wrapped their arms around her waist, supporting her weight. Then, instead of the power flowing in, it switched midstream, flowing *out* of Ava as Emma took a step forward, her eyes focused on their father.

She winced, and Ava knew the pain in her head, knew they were all feeling the same thing—the agony of turning against him.

Borré held Emma's gaze, glaring at her angrily. "You will be punished for this," he spat.

Emma lifted her chin, ignoring the blood dripping off it as she focused her power on him. She staggered.

"Emma?" Their roles switched as Ava supported her, feeding her, even though she was barely able to keep her own feet under her. Others joined their circle—Jae, Caleb, Tiernan, and Tyra—all sharing their power like a circuit feeding Emma's gift. Her anger, her pain, raced through the circuit in return, echoing in Ava's heart and mind.

"You don't have to do this," Ava shouted over the wind. "We can stop him now."

"Nothing will stop him," Emma mumbled. "Nothing but me."

"Emma!"

Emma looked at her, eyes sad. "You're not a killer," she said. "I am." She turned back on her father, gathering their power. It swept through Ava, gaining speed, until Emma let it out with an angry shout that shook the walls.

Ava barely drew a breath before darkness claimed her and she collapsed to the floor.

"Ava?" The quiet voice cut through the fog and darkness and sliced into her skull.

She winced and pressed her hands against her temples, mumbling something she hoped translated to "be quiet" or "leave me alone." She couldn't be sure because nothing seemed to be working properly.

"Ava, come on. You need to wake up."

She tried to roll over but stopped immediately when the motion sent another stab of searing agony through her head. Slowly, she lowered her hands and opened her eyes a tiny sliver. Light was all she discerned at first—blinding, painful light—but she fought the urge to squeeze her eyes shut again and blinked, willing her vision to clear. Eventually, Talia's face came into focus.

"Hi there," she said. "How are you feeling?"

"Terrible," Ava mumbled, closing her eyes again.

Caleb? Where?

He took her hand in his, and she calmed.

"Well, let's see what we can do about that, shall we?" Talia said, and Ava was absently aware of Talia touching her head, her palms warm and gentle against her scalp.

Slowly, the pain faded to a low throb, and Ava sighed in shaky relief. "Thanks."

"Don't mention it. Do you think you can sit up?"

Ava nodded slightly. Before she could attempt shifting her body again, a low thrum of mechanics hummed, and Ava's head rose. When she opened her eyes again, she saw Talia standing to the right of her bed and Caleb to the left. "Am I in the hospital?" she asked. "What happened?"

"You don't remember?" Caleb's voice was quiet but anxious.

"No, I . . . there was . . ." She closed her eyes and searched for the memories. "We were fighting, then Sophie . . . Emma—" Her eyes flew open. "Borré?"

"Dead," Caleb said, squeezing her hand. "He's gone, Ava."

She nodded, the images floating back to settle in her head. Borré . . . Andreas . . . Max, Lucien, Isaiah, Sophie. Emma's hand, so small and cold in hers.

Emma.

She sat up straight, ignoring the pain that shot through her body and focused behind her eyes. "Is Emma okay? She was trying to—"

"Ava," Caleb's voice cut through her as he lifted her hand to his lips. "I'm so sorry."

"No."

"We tried everything we could," Talia said, her eyes tearing with sympathy.

"No, that's not right," Ava shook her head violently. "No, that can't be right. We're hard to kill. Tiernan said we were hard to kill."

"But not impossible," Talia murmured.

"I thought that about you," Ava told Caleb. "You were shot and . . . and bleeding. You should have died, but they brought you back." She turned on Talia. "You can bring her back. Get the other doctors. Between all of you, you can figure i—"

"It's too late, Ava." Talia shook her head. "From what we can determine, the need Borré placed in each of you for him, for his gift . . . it worked both ways. You needed him to ward off your symptoms, but harming him would have the opposite effect. It was his defense against any of you turning against him."

"But—she saved me," she whispered. "She saved us all." Tears pricked at her eyes along with a wave of realization. "She knew what would happen. If I killed him, she knew what would happen. She took it on herself. She—"

Caleb said nothing but drew her close, his arms and his gift holding her tightly as Talia left the room and Ava gave in to painful, tortured sobs.

It was strange to think of New Elysia having a morgue. Although logically, Ava understood that people in the city did die—not as often as humans, but eventually it had to happen—it still seemed odd, for some reason. In actuality, the morgue wasn't like any that Ava had seen on television or in the movies. No walls of stainless steel drawers and toe tags and examination tables. It was a simple room with a simple bed, dimly lit, with a counter along one wall and rows of drawers underneath.

What could you possibly need to store in a room that's sole purpose was to house death?

Caleb held her hand tightly as Ava walked on shaky legs to the bedside.

Emma's face wasn't covered. The sheet was tucked neatly beneath her bare arms, her hands at her sides and her fingers curled slightly into themselves. She looked like she was sleeping. She looked like she was alive, but when Ava closed her eyes and reached out with her gift—she couldn't resist, had to *know*—there was . . . nothing where Emma used to be. She was gone.

"Do you want me to stay?" Caleb asked quietly. "Do you want to be alone?" He reached out tentatively and touched a strand of her hair.

"Stay, please," she said on a shaky breath. She touched the spot in the middle of her chest where her pendant hung, beneath it a burn she'd asked Talia not to heal. A reminder. "I'm okay. I just—" She looked down at Emma and touched her cold hand, finally taking it in her own. "Thank you," she whispered. "I'm sorry." Ava shook her head.

Sorry for what?

So much, really, but it doesn't matter anymore, does it?

"I wish things had been different," she said finally, tears filling her eyes and overflowing when she bowed her head. "I wish we'd had more time. I wish we could have really gotten to know each other. I wish we could have been sisters . . . like you always wanted." She squeezed Emma's hand one last time before laying it carefully back on the starched sheet. "Thank you," she said again.

She led Caleb out of the room and didn't look back.

EPILOGUE

One week later . . .

The Council chamber was packed as Ava made her way to the seat Caleb was saving near the front. She excused herself, stepping over a half a dozen people, before collapsing next to him.

"Thought you were going to miss it," he said, throwing an arm over the back of her seat.

"Got caught up with Sophie," she replied. "She and Isaiah are heading out tomorrow."

Caleb nodded and squeezed her shoulder once.

It was tough to lose her sister and brother so soon after finding them, but Sophie wanted to get Isaiah back to school. She'd been in touch with his adopted family, and she'd be staying with them while she figured things out.

Ava had wished her luck.

Sophie had said they'd keep in touch and would probably visit over the summer break, and Ava was happy about that. Although she'd been spending some time getting to know her new family, her bond with Sophie had been the strongest. Especially now that Emma was gone.

Emma.

Ava found it difficult to put her complicated feelings about Emma into words. She'd betrayed her, manipulated her, used her, but in the end, she'd also given her life for her—for them all. Emma hadn't been perfect. She'd been broken and twisted by their father from birth, but when push had come to shove, her loyalty to Ava and her inner conscience had overridden all those years of manipulation and abusive training.

Ava felt sorry for her. She was grateful to her. She even had to admit she loved her, in a way.

She *missed* her, as strange as that was. The absence of her gift was like an empty space inside Ava. She wondered if it was the same for all the Twelve, or something unique because of their particular bond. Maybe it was simply plain, ordinary loss, and over time, she'd be able to remember Emma without feeling the ache of oncoming tears.

Maybe.

The door at the back of the chamber opened, drawing Ava out of her thoughts.

The Council members filed in and took their place at the table.

Ava smiled when she caught Gideon's eye as he took Andreas' vacated seat.

Elections would be held in the fall, but for now, the current Council would oversee the restructuring of the city and of the Law. They had already presided over the trials of the surviving Twelve. Those who had aided in defeating Borré had been pardoned. The others had been imprisoned.

Except for Sloan. With a little encouragement from Isaiah, he had returned to Allenmore to turn himself in. He would plead guilty and accept whatever sentence the human courts handed down for the murder of Officer Simmons. He'd spend thirty or forty years behind bars, his Veil altered to give the illusion of aging. A life sentence was a drop in the bucket for Race, but at least he was eligible for parole. Ava knew, however, even when he was released, he'd never walk free again.

Madeleine cleared her throat, and Ava sat up a little as the Council chamber grew silent.

"For centuries, we, the First Race, have lived according to the Law our forefathers put forth," she said, her voice ringing out, loud and clear. "We have lived by the credo to aid humanity in whatever way possible but have learned to maintain our secrecy if we are to protect ourselves. Recent events have challenged those ideals and led to an uprising that, if it had succeeded, would have destroyed everything we hold dear."

Ava saw a few nods, heard a few murmurs.

Madeleine gripped the back of her chair and lifted her chin, always the leader. "Our recent alliance with the Guardians has shown me, and I believe shown you all"—she waved a hand to encompass the crowded room—"that our current mandate regarding Half-Br"—she pursed her lips and shook her head slightly—"regarding Race of *mixed heritage* is outdated and misguided. I believe, and the Council agrees, that the Law must be amended on this issue, and that these people—our brothers and sisters—should be welcomed and trained, taught to use whatever gifts they possess for the good of the Race and of the world as a whole."

Applause broke out, a few whistles cutting through the cheers as people jumped to their feet.

Madeleine waited, a small smile on her face, until she lifted a hand to quiet them. "In addition, we believe that secrecy might no longer always be in the best interest of the Race," she said. "Humans are growing, learning, some are quite"—she caught Ava's eye—"impressive. We believe there may be situations where revealing ourselves to certain trustworthy and carefully vetted humans may prove valuable, especially when it comes to seeking out Rogues and others who may wish ill on our people—human and Race alike.

"Over the coming months, the Council, along with a special committee, will be creating an amendment to the Law addressing these issues, to be put to the Race—the *entire* Race—for a vote in the fall." Madeleine swept the room with a soft look. "I hope—I pray—that you will consider these things carefully as you consider your vote. The future of our people is changing. I believe it will be for the better if we all work together." She locked eyes with Gideon, her cheeks pinking slightly as the room erupted in loud applause and cheers once again.

"Well, that was interesting," Ava said once the Council had filed out and they made their way toward the doors.

Caleb shrugged. "It's what we expected. She said what she told us she would."

"Not that." Ava took his hand. "I mean the little moment between your mom and dad."

"Moment?" He glanced back over his shoulder at the empty Council table. "You think?"

"Oh, there was *definitely* a moment," she said with a nod, stepping outside as Caleb held the door open. "Think about it. Everybody's told me how the bond is forever. They obviously still feel it—still love each other—and now there's nothing really standing in their way."

"Except themselves," Caleb said, throwing an arm over her shoulders. "Decades of stubbornness are hard to get past."

Ava slipped her hands under his coat to hold him around the waist. "Oh, I think they'll figure it out," she said. "You've always said I should trust my intuition, and I have a definite feeling about those two." She didn't imagine the slight smile lifting Caleb's lips.

She was about to suggest they find a quiet corner to talk—and *things*—when her phone buzzed in her pocket. She smiled at the caller ID. "It's my mom," she said, pressing the connect button. "Hey, Mom. Was the flight okay?"

"Bumpy as all get out the last hour, but we got here in one piece," she replied. "Did Lucy make it back to school?"

"Katherine drove her herself," Ava said, swinging Caleb's hand joined with hers between them. "She should get back to Allenmore sometime tomorrow night."

"Good, that's good." She paused, and Ava was about to end the call when she asked, "Will you be home for the Fourth of July?"

"Uh . . . I'm not sure yet."

"We're planning a family barbecue, and I thought maybe we could celebrate your birthday at the same time," her mom said in a rush of words. "I already talked to Grandma and Auntie Kay, and it looks like the whole family's coming. I know they'd all love to meet Caleb."

Caleb snorted, and she nudged him with her elbow.

"Not really sure what we've got planned yet—"

"Oh, come on, now. Surely you two could get away for a long weekend?" Sarah tutted reproachfully. "The family hasn't seen you in *months*, Ava."

"I've been kind of busy, you know, saving the world and stuff," she mumbled.

"Not by yourself, sweetie. I don't care what kind of superpowers you have, there's no need to get cocky."

Caleb burst out laughing.

"I've really got to go, Mom," Ava said. "We'll try to make it for the Fourth, okay?" When Caleb raised his eyebrows at her and prodded her with an elbow, she sighed. "We'll definitely be there."

"I knew I liked that boy for a reason," Sarah said.

"Hey! How do you know it was him?"

"A mother knows," Sarah said, like a wise old sage.

Ava found it irritating and a little bit endearing.

"Talk to you soon, sweetie."

"Bye, Mom. Love to Dad." She hung up and glared at Caleb. "I think my mom likes you better than me."

He smirked. "Can you blame her?"

She pushed him away but moved closer a second later. She scanned the thinning crowd. "Have you seen Tiernan lately? I haven't talked to him for days."

"He was in the meeting, but he left before it was over," Caleb replied.

Ava frowned. "Maybe Evan can help me find him."

"Ava, leave it alone." Caleb pulled her close. "He probably just needs some time to himself."

She pulled free and turned back toward the central building. "I only want to check on him."

"Tiernan can take care of himself."

"I know that. I just . . . we've been through a lot together, you know? I want to make sure he's okay." She looked up at Caleb hopefully, and after a minute, he pulled her close and kissed her gently.

"I'll find you later, okay?" he said.

"Yeah. Okay."

It took some doing, but Ava found Tiernan just outside the city, seated on a boulder on a rise overlooking the valley.

He didn't look up as she approached but scooted over to give her room to join him.

She tore apart a yellow flower, letting the petals fall to the ground, and glanced at him sideways. "So what are you going to do now? Go after the missing Rogues?" The pit Ava had created was empty once the Protectors had gotten back to it, the Rogues on the run once again.

Tiernan looked off into the distance and shrugged slightly. "Nah. I told Madeleine I needed some time off."

"Time off? *You?*" Ava laughed. "What are you going to do? Work on your tan?"

Tiernan just shrugged again.

Ava sobered and touched his hand lightly. "What is it? What's wrong?"

He seemed to chew on the question before answering. "I don't know. I've been at this a long time. Maybe it's time for a change of pace, you know?"

"Where will you go?"

"I'm not sure. Maybe back to Europe for a bit. Or I have a place up north. Haven't been there in a while. Might head there."

Ava felt a sudden prickle of tears, and she linked her arm with his, leaning her head against his thick bicep. "What am I going to do without you, though? You're my best friend."

Tiernan scoffed, but he didn't shake her off. "You have Lucy. And Caleb."

"Okay, then, my best friend who could crush a man's skull in his bare hands."

"That's disgusting."

"Shut up."

"Seriously, you've become kind of bloodthirsty. I think you need therapy."

"Tiernan!" Ava laughed through her tears, and after a moment, Tiernan gently pulled his arm free.

"You'll be fine," he said. "You're always fine." He smiled at her and lifted a hand to wipe the tears from her cheek. He rubbed the wetness between a thumb and forefinger, his green and blue eyes focused on hers.

It hit Ava how those eyes had once struck terror in her but were now associated with a person she held so dear.

Tiernan opened his mouth as if to say something but shut it a moment later, shaking his head as he stood and brushed his hands on his pants.

Ava realized he had a rucksack sitting at his feet, and her heart stopped as he hoisted it onto his shoulders. "You're going now?"

"No time like the present." He started toward the forest.

"But . . . what if I need you? Can I call—"

"No cell," he said quickly. "Katherine will know how to contact me if there's an emergency."

She stood, wringing her hands, her heart racing. "Will you be back?"

He slowed but didn't stop. "Not anytime soon."

"That's not never," she called out stubbornly.

Hopefully.

Tiernan looked over his shoulder and grinned. "Never is a very long time." He lifted his hand in a final wave, and he was gone.

Ava stared after him until his imprint vanished as surely as the rest of him. Wiping her tears, she turned to head back, smiling when Caleb's gift announced his arrival a few seconds later.

He materialized a few feet in front of her, his smile falling when he spotted her. "What's wrong?" He hurried over and cupped her face. "Are you hurt?"

"I'm fine . . . it's just." She shrugged. "Tiernan's gone."

"Gone? Gone where?"

"Away, for a while," she replied, leaning close as he put an arm around her shoulders, and they started to walk back toward the center of the city. "Said he needed a change of pace."

"I can understand that," he said quietly.

"I feel bad for him. He seemed so alone."

Caleb was quiet for so long that Ava prodded him with her hip. "What's up?"

"You really don't know?"

"Know what?"

"How Tiernan feels about you."

"What are you talking about? He's my friend."

Caleb shook his head, his gaze staying locked on the ground. "He *is* your friend. And he's mine, too. Which is why he had to leave."

Ava's heart sank as the reality of what Caleb was saying hit her. "You think he—"

He squeezed her closer and kissed the top of her head.

"But he never said anything."

"Have you met Tiernan?" he asked, lips quirking slightly. "You think he'd actually talk about his feelings?"

Ava winced. "Now I feel even worse."

Caleb stopped and pulled her into a hug. "Which is another reason why he'd never say anything."

"So why did you?" she grumbled, smacking him lightly on the chest.

"Because, Miss Intuition, I assumed you'd already figured it out!"

"Nope," she said quietly.

"Nope?"

"Nope."

"Sorry." He kissed her again and took her hand. "He'll be okay, Ava. I promise. Tiernan's been through worse."

She nodded, but the sadness hung over her as they walked through the city. She would miss him. And she hoped he would be okay. That someday he'd come back or they'd cross paths.

"There's plenty of time," Caleb reminded her. "You'll see him again."

"I thought I told you a long time ago not to read my mind."

"And I thought I told you I can't read minds," he said with a laugh, his eyes twinkling. "I've just gotten a little better at reading you."

They continued toward the center of town in silence, their joined hands swinging between them.

"So what now?" she asked.

"Now?" He tilted his head up, considering. "Now, I'm thinking a lazy evening watching a boring movie . . . maybe some Chinese food—"

She shoved him, he laughed, and her gift seemed to laugh with him.

"You know what I mean," she said, resisting a little—only a little—when he pulled her close and wrapped his arms around her.

He leaned down to nuzzle her cheek and breathe into her neck. "Now, I kiss you, then we go to my place, and I give you something I've got hidden in my top drawer."

"Something?" She let out a shaky breath and tilted her head as he trailed his lips over her skin. "What kind of something?" She shuddered at the scrape of his teeth and the gentle, teasing bite on the juncture of her neck and shoulder.

Caleb pulled back and smiled softly. "Something I've been saving for a special occasion. Or at least until we weren't running for our lives." He rested his forehead against hers, all teasing gone. "I meant it when I said that I wanted you forever."

Ava's stomach flipped, and warm, tingling electricity swept through her. Whether it was her gift, or simply adrenaline, she wasn't quite sure. She smiled and placed a palm on his cheek. "I meant it when I said yes," she said.

His smile widened until his eyes—his beautiful blue and green eyes—crinkled at the corners. "Good," he said, and he leaned in to kiss her properly.

Ava wasn't sure how long they stood there in the middle of a city street, making out as if breathing was an unnecessary inconvenience. She wasn't sure if Caleb would give her a ring that night, or if they would end up watching a movie and eating Chinese food. She wasn't sure about a lot of things. But she knew, in that moment, that whatever lay ahead, Caleb would be right there beside her. And as she drew closer to him, breathing him in, tasting him, feeling their gifts winding together—exuberant and free—she knew that was enough.

It was more than enough.

BOOKS BY T.M. FRANKLIN

The MORE Trilogy
MORE
The Guardians
TWELVE

The Talisman Chronicles
WINDOW
TIMEPIECE
GAUNTLET
MANTLE
SHIELD
PRISON

How to Get Ainsley Bishop to Fall in Love with You

Short Stories

A Piece of Cake
Unscheduled Departure

ACKNOWLEDGMENTS

First and foremost, I must thank Tiffany Nichols, the first person other than myself, who read *MORE* and assured me it wasn't horrible. Thank you so much for all your help, Tiff.

To my fabulous editing team: DJ Gann, Jennifer Matera, and Andrea McKay—you all were a pleasure to work with. Thanks to my wonderful formatter Lindsey Gray, who made this second edition so pretty.

Special thanks to those who made publishing this book possible: Sydney Logan, Kathie Spitz, Shay Donovan, Jennifer McGuire, Jenny Pedroza, and Amanda Hayward. And of course, big thanks and love to Jeanne McDonald and all the lovely ladies at Enchanted Publications.

To my family, who left me alone (for the most part) when I was huddled over my laptop typing frantically—thank you and I love you.

To my longtime readers, who've followed me into this new adventure—thank you for the faith. It's impossible to express just how much it means to me.

ABOUT THE AUTHOR

T.M. Franklin writes stories of adventure, romance, & a little magic. A former TV news producer, she decided making stuff up was more fun than reporting the facts. Her first published novel, MORE, was born during National Novel Writing month, a challenge to write a novel in thirty days. MORE was well-received, being selected as a finalist in the 2013 Kindle Book Review Best Indie Book Awards, as well as winning the Suspense/Thriller division of the Blogger Book Fair Reader's Choice Awards. She's since written three additional novels and several best-selling short stories...and there's always more on the way.

Connect with T.M. Franklin

Web site: www.TMFranklin.com
Facebook: www.facebook.com/TMFranklinAuthor
Twitter: twitter.com/TM_Franklin
Email: TMFranklinAuthor@gmail.com

Made in the USA
Charleston, SC
13 February 2017